The

Triumvirate

Mary SanGiovanni

Prologue

From a video, lost: A man sits in a chair at a desk. His auburn hair threaded with gray, is neatly combed, and covers a good portion of his head. Also neat is the trimmed beard and mustache. He draws in a sudden sharp breath through dry, cracked lips. His eyes grow wide. In the background, the sound of a few footsteps draws closer to the camera and then recedes.

On the tape, a soft and sexless chuckling close to the mike causes the man to visibly tense in his chair. The picture dissolves into static along with the sound. Through the crackling "snow," the man's form, wide-eyed, leans close to the camera.

"They're here, I think. Outside," the man whispers. A flash of clear picture shows a trickle of blood from the corner of his mouth. To a watcher, there is little doubt that this is a man at the end of his chain, a man with a one-way ticket. He has kind eyes and it's a shame.

"—always watching, waiting," the man on the tape is saying. Through the static, a watcher paying close attention might notice the camera panning the room. What can be made out of the room suggests tidiness not for tidiness' sake, but because the man owns

little to clutter up the room. As it sweeps past a doorway, three silhouettes fill the space for a frame but are gone in the next.

The camera pans back to the man. He takes several large gulps of Scotch and settles back into his chair. Then he adds, as an afterthought, "I've told you all I know. All anybody knows. I daresay, that may be all anyone has ever known about the Hollower. And I can do no more."

The static clears. Cut scene to the man's motionless body, slumped over on a bed, a rough exploded mess of red and gray and white replacing the visible back portion of his head.

Faintly, a watcher can hear high, strained laughter.

***

In room 211 at Lakehaven Psychiatric Hospital, an old woman in the neat blue and pink floral dress sat in her chair and stared out her hospital room window at the night sky. The moon was a round, pale wheel of cheese tonight, bright enough to see even through the hazy cloud cover of her cataracts. Tonight was clearer than most others, outside the room and inside her head. She could think. It was cold in the room; she was old and thin, with old, thin skin, and cold went through it and got up inside and stayed there, most nights. The blanket over her lap helped. It had fire colors and was fluffy and warm. She couldn't remember who had given it to her. She'd have to ask Harvey.

The Triumvirate

Tonight there was a different kind of cold in the air. It had been this different-cold since the doormen came. She remembered a flash of light, but at the moment, couldn't remember where she had seen it or when. She thought it might be Thursday. She'd cook chicken for dinner that night. Her Harvey loved chicken, especially roasted chicken.

She loosened the bun on top of her head and her hair, cobweb-fine and sterile-white, drifted down like snow to her shoulders.

Low sirens sounded from down the hall, by Helen's old room and by the elevators, reminding her of the war. She made a little click of disapproval with her tongue. They would wake up Mrs. Meyers with their siren-talk, and once Mrs. Meyers got to ranting about the noise keeping her awake, there'd be no end to it. She could do without that insufferable woman's whine for the night, thank you very much.

She was reminded of their house in Brooklyn, before they'd moved out to Jersey. The woman who lived next door was a lot like Mrs. Meyers. She supposed everywhere had at least one person who was a lot like Mrs. Meyers.

The sirens sounded closer, under the bed now, then out in the hall, then out the window, broadcasting down from the moon. She could understand some of it, not as words but as impressions and feelings. She understood the ever-present hate and hunger that were a part of their make-up, she understood their power which was unlike the others' who had come before, and she understood that there was an objective beyond hunting. So they were there with a mission, a specific purpose. She was not so worried. They had never fed on her. She never worried, and so she gave them nothing to feed on. And she didn't think their mission involved her. She wished they'd come in from the Convergence and use words, though, so she wouldn't have to strain to understand. She was old, and it was hard enough most nights to remember the words of her own language for herself. Sometimes talking was lost to her. But she supposed it cost nothing to listen. She'd understand what she could. It wasn't like they were talking to her, anyway.

She felt them out there in the hall, there but not there, and she also felt that they sensed her, too. She supposed they did it on purpose to rile her, but they began giving off the most horrible notions about others. Helen, for one, and what they had done to her. What they had gotten her to do to herself. The old woman shivered. She had liked Helen. What happened had been terrible. And they were hurting someone named Lauren that she thought she should know, but could not remember at the moment. Others. Others that she was fairly sure she didn't know. But then, often lately she confused faces in her mind, and forgot names.

She listened in the dark, pretending to watch the moon out the window, pretending she didn't know about them moving through the halls, preparing, watching, hunting. Maybe they would pass her by. The ones before often did. She wasn't worried, not really, but they nettled her. They made her feel like a balloon on the verge of popping. Maybe they would leave her alone. They had a lot of killing to do.

She couldn't understand most of the siren language, which wasn't really siren sound at all but something that cruder senses perceived that way. Still, she picked up enough to know they had begun. She felt sorry for the people they had killed the way she felt sorry sometimes for little animals that got hit by cars and people in faraway countries with nearly unpronounceable names (the people and the countries, she thought) who were going to war, and the children on those commercials with the man who looked like Santa Claus asking for quarters for them. She felt sorry for all the races the doormen hurt, but she felt most sorry for Lauren, who was nice to her and smelled like springtime.

Yes, Lauren! She remembered now, silly her...well, at least that Lauren was nice. She had trouble recalling her face, but thought she might be blonde, like springtime daffodils.

Her mother would know. Her mother was always good about putting faces and names together. After she got out of school tomorrow, she'd ask her mother about it.

The doormen made no footstep sounds and cast no shadows. They suddenly just were, three silhouettes in hats and coats standing in the doorway, tall like Harvey had been when he was alive. They were sneaky like that. They split the layers of reality and slid in between them. She'd seen them take people with them in between those layers.

When they were there, the clouds in her eyes went away. She thought it was because she was seeing them inside her head instead of through those filmy orbs, but to her, it felt like regular sight.

Each tilted its hat to her and she scowled, pulling her blanket up tighter around her.

"We know you sense us," the middle one cooed in a number of stolen voices braided together.

"We are going to kill her," the one on the left said. "We are going to kill them all. You will not cause us any undue delay in this regard, right, Claudia?"

"It's better when you use our words. Your siren words hurt my head," she said with a petulant huff. "Too many shapes."

"That's a good girl," the one on the right told her.

She could feel their hate like tidal waves of cold. The cold passed through and got right up inside her, most nights.

"I'm not your girl." She thought of Harvey, and wondered when he'd be home from work. She hated when he worked late.

The one to the left tilted its faceless head. "When you do that, we lose you. When you shift thoughts. Shift time. Shift understanding."

"I'm an old woman," she said. "I'm sick."

She sensed that even so close to this world, they did not understand what was wrong with her. They did not understand "sick." Much of the time, she didn't understand what was wrong with her, either, but she suspected it was what kept them from tearing into her mind and soul like they did with all the others.

"There," the one on the right said, "we found you."

"Go away," she told them. "Your snow is a bother to an old woman."

They moved on toward Helen's old room, and the clouds moved in and knitted over her eyes again. The old woman could hear the chorus of their broken-glass laughter, loathsome and insane, long after they were gone.

Mary SanGiovanni

Chapter 1

Detective Lieutenant Steven Corimar's stomach had been twisted up ever since he got the call. He knew the address—the street, at least. He'd been there before, a couple of years ago, though he'd really believed he'd never have to go down that road, figuratively or literally, again.

On their route there, the unmarked police car slowed, just for a moment, in front of another address he recognized—that of an old friend. Steve suspected that maybe subconsciously, passing that house might give him strength, as its inhabitant had once before, in dealing with whatever he was going to find at the crime scene.

The strength didn't come. No one lived there anymore. No one had lived there in a good four years; not since the night its last inhabitant had sacrificed himself to save them. The house soulless now. Its window eyes were dark and empty, its mouth shut tight on rusting hinges. The lawn, like a shaggy, unwashed beard, tangled in itself. Something about the houses in Lakehaven remembered tragedy and drew it close like a shroud; he'd noticed that in his years on the force. Those houses whose inhabitants died were invariably left to fall apart, as if even the bankers who saw money value in blades of grass and hills of dirt knew that the land on which the houses stood was worthless. Even poisonous. Bloomwood County, New Jersey was like that. Lakehaven, Wexton, that long-abandoned ghost town of Thrall—all possessed of real estate soured by misfortune and death, terrible memories and terrible secrets.

Steve suddenly felt very alone. The car moved on, and if Detective Bennie Mendez, sitting in the passenger seat, wondered at his taking the long way or noticed Steve's barely perceptible shudder, he didn't let on.

Because Steve recognized the street where the crime scene was, he thought—no, he was sure—that he would also recognize the bodies. That particular street wasn't just soulless; it was one of the cursed places, haunted in its own way, clinging to the death and pain that seemed to wash over it with the persistence of a tide. Steve knew it for what it was—a place that would have destroyed forever the sleep and peace of that mild suburban New Jersey neighborhood if the full horrors that existed beyond it ever managed to cross over.

"Erik and I can tell you, this Hollower is different. Meaner. Stronger.... It's called a Primary."

The call had come in while he and Mendez, partnered for the last few years, were sipping morning coffee. Above them, a mottled steel sky bit back bitter rain, its displeasure with the world a thick humidity that sheathed everything in a clammy second skin. Steve had been hoping for a quiet morning. He knew Mendez had been up with his little daughter and her ear infection all night, and he himself hadn't slept well, either. Gordon had been touchy and distracted the night before, pushing him away. Usually upfront with his thoughts and feelings, he'd been unusually reticent, insisting he was just tired and wanted to go to sleep, but Steve knew better. Gordon was nothing if not loyal, so Steve was sure it wasn't someone else. But Gordon was also fairly open, and a family reunion was coming up in Oklahoma that Steve had been dodging the topic of for the last week. Gordon understood Steve's reluctance to go, to be introduced to his family as a romantic partner. It hadn't been too long ago that Steve had been in a place of tentative and fragile self-acceptance, following staunch public denial, and Gordon's family had been somewhat less than openly accepting of his lifestyle in the past. There were a couple uncles, a grandmother and an aunt that would be quite sure to tell them that "the Bible said men ought not to lay with other men," and other such pearls of wisdom. It didn't seem to bother Gordon much, but Steve still got a little hot and nettled at such careless homophobia. So it hadn't been discussed since Gordon had initially brought it up, the impending event simply a scrawl across a calendar square that he had so far been careful to dance around.

Of course, that didn't make it hurt any less that Gordon had uncharacteristically shut him out since, to the point of distraction. Steve would have to bring it up sooner or later because if Gordon did, he had a feeling that would make things worse.

The code coming in from dispatch over their radio had disrupted his thoughts. It was a 10-93—two individuals found deceased on the scene. The address was an abandoned house at 63 River Falls Road, a place that had once been home to a suicide victim, a few years before. The bodies were as yet unidentified.

Mendez had raised an eyebrow, watching Steve carefully for his reaction. It was the address Mendez recognized, just as Steve did himself. The address once had been significant to Mendez's wife, Anita, who had closed a very strange case there, and it had been significant to Steve, who had tied it to a disappearance and a number of other deaths. What Mendez had gleaned over the last four years from both wife and partner had come in reluctant mutterings—late night pillow talk after nightmares from Anita, and things she said in her sleep, and beer-soaked confessions after shifts from Steve. But Mendez had been a detective with Lakehaven's police force much longer than Steve had, and he knew when to ask questions, and when to wait for the answers to come to him. He didn't push Steve about what had happened at 63 River Falls Road or at the Oak Hills Assisted Living Facility a year after, and Steve didn't volunteer what he knew about either.

Mendez did know something about...*them*, and the numerous lives they had destroyed, but he also *didn't* know. He couldn't understand fully without ever having had those chill non-fingers poking through into one's life and manipulating, changing, invading one's most personal fears.

Steve drove to the address. Mendez, a creature of gut instinct, kept mostly silent and Steve was glad for that. They were past

14

needing to fill the silences—that seemed the first benchmark of a successful partnering, whether romantic or professional.

The front lawn of 63 River Falls Road was swarming with crime scene folks and uniformed officers keeping the curious neighbors at bay. The police force, and therefore, the team of crime scene techs, numbered few, despite recent expansions to both; Lakehaven had been primarily a peaceful vacation lake community until the late 1970s, and crime until the last decade or so had remained relatively low. Steve's personal experience though, especially in the last four years, jived more with the crime scene before him now. Suicides, homicides, unexplained disappearances, and bizarre accidents were on the rise in the county as a whole, and Steve was part of the new wave of officers being trained to close cases either by traditional hours of police work, or in occasional instances, to "spin, sign, and forget." It was the latter Steve hated. He didn't like loose ends.

The job wasn't a mine field of murder, like it might have been in Newark, say, or Plainfield or Camden. No gangs here, or drug dealers with weaponry that made the cops' hardware look like water pistols. But it was becoming increasingly common for Steve to roll up on scenes of milling officers holding foam cups of coffee, looking tired in their day-old rumple of clothes, strips of yellow police tape, the soft buzz of discovery and speculation and quite often, sad surprise, and following the sense of disconnect and cold proficiency to its source, a body or bodies swathed in blood and odd circumstance.

Steve and Mendez parked across the street. They flashed badges at a nearby uniformed officer Steve didn't recognize and he waved them under the police tape.

"That damn house again." Steve caught the woman's voice from a clump of sixty-something neighbors huddled at the curb, and that heavy sick feeling rolled along the bottom of his stomach. "Something's always happening in that damn house."

"They should just tear it down," a man's voice replied in agreement.

They were right, Steve thought. Something *was* always happening in that damn house. Someone was always dying.

They found Frank Kimner in the hallway, and he sent them up the stairs and around the banister to the master bedroom. Sussex County CSU was clearing out, and Eileen Vernon, the state medical examiner, was crouching by the bodies of two young people, a male and a female, lying face-up on the floor in the center of the room amid thick halos of blood. The bulk of Eileen's gray-black hair was pulled into a messy knot at the back of her head. Her long rubber gloves, streaked in crimson, were examining what looked like bite marks on the throat of the male.

Savage slashes in the cheeks and jagged, teeth-bearing extensions of the mouth, empty eye sockets, and demolished pulp where the noses were made the faces difficult to recognize, but Steve knew these people. He fought the gorge rising in his throat and the tears that washed his vision in a blur.

"Damnedest thing, stud," Eileen said to him. Her usually upbeat and flirtatious, flat-A Jersey voice was low. "It's just their faces."

"What do you mean?" Mendez, seeming to sense Steve's hesitation to get closer, took the lead.

Eileen looked up. "Mendez! My Latin love machine. Well, see here—" she pointed to the hands of the male. "Little defensive wounds here and here. And on the woman here, this gash on her forearm, also suggestive of defensive wounds. But otherwise, all the damage to these bodies was focused specifically on their faces and throats. The throat wounds ultimately led to the bleed-outs, but...it's just strange. Throat wounds seem almost secondary—like collateral damage. Claws digging into the necks to get at the face and destroy as much of it as possible."

"They look like animal bites. Like, what, a wolf? Dog?"

Eileen shrugged, casting a concerned glance at Steve, who still hung back, still silent. "Looks like. Wounds definitely have the ragged edges of teeth—not human teeth, either. But wounds consistent with animal attacks generally involve damage to the other soft parts—limbs, stomach, intestines, that sort of thing. Jugular maybe, to take the prey down, but otherwise, animals eat where the meat is fullest and fattest. There are no other wounds anywhere on the bodies."

"Hmmm." Mendez looked around the room. Steve did, too. The house, minimally furnished and covered in a snowfall of fluffy dust, had stood abandoned since the death of its prior owner, Max

Feinstein. There was the debris of neglect, but no real signs of struggle—at least, nothing that indicated the kind of animal attack that could kill two people. There were no signs of animal presence, either—no fur, no droppings, no splatters of dried saliva. The dust that formed a thin film on parts of the floor was undisturbed by paw prints or sweeps of a tail.

Steve's gaze kept returning to the mangled faces of his friends.

"Looks to me," Mendez said after a time, "like they didn't live here, at least not legally, and nothing in the room except the blood would suggest they were killed here, but then...nothing in the house suggests this is a dump site. So...what happened?"

Eileen winked at him. "That, you sexy hunk of brains, is your job."

"The bodies haven't been identified?"

"I know them," Steve said quietly.

Mendez and Eileen looked at him. "He speaks," she said, but the humor was swallowed up by the concern in her voice and on her face. Mendez watched him expectantly.

"The girl," Steve said with a shuddery sigh, walking to within inches of the drying blood, "is Dorothy Weatherin. Her boyfriend there is Jake Dylan. They lived together in a house on Cerver Street."

"Any idea what they would be doing here?" There was an element of caution in Mendez's tone, as if he expected the question might set Steve off somehow.

When Steve said, "No. No idea," he spoke the truth, or thought he did. Any reason to be in this house had been killed four years ago, and it was the belief of those who had survived that night—he and Erik, Dorrie and Jake—that places like this house on River Falls Road and Oak Hill Assisted Living could and should become the stuff of repressed memories.

***

It had become a kind of weekly thing for Steve to meet his friend Erik McGavin at the local bar in Lakehaven, a long log wood building called Olde Mill Tavern, on Wednesday nights. Steve usually had the day off on Thursdays, and Erik, an ex-coke addict, sponsored the newly recovering and ran an N.A. meeting on Wednesdays. He didn't drink alcohol—he'd told Steve once that it felt too close to cheating on his own sobriety—but he sat at the end of the bar, people-watching and drinking Diet Cokes. The low lights and noise and activity of the bar seemed to soothe him, to make him feel connected to the rest of the world. After their friend Dave Kohlar's death a few years before, Steve had taken to joining him. Gordon liked Erik, but he never went along on these nights. He knew that Steve and Erik and Dave and others (Jake, for one, and Dorrie, for another) had shared a painful, scary experience once, one Steve didn't talk about and Gordon seemed to know better than to ask about. He accepted that the experience was a kind of bond that needed periodically to be acknowledged by company, and by deliberately not being verbally acknowledged at all.

That Wednesday night, when Steve sat down at the bar on the empty stool next to Erik, his friend studied his face a moment, and in his quiet, unobtrusive way, said, "Want to talk about it?"

Steve ordered a beer and when the bartender had turned away, Steve sighed and said to Erik, "I'm not even sure where to begin. Two deaths, likely animal attacks except for some odd aspects that don't quite fit."

"There's more."

"Yes. The bodies were found," Steve said, taking a deep breath, "in the upstairs bedroom of 63 River Falls Road."

Erik's expression changed very little, but the color drained from his cheeks.

Steve's beer came, and he drained half of it before adding, "The bodies were Jake and Dorrie, Erik." He chanced a quick glance at his friend. Erik closed his eyes and seemed to be counting to himself. He opened them slowly.

"You said it was...animal attacks?"

"With odd circumstances."

"Odd how?"

Steve's voice dropped and he looked at Erik pointedly. "Their faces. Just their faces were torn up. And their necks. All the damage was concentrated there. No sign of animals having been anywhere in the house."

"Their faces?" Erik sounded hollow and weak.

"Yeah." Steve finished off his beer.

It seemed like a very long time before Erik said, "Please make it mean something else."

"What?"

Erik looked at him. The normally stoic facade was slipping around his shining eyes. "I know it sounds selfish, but...we killed it. We killed two of them, for chrissakes. I don't know if I have it in me again. So please, please tell me it's anything other than what it sounds like."

"Erik—"

"Use forensics or fingerprints or...or paw prints or whatever. Hair. Fibers. Something real—"

"Erik, I—"

Erik grabbed his arm. His grip was strong. "Please, Steve. I can't. I just...can't. Not again."

Steve didn't answer. He wished he could, but in the face (*or lack thereof*, he thought with grim and sour amusement) of the evidence, it sure seemed like that unspoken answer between him and Erik was the right one. He wasn't so sure he had it in him to face another one, either. The last one had nearly killed him.

The two finished out their evening in relative silence, both of them thinking but not quite able to express their certainty that somewhere, somehow, a rip between dimensions had opened up again. And a predator, a new Hollower, had started stalking and feeding in this world.

***

When Steve got back to his apartment that night, Gordon was already asleep. That was okay; Steve didn't feel much like talking. He made his way across the darkened living room to the long hall. He could hear Gordon's light snoring and beneath that, the buzz of the TV. Gordon set it on a timer; he liked the voices to keep him company on those nights when Steve had to work late.

Steve passed the bedroom, whose door was slightly ajar, and made his way to the bathroom. After relieving himself of the last of the beer, he washed up and looked in the mirror. The face staring back at him was tired. It was a strong face, a square-jawed, handsome face, but the eyes... the eyes looked sad. Scared. Exhausted. He sighed.

In the bedroom, he shut the TV off in passing and undressed in the dark, feeling over the pile of clothes for the black sweat pants he usually slept in. In the bed nearby, Gordon's breathing was reassuring, real. He had come to find it comforting, just as he had come to find the warm existence of him in bed next to him reassuring. Gordon seemed to find it funny: a big, strong cop like Steve finding comfort and security in Gordon's slighter presence. But Steve had seen things since he'd been a cop in Lakehaven that made him, for the first time since childhood, recognize the importance of having something—some*one*—real and steady to hold onto.

He looked at the dark silhouette in bed and decided to tell Gordon in the morning that he'd go to the family reunion—that he'd be honored, in fact, to go. Gordon loved him, and he was pretty sure he loved Gordon back. Steve knew he was incredibly lucky to have someone like Gordon in his life. He could tune out a few homophobes over hamburgers and hotdogs and, God-willing, a lot of beer if that would make Gordon happy.

Steve was just about to climb into bed when he heard a faint, high sound like a siren in the distance, followed by a thump and a moan in the hallway.

He glanced at Gordon, who remained sleeping. He reached for the gun he'd left in its holster on top of his stripped-off pants. He could feel his heart thudding against his chest as he crept through the dark toward the hall, but he refused to admit the thoughts that crept around the corners of his mind. It was not, could not, would absolutely NOT be a—

In the den at the other end of the hall, a den he would have sworn was empty when he'd passed it less than half an hour before, a blue-gray glow and inaudible mumble of voices suggested the TV in there was on. Despite the jarring suddenness of that idea, the clamp around his heart and lungs loosened a little. A thump and a moan echoing down the hallway made sense if some electrical surge or fried TV wire had caused the thing to turn on. An arbitrary channel pouring its surreal and graying glare of once-removed reality into his very real den could be explained that way, unspun by any ill-fitting forced logic. Just the TV. Just a wire short-circuiting. He lowered the gun, moving with more confident steps toward the den.

He stopped short just in the doorway, the clamp tightening down hard again on his heart and lungs, because the noises weren't coming from what was on TV. They were coming from what was tugging and wriggling and lurching its way *out of the television.*

Where the screen had been there was a space like a window; beyond the wriggling thing in the foreground, Steve could see glimpses of a dark purple sky punctured all over with alien stars. From the other world embedded impossibly into the circuitry of his flat-screen television, the thing struggling to pull itself through looked encased in sausage skin; it was slick with some fluid that seemed to be rapidly drying and crumbling off the surface at its exposure to the air of the den. Beneath the slickness was a mottled black and pink skin, thin over spiny vertebrae that writhed out into Steve's world in long, tapered appendages. These tentacles seemed randomly connected to a round mass of the same color and greasy appearance. The mass opened and closed a series of gaping holes around the tentacles that sometimes threw up obsidian orbs like eyes, and at other times, thin cactus-needle teeth. It had a rank moldy, swampy kind of smell, like organic things left out in the rain too long. It moaned again, retching from one of those sometimes-mouths a black fluid onto the rug that smoked and sizzled in little patches.

Steve had forgotten himself completely in staring at the atrocity stuck halfway in and halfway out of his television.

However, the tension holding him up was starting to strain his muscles, and he could feel his legs weak and shaking beneath him. His grip around the gun seemed dreamlike, its usually cool and reassuring solidity now completely without weight or substance.

"Oh shit," he whispered, unable to take his eyes off the thing. His brain willed him, screamed at him to raise the gun, to fire, and following that was the absurd argument that in doing so, he'd wake up Gordon. So what? Shouldn't Gordon be awake? Shouldn't they both be running like hell out of the apartment?

The desire to protect Gordon finally overrode his paralysis and he lifted the gun and fired into the squirming mass which had wrapped a tentacle around the leg of the coffee table and had hefted most of its bulk free of the TV. It roared, ostensibly in pain, and flopped to the floor.

The television had been a 60-inch flat-screen, and the creature on the floor in his den had filled the bulk of that. Now that it was free, Steve could see that the central mass extended outward behind it in a tail reminiscent of that of a lobster, sheathed in the same greasy, mottled skin. There, though, no eyes or mouths opened, but rather, a number of thin, jointed insect legs slid its bulk forward. The tentacle that was wrapped around the coffee table leg splintered the wood, and the flat top crashed forward onto the floor in front of it. It roared again, and Steve thought the sound was more anger than pain. All the slits in its body opened in unison, revealing numerous black, hateful, soulless eyes which focused their rage on him.

Steve fired at it again and again, emptying his clip into it until the gun clicked uselessly in his hand. He dropped it at his feet. He was about to run for the bedroom when a familiar laugh riveted him again to the spot. It was an entanglement of voices both male and female, discordant and cold, like a music box smashed hopelessly off-key.

That voice muttered words in a language Steve couldn't place, a language whose context suggested layers of sinister meaning. Then, in English, the voice said, "Now, you die."

Steve turned slowly in the direction of the voices, and the last of his strength gave out. He sank to the floor by his empty gun.

Three identical Hollowers stood in the kitchen, so close that they nearly blended in and out of each other. They had taken on the form so hideously familiar to him now. They each stood about six feet tall, humanoid in shape, their hairless heads each wearing a black fedora hat. They were clothed in black featureless clothes beneath long black trench coats, with black gloves and black shoes simulating hands and feet. These clothes had a surreal cast over them like a frost, a kind of quality that suggested their presence only half in this world, their consuming hunger and hate a biting, stiff, skin-cracking frigidity. Most terrifying to Steve were the flat, perfectly blank expanses of white where faces should have been, still capable of expression but utterly devoid of emotion or anything close to resembling pity or empathy.

The first of them raised a glove and tipped its hat to him.

Before Steve could scream, something hot and strong as steel wrapped itself around his neck and yanked him forward. The pain was immense, the tight band around his neck digging a hundred tiny spikes into his skin, the pressure choking off the air. He clawed at the tentacle but couldn't get a finger hold to loosen its grip. The creature yanked him forward again and for a moment, the world went out of focus in a bright, sharp cloud of pain. He could feel the pressure and heat building up in his face, his mouth working in futile and soundless gasps to try to draw in air. He struggled to get his legs in front of him and kick at the body of the thing now that it was within his range. His foot sank into the damp sponginess of that alien body. For a moment, the grip around his neck loosened and again Steve saw the world through twinkling of fuzzy pinpoints of light, his bruised throat rasping for air, before the tentacle tightened again.

The last thing Steve saw before both worlds in his view went black for good was the series of slits swallowing those terrible empty eyes so that myriad teeth could sink into the flesh and bone of his face.

Behind him, the Triumvirate had already gone.

Mary SanGiovanni

Chapter 2

It had been a fear of Ian Coley's ever since his mother's suicide that he would inherit the insanity that killed her. Every time he momentarily forgot the name for something, every time the dreams seemed a little too real and he woke up confused, every time the anxiety defied any real sense of rationality or logic, there was a quick flash of panic that he would end up like her. For the last few years of her life, she had hated being confused, hated that twilight state that had held her in a fever-dream of her own mind.

Ian's father had died when he was three, and he had very little memory of the man beyond a bristly dark mustache and the scent of Old Spice. His mother, he knew, had loved his father very much, and even after the schizophrenia had begun to set in, even after the voices and the newspaper duct-taped to the windows and the precise arrangements of soda cans and the complex symbols in bas-relief built up and out from the walls in plaster—even after all that, the one thing that could rally her sense of logic and reality was mention of his father. Ian wondered sometimes if his death was the beginning of her unraveling.

He wondered sometimes, too, if her death might have been the beginning of his.

It wasn't just the bad dreams that made him worry—everyone had bad dreams—or the anxiety that seemed to wrap its icy fingers around the better part of a day's thoughts. It wasn't the whispering he thought he caught from the corners of rooms, or the multi-voiced laughter he sometimes heard in a bar or restaurant or on the street. He could write off all these things if he had to, package them into neat little parcels of anxiety tied tightly with logic and fact and carefully over-thought reason.

The men without the faces, though—that he couldn't explain. And that, he was sure, was the first truly undeniable sign that he had inherited his mother's insanity. That scared the hell out of him. If a guy lost a leg or an arm, he understood it felt horrible, at first. The phantom itch, the phantom ache, followed by rebuilding one's sense of self and relearning to function without the limb or appendage. But what itched or ached when a guy lost part of his mind? How did one go about mentally restructuring one's thoughts and feelings? How did one learn to function as a normal person in a world encroached on by things others couldn't see or hear?

Sometimes in the dark that went beyond the thickest part of night, when these thoughts threatened to bury him alive and alone, he could begin to see why his mother had chosen an even deeper darkness, a final quieting of fears and a simple oblivion peace.

He'd taken over her home on Franklin Avenue once she'd been admitted to the hospital, since she'd been so adamant that "those alien bastards with the human masks" who ran the bank not get a hold of her home and possessions. He'd kept most of her things, having little possessions of his own beyond an Ikea Grono lamp from his dorm room, some clothes, and a small TV, and having no money to replace what was already furnishing the home. He'd had to take apart all those copper wire and soda can structures she claimed kept the men from other dimensions from getting through. He'd chipped off the plaster symbols on the walls and painted over them. He took the newspapers down from the windows and he'd cleaned the hard, gray layer of neglect off the surfaces of the kitchen and bathrooms. But he'd kept her bedroom exactly as it was, newspapers, plaster symbols, soda can towers and all. Her jewelry, what little there was, lay in a small box on her dresser, along with pictures of his father just after Viet Nam and at their wedding. There were baby pictures of him, too, and one he assumed was sent to her from his graduation, although he couldn't recall anyone being there in the audience who knew either him or her well enough to send her pictures. When she died, he'd kept the box of her possessions sent to him from the hospital, unopened, on the bed in that room as well.

He supposed when he really thought about it (which wasn't often), there was a part of him that had been waiting for her to get better and come back, to reclaim that home and those possessions she seemed to hold so dear. After her death, the pervasive thought that he had somehow failed her, failed to protect her from the monsters she saw everywhere, prevented him from clearing out the bedroom of those same precious things. If he thought even deeper about it (which he almost *never* did), he would have to admit that some part of him thought that by keeping it all, by some day working up enough courage to really examine the shrines to her madness, that he might be able to understand her. And maybe, he could understand himself, and what might happen to him....

He'd started seeing the men without faces about a week or so after his mother's funeral, a month or so before. He had been taking advantage of the unusually warm mid-May weather, reading on the porch of his mother's home, when he'd felt he was being watched. He looked up, but no one was there. He looked as far as he could strain his neck down either side of the street, but still, no one was there. His gaze quickly swept the porch. Still no one. He went back to reading.

He hadn't heard approaching footsteps or noticed any movement, but that feeling of being watched had been strong enough to lift his head again. Across the street, three figures stood close together. The near-luminous white of their faceless heads stood out against the crisp black of their clothes and hats. The first one tilted its head as if in quizzical thought, while the third raised a black glove and pointed at him. That pointer finger made slow, small circles in the air between them.

Ian frowned, setting the book aside, tented on the table next to his bench. He opened his mouth to speak then closed it, unsure what to say. There was a certain air of surreality about them, as if they were in a layer of space resting against this world instead of moving through it, but he was fairly sure—both brain and eyes in agreement—that they were there. And yet, he felt just as sure that nothing else in the environment around him knew of their presence but him. Even the sidewalk beneath them and the air around them were oblivious to them.

Which was a crazy thought, he knew. Crazy, even for him. Crazy, like his mother. But true.

In the middle of the street between them, the air wavered. The sizzling smell of ozone coated the back of his throat. It looked as though waves of heat were rising from the pavement to distort it. In the center of the bright, rippling spot, a shadow began to form, smoky at first but gaining more definite darkness. As Ian watched, the spot took on an oily quality that reflected swirls of color and seemed to pull in on itself, forming an indent, a kind of hole that tugged at the space in front of it.

"Oh wow." Ian rose slowly, his mind and body in agreement once again that he should move away from that swirling black. Instead, he moved closer, hovering at the top of the porch steps. The whirling spot made him think of black holes, pulling and sucking light and color and the very fabric of the universe into it, deeper, dragging it through and out into someplace alien, someplace cold and deadly and—

Ian shook his head, feeling confused and a little dizzy. Crazy, yes, but those weren't his thoughts. They were—

He looked up at the figures beyond the building vortex. Their voices swirled like the colors, in and around and through each other, around his ears, in and out of his head, male strains and female strains, a terrible chorus of hate.

"You are going to die," they told him, "just like your mother. Die. Die. Just like your mother...."

Ian squeezed his eyes shut and covered his ears, blocking out the vortex, blocking out their terrible voices. He could feel the tears slip beneath his lids and wet his cheeks, sudden and unbidden, and a terrible panic seized his chest. *No no no no no....*

Their laughter was jarring, like breaking glass. He opened his eyes slowly. The three figures were gone, and so was the dark vortex they had opened up. No trace of either remained. Ian stood where he was for several minutes after, focusing on his breathing, willing his heart beats to slow down. He squeezed his eyes shut and opened them twice more, as if wringing the things he'd seen like dirty water from his mind.

"Just like your mother...."

The trail of painkiller bottles she'd stolen somehow from the hospital supply cabinet (they'd never found the key she used) sprang to his mind's eye.

He closed his eyes. Squeezed. Opened them.

The smears of blood on the staff elevator's shiny metal sides and on the floor buttons.

Closed his eyes. Squeezed. Opened them.

The bloody hand-print on the basement's rough wall. The smear across the morgue door. The matches.

Closed his eyes. Squeezed.

The razor and the ceramic bowl in which she'd burned what she could manage to cut off her face before the blood-loss and painkillers made her woozy.

Squeezed.

The smell. The irregular pools of blood, black in the dank basement, swirling (like a black hole) with dirt and plaster dust. Her crumpled body, dangling. He'd been there. They knew she'd only come to him if she were having an episode, and they'd called him. They'd let him join the search. He was there when the hospital staff found her. He'd seen it all, taken it all in, and he didn't think he'd ever be able to squeeze it all out of his mind for good, for ever.

He opened his eyes, and when he did, his vision was blurred with tears. He sniffed, and wiped his eyes with his sleeve.

He backed slowly toward the bench and picked up his book to bring it inside. He was about to close it, the contents forgotten, when he noticed the red from the corner of his eye. He looked down at the page he had been reading. In thin, spidery red script across the black and white of the printed page, someone had written:

At daemon, homini quum struit aliquid malum,
pervertit illi primitus mentem suam.

He dropped the book, wiping the fingers that had touched it on his jeans.

His mother had taught Latin once among other ancient languages, when her mind was still good. Her mind had once been *very* good. She had taught Ian all kinds of things, given him a love of literature and music, of science and logic, but most especially of languages. She had once been a woman possessed of a bountiful wealth of knowledge, and she'd passed as much of it as she could on to Ian, who had shown a remarkable ability to absorb and remember anything so long as he could visually see it.

That had especially included ancient languages, which had formed the basis of secret conversations between them.

He understood the words in the spidery red script.

But the devil when he purports any evil against man, first perverts his mind.

***

For over a decade, the number of patients in the Sisters of the Holy Rosary Hospital's mental health wing had been growing too large in proportion to the funding and facility space to house them and the staff to take care of them. Bloomwood County saw the scandals of Greystone Hospital and heard the rumblings of budget cuts and subsequent poor care in several of the large asylums along the east coast, and decided that a new facility should be built to house the overflow of patients. This was suggested for altruistic reasons and funded for practical ones, not the least of which was avoiding investigation of mistreatment of patients at SHRH due to lack of staff and space.

Built on a private pond connected by a river to the main lake itself, Lakehaven Psychiatric Hospital rose two stories from the surrounding woods. The staff members were, for the most part, courteous and caring individuals, highly qualified and sufficiently experienced. The patients transferred from SHRH were mostly harmless. So it was difficult for one to pinpoint what made the hairs on the back of the neck rise while looking at the place, or made one shiver even on the warmest of days, but it was impossible to deny. It had been built with what had ostensibly been considered soothing gray stone. However, its dark turrets, massive oak front doors, barred windows, and rather unforgiving facade suggested a sinister history before it had time to have gathered one. The place looked daunting as much for its sterile, brand-new, equipment and thorough efficiency as for its contrasting patina of age—the uneasy understanding that lingered in every well-lit corner between insanity and consequence for that insanity.

Lauren Seavers, RN, believed something was off in the very building itself. She had never been bone to find hospitals scary—her job testified to that—and it had been years since the patients themselves could really shock or frighten her. But LPH, with its new-building smell, its bright walls and even brighter lights, had begun, over the last month or so, to make her uncomfortable. She wouldn't have admitted it out loud for fear of sounding ridiculous, but she suspected it was causing the bad dreams.

Lauren had worked the night shift for the last three months. Since Barry had broken up with her, she found she couldn't sleep well anyway, so she had volunteered. It kept her busy, kept her mind off of the distinct lack of his phone calls and texts, his arms, and his presence in the bed beside her. And the shift in her sleep schedule didn't make too much of a difference at first. But as it caught up to her, she found herself sensitive to suggestion about the place, and that found its way, magnified and distorted, into her dreams.

In those dreams, she was in a house somewhere in the suburbs, a place she didn't know in real life but seemed to know in the dream. She was not alone. There was a bone-thin blond woman, a tall, dark-haired woman with long legs in tiny shorts, and a blond man holding a drink. There was also a couple, a zaftig young woman and her boyfriend. None of them had faces. They stood in the shadowed corners of the room as if watching her with those empty and glowing expanses. They pulled away from her if she tried to touch them, and if she talked to them, their heads would twitch and vibrate rapidly, or turn suddenly from side to side as if they were looking for something in the room. She'd follow their blank-faced gazes toward what she thought they might be looking at, and invariably, there would be a tunnel. Sometimes the mouth of it would appear in a wall, or from the hallway, or once, where the window had been. And without fail, she'd feel compelled to follow it and see where it would lead. Often in the dreams, the tunnel would lead her through catacombs where carved rock would curve around and over her, making her feel buried alive and miles from anywhere safe. That feeling would drive her forward, that barely contained panic that if she didn't, she'd be stuck down in those catacombs forever.

Sometimes there would be voices in those catacombs, close to her ear. Male and female voices intertwined, they would whisper horrible things to her, things about death and rape and dismemberment, about her cousin, and about a patient she had recently lost. Talk of her cousin and her patient, Mrs. Helen Coley, bothered her more than the sum of other horrible things they said, because they weren't generalities of horror, but real and specific. The voices blamed her, accused her, told her all the suffering both her cousin and Mrs. Coley were subjected to that she could have stopped. She hated that part the most.

In those dreams, the tunnels and the voices always led her to Lakehaven Psychiatric Hospital.

As she crossed the threshold from the rock tunnel to the sterile tile of the second-floor hallway just before the nurses' station, the voices would break off as if someone had cut off the transmission. She'd be alone.

Only, that wasn't quite right. She knew that the same way she "knew" the house where she had started. She wasn't alone.

The patients' rooms looked empty as she passed them, one by one, the bed sheets turned back and rumpled impressions on the mattresses and pillows where patients should have been sleeping. Windows were open, and cool breezes brought noises like voices and crying from the outside. When she reached the end of the hallway and looked in the last room, there was a complex symbol on the wall, branches and diagonals of which extended outward. Blood dripped from its sharp, upturned limbs and formed a blackish puddle on the floor.

That was when she heard the sirens. One long, low wail was joined by another and another, strange cries from unseen patients, in the rooms she had just passed. And as she tried to run, her legs felt like lead moving through water. She couldn't count on them to move her fast enough or take her away from those rooms; they took her instead toward room 205 which, in the waking world, had once been Mrs. Coley's room. The sirens had seemed to start from that room. When she reached it, there was no one there—at least no one that she could see. The walls were wallpapered with drawings and clippings from magazines, interspersed with old photographs. Streaks of blood were smeared across it all. On the bed, the sheets had been drawn up again over a humanoid shape. Before she could move into the room, the sheets would burst into flame, the shape beneath writhing and screaming. Long, slick black appendages like spiny tentacles lashed out frantically from beneath the sheet as it turned black, burning through cotton and flesh and deeper, into meat and blood.

She'd wake up sweating, heaving out breaths that had tried desperately and failed to be screams.

Those dreams had started about a month ago with Mrs. Saltzman and her talk of the "doormen."

Mrs. Claudia Saltzman of room 211 had seen her fair share of psychiatric wards, having been transferred from Sisters of Mercy to Sisters of the Holy Rosary, and finally, as with many of her fellow patients, to LPH. She had moderate dementia which seemed to wrap her up in a fragile little cocoon of near-catatonia at times. She wore a neat blue and pink floral dress over a body endlessly creased with age and pale, papery skin. Her hair, cobweb-fine and sterile-white, she wore bound in a loose bun atop her head. When the oubliette of her mind opened on occasion to let rationality shine down, she could be incredibly smart and funny. It was hard to tell, though, from the gray-blue eyes, slightly cloudy with cataracts, what kind of day it was going to be; it was more apparent in her speech, and the expressive and delicate little ribbon-mouth.

She was old and smelled like mint and antiseptic, but Lauren liked her. She suspected Claudia Saltzman had been one wild, sexy woman in her youth—the kind who never would have stood for a man like Barry, or taken the lies and cruel words over and over. Lauren thought Mrs. Saltzman had once been, in her youth, the kind of woman Barry would have left *her* for—the kind that knew her body, her power, and her charm over others as a simple matter of course, and if others didn't like it, she just didn't care.

There were a great many things Mrs. Saltzman seemed not to care about these days. It wasn't so much that she had forgotten them. It was more like reality, to her, was a paint color into which someone (or something, if one were to hear her tell it) had spilled tendrils of alien colors. They changed the color of her own reality where they mixed, and as time wore on, less and less of that pure original color from this world was left unblended by her new world-view. For the most part, the old woman seemed okay with that. Trouble was, the pure colors fading from that world-view contained the parts of life that reminded her to eat and sleep and bathe. So LPH tried to pour traces of that pure color back into her life through pills and nursing care.

A particularly bright odd hue of Mrs. Saltzman's new spectrum, the doormen, had been old when this world was young, she told Lauren. This time they had come through a hole in space that she thought but couldn't say for certain might be located in the elevators that went up to the Electroconvulsive Treatment floor. Mrs. Saltzman was in the Geriatric Psychiatry wing south of that elevator, and claimed to see them in the hallways late at night sometimes. She claimed to often see them going in and out of room 205.

Lauren supposed that Mrs. Saltzman's hallucinations were a way of explaining what she at least marginally knew about ECT and the attendants that prepped, delivered, and returned patients undergoing such treatment. It was her experience that many of the patients who were cognizant enough of their situations and diagnoses initially feared ECT, and with Mrs. Saltzman's situation, it was likely that truths were mixed with her hallucinations. The old woman would claim that sometimes the elevator doors would open and she'd see flashes of light and see the doormen coming and going with a patient from Mood Disorders. She'd even stated they had taken Mrs. Coley with them in their comings and goings a few times.

Sometimes she'd hear sounds like sirens.

"That's how they talk to each other," she told Lauren one night. "It's their language." It was about a month after Mrs. Saltzman said they first crossed over through the elevator and the bad dreams had started—three nights after she claimed they had begun "pinching the Convergence," whatever that meant, and killing and feeding. She was sitting in a chair by the window, a crocheted blanket of red, orange, and yellow folded neatly over her lap, and her hands folded neatly on top of that. She was a small, graying thing, dust dervished up into a person for a time, her hold on form tenuous. The clouds of her cataracts reminded Lauren of clouds in a blue sky.

"How who talks, Mrs. Saltzman?" Lauren flipped on the small light near the bathroom—sometimes flooding the patients with bright lights during these night hours only served to agitate them—and moved across the room to her patient. She handed the old woman her capsules of Memantine. The old woman took them and swallowed them. Both knew the capsules would do little to separate those colors of her reality, but they did seem to help slow those colors from mixing entirely.

She took the old woman's blood pressure, checked her eyes and throat, and asked her the perfunctory questions of well-being and comfort, before Mrs. Saltzman replied, "The doormen. You know, from the elevators. The siren sounds—that's how they communicate. I think it's how they pronounce the sculpture words."

"I see," Lauren replied soothingly, although she did not see. The nurses were neither supposed to play into nor try to deconstruct the patients' delusions. "Kalia says you didn't eat much of your dinner today. Why is that?"

"Who's that?"

"The day nurse who comes to check on you."

Mrs. Saltzman made a face. "I think I can understand some of what they're saying. When they talk to us, of course, they use words. We'd never be able to pronounce the three-dimensional words, even in the siren language. But I still think I can catch a little of what they mean."

"Come now—let's get you back into bed." Lauren took Mrs. Saltzman's arm and guided her gently to her feet. The old woman was surprisingly steady. She got into bed without help, and Lauren went back and retrieved the blanket from her chair. Since moving to LPH, she refused to go to sleep without it. It was a present—a guilt gift, they were called secretly among the staff, from some relative of hers who sent checks but never came to visit.

"There now...are you comfortable Mrs. Saltzman?"

"Yes." She turned over on her side, away from Lauren, already slipping further into her own head.

"Okay, good. Good night." Lauren got as far as turning off the light by the bathroom when Mrs. Saltzman said something she couldn't quite catch.

"What was that?" She turned back to the old woman and found her sitting up in bed, those clouded eyes fixed on her.

"Be careful. They want you dead. The doormen...." she slid back down under the covers and turned away. "They killed Helen Coley. They know about your cousin and what he did. And the doormen want you dead as they are. They want to watch you die."

Lauren hovered in the doorway, her stomach turning a little. "Wha—what? Mrs. Sa.... I...."

"Go to sleep," the old woman murmured. She started humming, and before Lauren had managed to shake the words off her and get moving again, the humming had dulled to light snoring.

Mary SanGiovanni

Chapter 3

Upon arriving at Steve's apartment, Bennie Mendez ducked beneath the yellow tape and dodged CSU and the other detectives until he found Gordon. A uniformed officer was taking Gordon's statement as he sat, pale and hollow-eyed, holding a mug with a shaking hand. As Bennie approached, Gordon looked up and tears resurfaced in his red-rimmed, dark-circled eyes. The look was one of apology; he claimed to have somehow slept through the attack. His hair was a mess, sticking up in bed-head spikes, and his round chin was shadowed and in need of a shave. Both were very uncharacteristic of so neat and well-put-together a man. Those things—the look of him and the look in his eyes—made it real, somehow, more real than what his captain had told him, more real than the voice messages from his pals at the precinct, more real than the yellow tape that had been strung across the apartment doorway. It was always like that for Bennie, seeing victims' loved ones in such states of grief. It reconnected in him what he necessarily needed to detach

Bennie had wanted this to be a mistake, a case of mistaken identity or a terrible clerical error of some kind. Hell, he would have even settled for a terrible joke in poor taste, if it meant being able to walk through a doorway he had come to feel was a second home to him over the last four years and see his partner sitting up, drinking a beer and A-OK.

"He's gone, Bennie," Gordon said, unashamedly letting the tears streak down his face. The quick glance to the body bag beneath the television led Bennie's gaze in the same direction. Bennie sank down on the easy chair across from Gordon, leaning forward to put his head in his hands. Other officers, noticing his presence now, walked by with soft words of condolence and pats on the back or shoulder.

He got up suddenly and forced his legs to carry him over to Eileen Vernon. She was packing up her kit, busying herself with the clasps on the case. He touched her shoulder. She looked up. He could tell she had been crying.

"Eileen," he said, and nothing else. Neither could speak for several moments. She hugged him, fiercely and tightly, and he hugged her back, glad not to have to look into her eyes, afraid his own *machismo* would crumble and he'd begin to cry himself.

"How?" he finally whispered.

She pulled away and, without looking at him, crouched down by the body. "Don't let Gordon see again." She unzipped the body bag, and for all Bennie had seen as a cop, he nonetheless pulled back in horror and revulsion.

Bennie recognized Steve's body by the tattoo of a Chinese dragon on his forearm that he'd gotten to celebrate his promotion to Detective Lieutenant and his moving in with Gordon, both major steps in his life. However, where Steve's face should have been was a tortured mess of torn-up flesh. His bottom jaw had been torn completely away, and the places where his nose and left eye should have been were shredded and swollen beyond recognition. The right eyelid was closed, but looked caved in, as if the orb it had once protected was no longer beneath it.

"*Dios mio.*" Bennie thought for a moment he might be sick. He took several deep, silent breaths until control returned and crouched down next to her. He winced at the edge-curled smell of early decomposition and the meaty smell of blood, and something else—something vaguely reminiscent of ozone.

"Not sure what the car battery smell is," Eileen said dully as she zipped the bag back up. "I'll let you know." A pause. "This is a lot like the last two, over on River Falls Road. Concentrated injury to the face and neck. Nowhere else. No one heard a thing." The last she said with a skeptical glance in Gordon's direction.

"Time of death?" He spoke before he realized he was really talking, partially just for something to say and partially because job instinct was beginning to take over. He might not be able to detach himself from Steve's death, but he'd be damned if he didn't catch the *puta madre* who killed him.

And he had been killed; no animal attacks here to speak of. Large bands of bruising around the neck denoted strangulation, likely as his face was being mutilated.

"Some time around midnight or 1 a.m. would be my guess."

"Murder weapon?"

"Nothing," Eileen replied, the unspoken agreement that it was murder acknowledged between them.

Bennie went to stand and Eileen grabbed his arm. Her grip was tight, her eyes shining and intense. "I want you to find the bastard that did this and take care of it. Make it right," she said in a voice barely above a whisper. "No questions, no details. Just make it right."

Bennie took a deep breath and let it out slowly, meeting her eyes for several moments before nodding. "I'll get him."

He moved away to talk to Gordon when he caught a glimpse of figures in the kitchen.

They weren't dressed like cops; they didn't move like cops, either, and that's what he noticed first about them. As he made his way toward the kitchen, he also realized that no one else seemed to notice *them*. No one spoke to them. No one even seemed to have need to move around them. He frowned. There was something unsettlingly familiar about the way they looked....

Their backs were to him. They stood at the sink as if conferring over something. All three wore long black trench coats, black gloves, and black fedora hats. All three appeared to be bald, the bloodless white of the backs of their necks reminding him very much of dead flesh. As he passed through the doorway into the kitchen, he felt a biting cold all across his skin, and revulsion crawling beneath it. The three turned in unison.

None of them had a face. Bennie felt the air rush out of his lungs and a ball of ice form in his stomach. He thought of Anita and Steve, of the cold cases in the file cabinet they were all supposed to forget about.

Anita talked in her sleep; once she had dreamed of something she called a Hollower. When he asked her, she had grown evasive, and that had been answer enough. Her experience on River Falls Road at that same house where they had found the bodies of those two young people was somehow connected to the experience that had left Steve beaten all to hell and those unsolved files he had once advised both Steve and Anita to spin, sign, and forget about. The Hollowers. He knew it, felt the connections all at once, firing off paths in his mind.

The Hollowers.

"You can tell her we killed it. It isn't coming back." That's what Steve had asked him to tell Anita. They had killed the *monstruo*, the one she had been so convinced had found her, so convinced was trying to kill her and the baby. He thought of Cora, three now, and finally understood her fear.

"What are you doing here?" Bennie flipped the safety off his gun.

The one to his left cocked its head as if considering his question. The one to his right looked off into the den. The middle one spoke to him—at least, that's what Bennie assumed was speech, although it had no mouth that Bennie could see, and the voices intertwined were both high and low, loud and whispering, seeming to wash toward his ears like a tide, coming from numerous directions.

51

"We have come to bring death," the middle one told him.

"You will not interfere," the one on the right added.

"I can't help that," Bennie said slowly. "It's my job to interfere in cases like these. To stop death when I can."

"You cannot," the middle one said. "This is only the beginning. It will not be stopped."

"I can't let you hurt any more people," Bennie said. He could feel their hate radiating off them in icy waves, an almost tangible, painful thing against his tense nerves. His hand was on his gun, and his mind, while he spoke to those things, was calculating the risk of shooting at them.

"You can't hurt us," the left one said, as if reading his mind. "We are ageless, and we won't die."

"Everything dies," Bennie replied.

"*No joda con nosotros,*" the middle one said, "or everyone who means something to you we will tear apart."

"What?" he asked, his heart racing now.

Don't fuck with us, is what they had said. The blank expanses of the three figures were fixed on him.

"Detective Mendez?"

He flinched and turned to find the officer who had been taking Gordon's statement standing in the doorway.

"Mr. Wrighston asked to speak to you."

Bennie turned back to the sink. The figures were gone. He swallowed, trying to calm his heart.

"Detective?" The officer sounded hesitant, confused.

Mendez turned. It didn't look like the officer had seen the figures at all. Mendez could see from his stance and the look in his eyes that he knew something had just happened to his superior officer, but that he didn't quite think it his place to question him at the moment. Mendez didn't give him an opportunity to change his mind.

"I'll be right there." He glanced back once more to make sure those things—the Hollowers—were gone. They were.

But as he passed back into the living room, he could have sworn he heard multiple strains of voices laughing softly behind him.

***

Over the last four years, Erik had seen a lot of death. It had started with the suicide of a man he had never met, a man named Max Feinstein, who used to live at 63 River Falls Road. Following that had been the deaths of Sally Kohlar and Cheryl Duffy and Dave Kohlar, and more recently, Jake Dylan and Dorrie Weatherin. There had been others—a number of strange cold cases and open cases that the police of Lakehaven, New Jersey had yet to solve. His friend Steve had told him about those. Steve had known they were connected, and in Erik's mind, it didn't take a great leap of faith to see how. For hundreds of years, the world he knew had been a hunting ground for beings that could straddle dimensions and bend the surroundings of this Earth to mimic the worst of one's fears and insecurities. The beings were terribly strong and full of hunger and hate. And everywhere they went, they caused pain and fear and so, so much death.

Max Feinstein had called them the Hollowers. They had driven Feinstein to splatter his brains all over the back wall of his bedroom. They had killed just about everyone he knew who had fought back. And they had taken Dave.

He'd had a lot of trouble with Dave's passing; he and Dave had gotten to be good friends in the time they'd known each other. Dave had helped him fight—the urges to go back to coke, the Hollowers, all of it. Dave had, in a sense, helped him find the strength to reclaim his life, to find a reason to hold onto himself. Dave had been the connection between them all. Dave had given his life to save them from an influx of evil the likes of which none of them could begin to imagine. To say he had trouble with losing Dave was an understatement, to be sure.

And he was having trouble with Jake's death, too. Jake had been his sponsee, a little brother of sorts in the family of those recovering from substance abuse. He'd felt protective of Jake, who, like all recovering addicts, had fought for a second chance at life. As his sponsor, Erik felt it was his responsibility to safeguard that second chance, and help Jake make the most of it. But he'd failed Jake, and he hadn't even known Jake was in trouble! Why hadn't they called, especially if a Hollower had been involved? And that was the plain truth of it, wasn't it? He and Steve didn't have to say it. They were brothers in another kind of family, one where survival meant words weren't always necessary. Gut feelings and warning signs and the horrific calling cards of monsters were enough to be sure. Jake had needed him and he hadn't been there. Maybe there hadn't been enough time. And if that was the case, it added a new and terrifying layer to the situation. The Secondary and the Primary they had fought before had toyed with them, stalking them for a time before amping their power to shroud him and his friends with dangers from their own minds. He and Dave had supposed it took time for the Hollowers to build enough power in this world to attempt death blows, especially against those who were alert, aware, and waiting. This Hollower, it seemed, was swift and deadly right out of the gate.

It didn't make sense. They'd agreed to keep each other in the loop regarding any possible return of the Hollowers. If Jake was being stalked, he would have told Erik. And if the Hollower was newly arrived in this world, how could it be so strong as to kill two of them right off without warning?

The answer was there in his head—had been since the last time they'd battled a Hollower to the death. It wasn't something he'd ever told the others, because to do so had seemed cruel. It was a secret he'd felt justified in keeping at the time. But what if he had been wrong? What if keeping that secret had left Jake and Dorrie unarmed?

Erik had been stuck alone for a while in a tunnel somewhere between this world and the Hollower's mind. In the sharp, carved contour of rock, Erik had seen other worlds.

There had been carvings, garishly painted, depicting the kind of sometimes self-inflicted mutilation and violence he had come to associate with the Hollowers. Those had been horrible—faces peeled from skulls, pounds of flesh cut away for some fervent need for peace of mind. There had been a horrible depiction of a child with pain-glazed eyes whose head was a bloody mess from the bridge of the nose down, surrounded by a mural of small lips and hanging mouths hung like hunting trophies. One in particular which had made him feel sick and cold all over was a carving showing a stampeding race of tripod-beings, their pyramid faces shrieking and wide-eyed as they fled down a hill while behind them, a strange and terrible city suspended in the sky sent terrible skeletal beings in a locust rain after them. The atrocities spread along a significant length of the tunnel wall, showing the beasts devouring pieces of the screaming alien things, raping and mangling and maiming them. Another portrayed a small village leprosied by dimensional rips from which long fingers curled out, along with the first curves of heads, the first scissor-blade of leg or the tip of a crab-like claw. Dead bodies, split open down the middle as if overripe, rotted in the grass in between the buildings.

He had known then, feeling the rough rock beneath his palms, that the fear and horror the Hollowers had caused were not limited to his world, nor were they even the worst these creatures could offer. Other worlds were terrorized, possibly destroyed completely. And as the carving with the pyramid-faced creatures suggested, the Hollowers were not the only nor the worst monsters to decimate an alien world. That other doorways and other invasions of unspeakable things was possible had proved too much for Erik at the time. But as he sat in his truck, watching the gold-orange of the setting sun glance off the hood, the possibility of something even more horrible than a single Hollower seemed very likely.

"You said it was...animal attacks?"

"With odd circumstances."

"Odd how?"

Erik remembered that there had been one other thing he thought confirmed the idea. In the years that had passed since, he'd dreamed of it often, each time reinforcing the certainty that it was a language of some kind. There had been painted and carved symbols amidst ancient pictographs that actually extended from the wall, curving and swimming in and out of each other. He was sure the third dimension to the writing was significant to its meaning and understanding, a language unpronounceable by human vocal chords, maybe capturing words and ideas utterly foreign to human experience. He didn't know when he'd first seen them what they could possibly mean, but translation suggested itself in vague concepts to him in his dreams, and the meanings were always almost unbearably sinister. It was an ugly language, whatever it was, full of cosmic taboos and curses and magic older than the known universe. It was a language of monsters and demons. He sometimes wondered—only during those dreams, where he couldn't help but wonder—if knowing what that language meant in its entirety could help or do irreparable harm.

A sudden, sharp knock on the truck door made him jump. He turned to see Bennie Mendez. When Erik had been knee-deep in a coke habit, he used to run into Mendez, who had been working in Narcotics then. It had been Bennie Mendez who had dropped his skinny, coked-out ass off at Trinity Methodist Church in Wexton for his first N.A. Meeting, and although Erik had never said it, he'd always felt that Mendez had probably saved his life in doing so. He had gotten to know Mendez better through Steve, and also through Anita DeMarco, who had helped him and Dave kill the first Hollower years before. DeMarco and Mendez had a little boy who was probably about three by now, and had gotten married not too long after he and Casey had, last year. Whether through fate or coincidence, Mendez had become interwoven in his life, and that was a good thing. Erik liked him.

Judging by the expression on the detective's face, though, he could see Mendez wasn't there to see him on a social visit.

He opened the truck door and slid out. "Hey, Bennie. How've you been?"

Erik noticed the slightest of tremors in the detective's hand when he brought it up to slide off his sunglasses. Mendez looked pale and tired, bruise-colored circles cupping his onyx eyes.

"Erik, it's Steve."

Before Mendez could even elaborate, Erik saw the world swim out of focus. He closed his eyes and began counting, concentrating on the hard earth beneath his boots.

Three, four, five.... Erik opened his eyes. "Is he okay?" he asked, knowing he wasn't.

Mendez's face confirmed it. After a moment, the detective said, "Gordon found him this morning in the apartment. He wasn't...we're not...."

Erik slumped against the side of the truck. "How?"

The detective looked at him helplessly. "Nothing conclusive," he said softly. "Looks like strangulation, but there was nothing at the scene to indicate what was used."

"How did he look?"

"What do you mean?"

"His...body," Erik said impatiently. "The shape he was in. The shape of the apartment."

Mendez shook his head, and Erik could feel his hands clenching.

"I deserve better than the police runaround, Bennie, and you know it. What happened to Steve? He was strong. He had a gun. Gordon was in the goddamned apartment, for chrissakes! Tell me what was off about the scene. Tell me what you won't put in the police reports."

Mendez looked somehow relieved to be able to say it out loud. "He—his face—"

"Fuck."

"Just like Jake. Just like Dorrie."

Erik closed his eyes, counted, then opened them.

Mendez paused, then: "There are some things I need to know, man."

Erik shook his head. "I don't know what to tell you."

"Yes you do. You asked about the state of his body for a reason. You know."

"I don't know anything that can help you."

"Erik, look—"

"I know where this is going. Ask your wife." He started to turn toward the house.

"You and Steve were close. I thought you'd want to help."

Erik turned back to him, suddenly angry. "I can't help!" he growled. "I couldn't help Jake or Dorrie or Dave before that, or Sally or Cheryl or anyone else, and I couldn't help Steve, when it came down to it. Nothing I could tell you matters, because there's always another one waiting. Don't you get it? No matter what we do, the door keeps opening."

Mendez replied in an even tone, "I talked to them."

"Them?" Erik frowned.

"There were three."

The world swam away from Erik for a moment. He thought he might be sick on the driveway. He swayed a little where he stood. "Three? You saw them? Are you sure?"

"Yes. Why?"

"We've only ever seen one at a time. A Secondary and a Primary. They hunted alone. And both nearly killed us all on their own." Erik walked back to his truck, mostly to have something to lean heavily upon while he thought about what Mendez had said. "Three?"

"They didn't try to attack me, but they threatened to if I didn't stay out of their way. I could hear them and see them, but no one else could. And they barely seemed to notice me, let alone anyone else. But they told me that they've come to bring death."

"Yeah, that's what they do. They sense everything, all your fears, your secrets. That's how they find you. And they use what they know to destroy you. I–" Suddenly, Erik felt the panicky need to get away—from Mendez, from the conversation, all of it. He started back up the driveway again. "I can't do this, Mendez. Count me out. Talk to Anita, look it up on the internet, scour Steve's desk, whatever you want, but for God's sake—"

"I talked to Gordon, too, after most of the other officers had left," Mendez said. Erik kept walking, and the voice behind him continued. "He wanted to apologize to me. Can you believe it? Apologize for not being there when Steve needed him."

Erik paused by the front door, listening.

"He said he never heard Steve being...attacked," Mendez continued. "Never woke up at all. He thought the officer that took his statement might have thought he was lying about that, but I believe him. I saw those fucking things, Erik. And they messed Steve up pretty bad. Gordon found Steve's body by the television in the living room. Huge bruises on his neck—which, by the way, was twisted in a way necks shouldn't be. Something had taken off half his face, too. You're right. Steve is—was—a strong guy. A guy with a gun. All I want to know is how those things could have taken him down like that, without anyone else even hearing."

Erik turned slowly. Something wasn't quite right. "Did the wounds look self-inflicted?" At Mendez's frown he hastily added, "I know, I know he didn't do it himself. But did the wounds look that way?"

"No," Mendez said, confused. "His bottom jaw was missing."

Erik felt the world slide out of focus and he closed his eyes and counted (a trick his sponsor had taught him to get through the urges to use coke) down to three before he could speak again. "That doesn't sound like their kind of damage. They can't physically touch you. They can't see you, hear you, smell you. They don't have senses like us. They can kill—they do it well—but the deaths usually look self-inflicted like suicides or like accidents. Not like ripping off jaws and destroying faces."

"Tell me what else you know about them. Is there a way to kill them? Is there even a way to figure out who they're going after next?"

Erik shook his head and looked down and away. He didn't know. Didn't have any fucking idea what these new Hollowers were like. Didn't want to know.

Softer, Mendez said, "I deserve better than the runaround, too, Erik. You know damn well what they did to Steve and all those others. You of all people know what they're capable of. But this isn't just about them anymore. These things aren't done, and that means this could affect Anita. My son. You, too—and maybe your wife."

Erik knew he was right. He stood there, unsure of what to say, and Mendez took advantage of the pause to press on.

"I know you all went through something I can hardly begin to understand. I know that whatever these things are, these Hollowers, they scare the hell out of Anita. They killed Steve. I get that you're scared. But I'll be damned if I let anything happen to my wife."

Erik could understand that. He loved his own wife, and if she were in danger—

A terrible thought occurred to him then. Three...there had been three that first time, when the dying siren wail of the Secondary had brought them through to claim its body. Three...and at least one of those had been a Primary, bent on revenge. Those three had opened and closed the rip between his world and, ostensibly, theirs. And that thought led to another: if those carvings in that tunnel had been right, the Hollowers weren't the only things that crossed through into other worlds. If these new Hollowers were somehow stronger than Primaries, could they be the ones who made it possible for things to cross over? Did they open and close rips in dimensions at will, and manipulate any of the lifeforms of alternate worlds? If so, just about anyone could be in danger, especially those closest to the humans who had dared to kill Hollowers in the past.

Erik sighed. "Okay. Okay, come on in. I'll tell you everything I know."

Chapter 4

No matter how Lauren turned it over in her mind, the plain facts were that Mrs. Saltzman's "doormen" couldn't know anything that Mrs. Saltzman didn't know. Insanity didn't give people psychic powers. And while patients talked, and it was possible that details of Mrs. Coley's death could have made their way, however distorted, back to Mrs. Saltzman, there was no way she could have known anything about Lauren's cousin.

No one in her current life knew anything about that. No one.

"They killed Mrs. Coley. They know about your cousin and what he did. And doormen want you dead as they are. They want to watch you die."

So what had the old woman meant? Lauren meant to find out—had to. Had to.

She had tried all that day to get some sleep by squeezing the memory of her cousin from her mind, but that just made the images and the accompanying anxiety stronger. She turned from side to side to back, flipped her pillow to the cool side, tried more blankets then less, and found that sleep just wouldn't come.

Sighing in frustration, she had fished for the remote on the night table beside her bed and turned on the TV. Then she propped herself up with pillows to watch.

A home movie played on the screen, a little girl with blond pigtails and a Cabbage Patch Dolls t-shirt and pants. She frowned, changing the channel. The movie played on that one, too. She jabbed random numbers and pulled up another channel, then another and another. The same home movie, the same little girl waving to the person behind the camera (her dad), running across the back yard, laughing, tugging on the arm of a shy little dark-haired, hollow-eyed boy turned in on himself, refusing to look at the camera.

She recognized the little girl. It was her. And the boy next to her was her cousin Dustin.

She didn't want to watch, but she couldn't help it.

The home movie went grainy for a moment, and when it cleared, it was black and white. The camera, held stationary, was likely set on a tripod, and focused on a bed where the little dark-haired boy she knew to be Dustin sat in his underwear. He looked small and scared, dwarfed by the pillows his legs almost long enough for his feet to touch the ground.

"Good, good...." a familiar voice said. Lauren hadn't heard that voice in years. After what happened to Dustin, none of the kids in the family did.

She pushed the Power button on the remote but the television stayed on. She leaned over her sheets and pushed the button on the television manually, but still it stayed on. She cursed softly, the picture blurring in front of her, and leaned back.

The little boy's cheeks were damp with tears. His skinny little arms wrapped around his narrow chest. "I don't want to do this," he whispered, barely looking at the camera.

"I'm teaching you to be a man. You want to be a big, strong man, don't you? Like me?"

The little boy on the television hesitated, then nodded quickly.

"Then do it. You know how."

The scene cut quickly to little Lauren and little Dustin sitting in their favorite hiding spot under the weeping willow tree in her backyard. She couldn't imagine where the camera might be or who would be filming it—in her memory of that day, they were alone.

She pulled the blanket tighter around herself, suddenly very cold.

"Fire would be the worst, no doubt. I also think I'd hate to drown," she said. They were at that age then of kids beginning to understand the violent world around them. They had been talking about ways to die with the morbid fascination and pseudo-boldness that children talking about forbidden or grown-up things so often had. Dustin, when she thought about it years later, had been more than harmlessly interested in the topic, and a part of Lauren always felt like those talks had maybe given him ideas in which way to end things.

"I dunno. I think it might be kind of peaceful, once you got past the struggling part. Me, I'd hate to get stabbed. You see people get stabbed on TV, and they always have this look like they swallowed this big sharp rock and it's rolling around inside them."

"Ick. I can't even get a paper cut without freaking out. I'd hate that." A pause, then the little blond head tilted in thought. "I think the way to go is something quick. Falling, maybe. You just break your neck or your back, and you're gone. You never even feel it."

"I think you'd feel it. Come on, landing on rocks or something? I think it would hurt. I wouldn't want it to hurt." His voice was soft. The camera focused in on his face, the faraway gloss of his stare, the thin lips tight to keep the sadness in.

"I'm telling you, you wouldn't feel it. My dad says once you break your neck, you can't feel anything."

The little boy didn't answer. He shifted his position on the rock and winced.

The little girl, knowing and not looking at him, said, "What do ya wanna play?"

"Dunno."

"Wanna play hide-and-seek?"

"Nah."

She picked up the fuzzy caterpillar she had been watching inch its way across a rock, and she pet it gently. "We could play Donkey Kong."

"Can't. It's at my house. My dad is home." The little boy said this with the slightest tremble of disgust in his voice. He shifted again and grunted like an old man."

"You up late again last night?"

"Yup."

"He's a monster."

"Who?"

"You know."

"No, he isn't. You can kill monsters with sunlight and fire and stuff. I can't kill him."

The little girl looked up from the caterpillar. "Does it hurt real bad?"

The little boy turned his head away, but not before a close-up shot showed his eyes were filled with tears.

"I don't want to talk about it."

"You should tell. Tell Aunt Maggie."

"I can't!"

"Tell my parents!"

"No! And you can't tell, either. Promise me."

"Dustin—"

"Promise me or I'll never talk to you again."

The little girl looked uncomfortable on the screen, but nodded. "I promise." She put the caterpillar back down on the rock. The little fuzzy body didn't move. "But if you don't tell, it's gonna get worse."

The scene cut away again to a small, rocky canyon not far from Aunt Maggie's and Uncle Mark's house. A tiny broken doll lay across the jagged rocks at the bottom. The camera flashed to an orange pill bottle with Aunt Maggie's name and address on it and Diazepam written on the label, then back to the aerial view of the body. A slow close-up showed the doll to be Dustin's broken body. The bones had been knocked loose with impact, as had his right eye, which sat drying out on his pale cheek. Trickles of blood ran from his nose, his ears, and his mouth. His shoulder was dislocated, and one of his legs was twisted up under him in a way no leg should ever look. A rib protruded from the striped shirt he wore. One of his sneakers, knocked off, was wedged between two rocks.

Overhead, the clouds raced by, indicating time. The scene darkened and lightened quickly, three times, and each time, Dustin's body looked worse. Animals had chewed on him. Bugs had landed, burrowed, laid eggs. Blood on the surrounding rocks was baked brown in the sun, and looked like spilled ink in the moonlight.

It had taken three days to find him when he'd gone missing. He'd left no note. The pill bottle was what the police had used to determine his death was a suicide—he'd only taken a few of the pills, but hadn't taken them as a means of killing himself, the police surmised—he'd only wanted enough in his system that he would have been drowsy enough to fall, or high enough to jump and just not care about the sharp rocks at the bottom.

He'd had a closed coffin at the funeral. Lauren had wanted to see him one last time, to say good-bye. No one had ever told her about the condition of the body, and she'd never thought to ask.

The broken, mangled figure on the rocks sat up then, and Lauren let out a choked little squeak of terror.

"Look what you did to me. I'm going to find you, and I'm going to do this to you, Lauren. Things are gonna rip pieces off of you when you're too broken to get away. Things are gonna lay eggs in you and chew their way out. I'm gonna find you, Lauren." The TV went dark.

She'd run out of the bedroom and had flown down the stairs, then cried on the couch until she'd fallen into an uneasy doze. In it, she waited for something thin and rotting to drag its skin bag of broken bones up her driveway, to reach a half-rotted hand to the doorknob, to pull itself up her stairs, the protruding rib knocking against each one. In the dream, the broken corpse of her best childhood friend would let in death in hideous forms to chew and tear her up. She woke with a start. She left for work early. She had to know what Mrs. Saltzman knew, and how.

If Mrs. Saltzman's doormen knew something about all that, then she wanted to know how and why. She wanted to know what they wanted, what it would take to make them stop.

The following night was a Friday—the weekly staff meeting for the night shift was the first fifteen minutes' priority, but afterward Lauren made her way down to 211. She found Mrs. Saltzman sitting, as usual, in a chair by the window with her blanket over her lap. She was looking up at the stars. She didn't turn when Lauren entered, but her humming broke off and she said, "Little pieces of the world at a time." She laughed, a high, hysterical, off-key sound, and finally turned to Lauren.

Lauren thought her facial features took a moment to swing around and match up with her head. She blinked, shaking her head slightly. The lack of restful sleep was catching up to her.

Mrs. Saltzman didn't seem to notice. She was back to humming, and Lauren suspected it was not going to be one of her lucid nights. Lauren spoke to her anyway. A nurse who had overseen her work when she first started had stressed that it was important to do that. Obviously, just because patients might be in a vegetative state, that did not make them vegetables; they were still human and deserved human compassion, dignity, and respect. Conversely, no matter what quirks or tremors or sudden outbursts or utter, eerie lack of those things might happen, she was still simply in the room with another person, another human being and no more. They were no more demons than vegetables. Small tricks for re-humanizing them served to keep that in perspective when natural empathy and compassion were difficult to summon during long, dreary, lonesome shifts. In psychiatric wards, these proved especially valuable lessons.

"Good evening, Mrs. Saltzman. How are you tonight?"

The old woman didn't answer.

Lauren administered medication and checked her over and changed the sheets on the bed, adding an extra blanket from the closet because the early April night was forecast to retain a last bit of winter's chill. All the while, she spoke to Mrs. Saltzman about small pleasantries and innocuous news about other patients on the floor. And all the while, Mrs. Saltzman hummed disjointedly and watched her with those opaque blue eyes, her arthritic, bird-bone hands trembling in her lap.

Lauren was in the midst of telling her about the new ice cream flavor the hospital administration had added to the menu when, as she walked by, Mrs. Saltzman growled at her.

She paused, startled but not particularly alarmed. "Well, that's not—" She reached out to touch her arm and Mrs. Saltzman surprised her again by jerking away from her. The old woman bolted up out of her seat and moved with surprising speed and agility away from her, to the wall across from the bed. Her lower jaw dropped and from deep in her throat came a sound like a siren.

Lauren gaped at her. A number of thoughts ran through her head very quickly. Had the old woman swallowed something that was making that noise in her throat? Had she swallowed some pills that gave her that strength, new but by all bets temporary? Or was it some new symptom of her illness? If it was the latter, it was something she had never come across in a dementia patient of Mrs. Saltzman's advanced stage.

When she found her voice again, she spoke to the woman seething and hissing and growling across from her. "Mrs. Saltzman, I need you to calm down. If something is hurting or bothering you, I need you to try your best to tell me what it is so I can help. I—"

"There is something you can do for me," the old woman said in a number of simultaneous voices that weren't hers. "You can die."

"What?"

"You let your cousin kill himself," the voices in Mrs. Saltzman's mouth told her. "You let your uncle hurt him over and over. You even told him how to end it. And you think you should be allowed to care for others? You think any single one of these meat bags in this place could ever really be safe with you? How could anyone trust you? You deserve for someone to let you die. To make you die."

"No...no, that's not true." Tears blurred her vision.

The bottom jaw dropped again, only lower this time, as if it had unhinged from her head and she meant to swallow up Lauren in one bite. The old woman's pointed little chin hung down between her sagging breasts, the cavernous maw lined with impossibly long teeth. From the depths of her throat, the siren welled up again, growing louder.

Lauren pushed the panic button at her belt that alerted orderlies and if necessary, security to assist with a potentially dangerous patient. She had never had to use it before, nor could she understand why she suddenly had to with an elderly dementia patient, but she used it now more out of instinct than any real training. The vibes of hate coming off Mrs. Saltzman were thick and freezing, almost palpable, and her gut told her the old woman who most days couldn't remember how to feed and dress herself and couldn't recognize the nurses was, at that moment, possibly very dangerous.

Mrs. Saltzman's head started vibrating so fast it blurred her features, though never broke the steady wail of that siren. Lauren cried out. When the head stopped moving, holes that took up the space where her eyes and nose should have been dribbled thick blood.

Lauren bolted for the door and swung out into the bright hallway, sliding and nearly crashing to the floor. She burst into tears then, clutching the door frame. It took her two, maybe three minutes to bring herself to look into the room again, to make sure the thing that had been Mrs. Saltzman was still a safe distance away from her. Behind her, the footsteps of the running orderlies began to fill the silence.

Inside the room, Mrs. Saltzman, fragile, small, and very, very old, dozed in the chair by the window. Peaceful little snores had replaced the siren. Eyes (although closed), nose, and mouth all appeared as they should. No blood. The sudden reversion to normalcy choked off the last of the sobs, but the tears still came. They were still streaming down her face when the orderlies, their voices a cloud of noise outside her head, rushed Mrs. Saltzman's room. They still wet her cheeks as she managed to explain she was okay, that she had just panicked, that she was sorry to worry them, and as she examined the confused and groggy old woman while they watched silently behind her.

But when they were gone and everything had settled down, in the newly-resumed silence of the hallway beyond the nurses' station and the shadowed rooms of the sleeping patients, the tears did not come. Even with thoughts of her cousin Dustin, the tears did not come.

It wasn't Mrs. Saltzman who knew about any of it. It was her doormen. They knew.

They knew it all.

***

Ian stood outside his mother's bedroom, his hands on the door. He thought what he needed might be inside the room.

At daemon, homini quum struit aliquid malum, pervertit illi primitus mentem suam.

His mother's demons were shut up inside that room. And he thought—no, felt throughout the very marrow of him—that answers about his own three demons could be found in there, too.

He paused. There would be ghosts in there, too.

Since that first afternoon when the demons had appeared across the street, he had seen them everywhere—at the ends of school hallways at work, in the produce aisle at the local grocery store, amidst the sunshine and laughter of the park down the street. They watched him, heads cocked to one side, and he could feel the radiation of their hate. They meant to kill him.

That Saturday afternoon, he had discovered that they had killed his mother, too.

He had run some errands—the bank, Walmart, Home Depot—and when he returned home, his front door was open. He frowned, glancing behind him then back at the door. He made his way up the steps, but couldn't see any immediately discernible reason why his front door should be open. He'd locked the door before he left; he was sure of it.

"Hello?"

No one answered. He put the bags down on the porch. "Hello?"

From somewhere inside the house, he heard children laughing. His heart sped up in his chest. He walked inside. For a moment, he just stood in the foyer, unsure what to do. He reached into his pocket for his cell phone, considering calling the police. It was break-in, after all, and even if the culprits were only children, he still thought it better to let the police handle it.

The phone buzzed in his hand, making him jump. He looked down, but there was no call, no text. He put it on the side table by the front door.

The laughter came again from upstairs.

"Hey," he said, his voice cracking. He cleared his throat. "Hey there. Whoever you are, you better get the hell out of here." A high-pitched giggle on the edge of hysteria floated down from upstairs. From his mother's room. His stomach turned. There was someone, maybe more than one someone, in his mother's room.

"I have a gun," he said, and then kicked himself mentally. A gun? What if whoever was up there called his bluff?

"Ian? Ian, honey?"

That sick feeling rose up into his throat. It was his mother's voice.

"Ian, come on up here, honey. I want to talk to you."

"Mom?" his voice sounded very small in his own ears. He took the first few steps and paused, confused. It *was* his mother's voice.

"Ian...."

He jogged up the rest of the staircase. The upstairs hallway was empty and it was dark, darker than usual. The door to his mother's room closed. "Mom?"

He crept down the hall to the door. "Who are you?" he whispered.

"Death," voices from behind him said. He wheeled around.

The three faceless things stood at the far end of the hallway, blocking his access to the stairs.

"Oh God," he said, slumping against the door to his mom's bedroom.

"Your God does not exist," the one on the left told him. There was no mouth to speak from.

Ian eyed the staircase and considered his chances.

The middle one laughed, and it sounded like the crying of children.

The right one said, "You will die like your mother. We will tear the life from you."

Ian reached behind him. His hand felt the cold metal of the doorknob. "How do you know about my mother?"

"We bled her dry," the middle one told him. "She tried to keep us out, and we cracked her open."

"We fed," the right one told him. "Her cans and wires and silly plaster stick figures couldn't stop us."

"You killed her," he whispered. "You killed her."

"In the end," said the one on the left. "And we will kill you, in time."

The one in the middle reached out toward the wall next to him and made a motion like it was grabbing something and pulling it toward itself. The wall groaned and leaned toward the three, plaster chips and chunks exploding suddenly outward. Ian jumped and yelped, skittering away from the hole. Leaning forward, he looked into it. It seemed to stretch out and down into blackness, and from the abyss, he could hear screaming. He thought he could also see movement rising upward.

"Oh...oh shit...oh shit...."

He looked back to where the three stood but they were gone. Scraping and growling and clicking accompanied the screaming now, and Ian wanted to scream with whatever was down there, but couldn't find his voice. There was a lump of fear in his throat that choked it off.

A mass of moving, fleshy parts drew closer, and Ian found both his voice and his ability to move. He tore away in the direction of the steps and took them three at a time, tumbling out the front door and tripping over his own bags.

He collapsed in a heap on his own front walk, has hand and arm scraped and bleeding. He panted for several minutes, waiting for his heart to slow and that sick knot in his stomach to loosen.

Nothing flew out the door at him. Nothing followed down the stairs. He heard some growling, but within moments, that subsided, and the screaming snapped off completely.

It took him a long time to get to his feet and go back into the house. He listened for several moments from the foyer, but heard nothing. He crept up the stairs slowly, peeking over the landing through the bars of the railing.

All trace of the hole was gone. Nothing had come through into the hallway. He glanced down toward his mother's bedroom door and noticed it was slightly ajar. As if noticing him back, it blew shut with a tight little slam.

Chapter 5

It had been beyond the scope of time since the Likekind had seen their Origin world. The Triumvirate were the last who could remember it, and even from their earliest collective Memory, it had been a bleak and dying world. Desolate and crumbling, shifting, falling into itself, the world had been made of the same as what was inside them, an emptiness that continually pushed and pulled and stretched. Their world was likewise always pulling apart and crashing together, tumultuous and hungry. The slow and ancient races, those less than Tertiaries, had not long survived there. The Likekind had opened them and picked them dry. Their desiccated physicalities were eventually swallowed by the scorched plains, their inside-frames spiking out of the ground, reaching upward into a red sky as if pleading for salvation. None came.

The Likekind had taken to the Convergence, the soft dark cushion between worlds where there were no *sounds*, no *sights*, no hateful physicality, neither someplace nor no place but the space in between it all.

Beyond it, there were other worlds to feed in.

The Likekind had never seen a dimension like theirs in any of the Outworlds beyond the Convergence. In their collective Experience, gathered, maintained, managed, and disseminated outward by the Triumvirate, none had ever found a world in which they could replace the Origin. This was of little to no significance to the Likekind. They were predators above all, and in most of the discovered Outworlds, they had power to sharpen their hunting skills by manipulating and reshaping those dimensions as needed.

They had found, on occasion, that some dimensions were unsuitable as hunting grounds. The natural inhabitants in some were of too little intellect to form the Emotions and Distortions the Likekind could sense and absorb. Sometimes the worlds contained other predators whose strengths and intellect made them impossible prey. Those predators and the Likekind hunted around each other, sharing worlds, circling each other carefully. Some Outworlds were made in such a way as to slow or maim the Likekind by solidifying them. And there were many empty dimensions, as yet to develop lifeforms at all, or whose time had long passed when anything could live in them.

The Triumvirate had come to a dimension central to many of the Likekind's and others' hunting grounds. The meats who populated it used a *word* for it—Earth. It was their original home dimension, and the Triumvirate were fairly sure they did not know others existed (except for the dimensions they called Heaven, Hell, and Dreams—these were indeed the alternate worlds closest in proximity to their own). This Earth had proved to be something of a dilemma. The Experience of Likekind in that world had reported many successful hunts of complex prey. Three notable enticements, Fear, Guilt, and Insecurity, had proved immensely capable of quelling the black holes inside for a time. But the meats had proved themselves more resourceful. They had killed some of the Likekind—a Secondary and a Primary. The latter had once been part of a previous Triumvirate, but had left specifically to hunt the meats that had destroyed its favorite Secondary. That it had been, it turn, destroyed as well was unacceptable. The Likekind wanted the wholesale slaughter of the world and a flooding of that dimension, followed by cutting it off from the Convergence.

Only a Triumvirate could make decisions regarding the Likekind's request, and only the Triumvirate could carry out the actions detailed. Only they could manipulate across dimensions and sense the unsensible. Only they could call on the Scions, the Zxom, the *varich-har*, or the *hinshing* at will. The decisions of the Triumvirate were final and unquestionable. Their execution was unchangeable and unstoppable. Even the ancient Ones Without Names, whose amusements were the chaosium of galaxies, whose very will, uttered or thought, had length, width, and depth, who had created countless Origins—even They abided the actions of the Triumvirate, including the pinching of the Convergence when necessary.

The current Triumvirate of Primaries had wielded this power with supreme efficiency.

In the Outworld called Earth, the Triumvirate had already decided that those meats responsible would be eliminated. It was yet to be determined whether they should then pinch the

Convergence and tear open the boundaries, flooding Earth with the deadly spawn of adjacent dimensions. Should that be the decided course of action, it would become necessary to seal off Earth's access to the Convergence forever. The colliding of dimensions would mean total annihilation; better to let the course of it wipe the place clean without the threat of such carnage leaking into good hunting grounds.

To set about completing such lengthy and involved actions, they first had to feed. They had found a structure which contained a number of meats to feed on. They had also found some of the meats responsible for the death of the Primary and had eliminated them. They had only come across one unforeseen issue—the interference of a meat whose mission, it seemed, was to protect other meats. The *word*, when they got close enough to the dimension to pick it up, was *detective*.

Their objectives did not include it, but they would kill it if necessary.

In the meantime, they would pay a visit to the one this interfering meat called "wife." They believed that would serve as a deterrent. And further, the "wife" creature had played a part in killing the Secondary. It was time to strip all that it loved away from it, and watch it crack open and die.

***

84

Bennie Mendez left Erik's house feeling like he'd been hit in the stomach with a sledgehammer. It was dark by then, and the shadows he had never thought twice about between homes, inside cars, and across lawns now had taken on a sinister suggestiveness.

Casey, Erik's wife, had been making dinner when they both walked in. Mendez had met her a few times before. She was a pretty little thing, too thin for Bennie's taste but lovely nonetheless in that sweet, girl-next-door sort of way. He knew Erik was crazy about her. From the smile and warm kiss she planted on Erik's mouth when she saw him, Bennie saw she was crazy about him, too.

When she pulled away and had a moment to study Erik's expression, her eyes immediately filled with worry, her smile sagging. "What's wrong?"

"Hollowers killed Jake and Dorrie. They just got Steve, too," he said with a heavy sigh.

"Wh—what?" She pulled away.

"There are three of them."

"But...you said—"

"We thought we closed the rip for good. I don't know how they got here."

She turned, distracted, and went back into the kitchen. Erik shook his head.

"What was that about?" Bennie asked him in low, confidential voice.

Erik halfheartedly tossed up his hands. "She can't handle when this happens. I thought...last time would be the end of it."

They followed her into the kitchen. She greeted Bennie as if seeing him for the first time, then went to the stove to stir whatever she was cooking in a large black pot. She didn't seem angry to Bennie so much as preoccupied. He supposed she actually was handling it as well as she could, and given the circumstances, she was holding up; he imagined hearing the Hollowers were stalking her husband again must be something akin to hearing cancer cells had returned. It would be another brush with death, one that this time Erik might not return from.

She said very little, getting a beer for Bennie and a Diet Coke for her husband as he explained how the first Hollower, called a Secondary, had tried to drive him back to doing coke. It had been using his shaky sobriety to tear him down, to make him doubt himself and fear the future. He told Bennie how Dave had been separately seeing the Hollower, as had his sister, who had some kind of mental wrongness Erik was never quite able to get a name for. In Dave's case, it used his sister and what Dave felt were his failings as a brother to hurt him. And there were others: their bartender, Cheryl, who was reminded over and over of a childhood trauma, and the boy Sean, who used to live across from the Feinstein house and who just missed his father very much. He remembered how good it felt just to find out he wasn't alone. It was coincidence ("Or fate, or design of some other power," Erik had said in a thoughtful murmur) that had brought them together and revealed their common enemy. They had realized they were stronger together. Together, they had a chance to fight back.

Anita, Erik told him, had become involved because she was handling Dave's sister Sally's missing person case, Cheryl's intruder break-in case, and initially, the Feinstein suicide. Much like Steve, she had put the clues together and had seen that all of them were connected, not just to each other, but to other cases, as well. Bennie knew that in her spare time, she had always liked to try to tackle the cold cases in the file downstairs, especially the weird files that the rest of Lakehaven PD was more or less able, in time, to put out of their heads. It made sense to Bennie; she had gone out to Feinstein's house the night the rest of them had gone to battle the Hollower because of the connection she found between those cases and many of the weirder, more unsettling cold case ones. There was undoubtedly a connection, Bennie thought, among all the victims of the Hollowers, past and present.

He was familiar with the ones Anita had been looking into. He had, in fact, cleared them off her desk when she went on maternity leave. Those file names sprang to his mind. He hadn't even known he knew them, but there they were: Carrington, Savannah—Homicide; Henshaw, Deborah—Homicide; Peters, John—Suicide; Feinstein, Maxwell—Suicide. And there were the new ones: Weatherin, Dorothy—Animal Attack; Dylan, Jake—Animal Attack. The picture that it drew, Bennie thought, was only a corner of the full picture, a mural of death, mutilation, and horror.

Erik told Bennie the Hollower had been strong—incredibly strong (Erik had scars on his arm to prove it) and it had nearly killed them, but in the end, they brought it fully into this world and Dave had taken it down. An injury, Erik noted pointedly, to its head—to where the face would have been.

The second Hollower, a Primary, had hunted in much the same way as the first. Anita was pregnant and Sean's mother had moved him far away; for some reason, the Primary didn't or couldn't get to the boy. Mendez remembered that it had tried to get at Anita; once she had bled and they both thought she was going to lose the baby, but it had been a trick. Anita hadn't slept well after that for most of the rest of the pregnancy.

The Primary, Erik had told him, was even stronger than the Secondary, though. Its hate fueled horrible attacks on the rest of them. Jake's family and relationship history drew him in. Dorrie had body issues, from what Jake had told him, but Jake loved her—he thought she was the most beautiful woman in the world. He and Dorrie had both lived on Cerver Street, near Cheryl's old house. They had found each other before Erik could reach out to Jake to help him. He hadn't wanted to get involved again, but...he'd sighed then, and looked Mendez in the eye. Mendez understood. There were times in life where one couldn't avoid getting involved, because to do so would strike against the core of a person that makes him or her human. Erik, at Casey's insistence, had sought Jake out and offered what he knew.

Steve had become involved for many of the same reasons Anita had, but with the added incentive of wanting to stop it from trying to kill him, too. His struggles with his sexual orientation were the prime focus of his attacks. When Steve had seen the old files that oddly coincided with his experiences, when he saw the reports of Sally's and Cheryl's deaths and new reports by Dorrie of an intruder, he went looking to Dave for information. Dave, Erik explained, had always been their center in this. He never wanted to lead them, but he seemed to go by gut instinct, and that instinct always proved right.

It was Dave again who had tackled the Hollower, the both of them tumbling back through the rip in dimensions it had opened up. That had resealed it. Dave was gone. Erik, Steve, Jake and Dorrie were the only survivors.

Now, this new group of three had killed Jake, Dorrie, and Steve. If the other Hollowers' behavior was any indication, the three would pursue the rest of them relentlessly. They wanted to bring death and pain. And likely, they weren't alone. Erik had been willing to bet a kidney that other victims right now were suffering and in danger of being murdered just as they were. Just as Bennie likely was, Erik pointed out, if he was able to see them, and they were able to sense him back.

Bennie suspected there was more, that Erik was holding something back, but for now, he didn't push. What he had disclosed, much of which seemed to be crossing Casey's ears for the first time as well, was enough to swallow for one day. She sat

89

and listened quietly, but Mendez suspected there would be one long and serious talk after he left.

As Bennie drove home, he fished in his glove compartment for any stray Marlboros. He'd quit years ago, and then again for good when Anita had gotten pregnant. But *a dios*, did he need one now.

It was an incredible story—monsters, dimensional portals, manipulations of the environment. But what Erik had told him jived with what little he could glean over the years from both Anita and Steve. And he'd had those unsolved case files for a while, too. Everyone in the department had taken a crack at them one time or another; just because they had been able, eventually, to put them out of their heads doesn't mean they hadn't ever entered in the first place. The trick was not to dwell. He thought (and he considered himself counted in this number) that most of the cops of the Lakehaven police department had looked through them out of curiosity, recognized a road ahead of fruitless obsessing, and put them back. Those files—the department had come to call them the Weird NJ files, because someone had been a fan of the magazine—had elements that made it so that no rational explanation would ever fit. The officers on the scenes of these cases had spun the events with as much "real-world" as they could, signed off on them, and filed them. This method of handling whatever was wrong in this particular area of New Jersey had been passed down from senior to rookie for decades. It was only questioned until that rookie landed a case for the file him- or herself.

His hand closed around a small tube—but it was a pen, not a cigarette. The next one felt more papery to him, and excited, he withdrew it from the glove compartment. It was bent, the tobacco stuffing protruding from the break like straw from a tiny decapitated scarecrow. He frowned, snapped off the broken part, and stuffed the filtered end between his lips.

That the number of Weird NJ files was growing was also something no one talked about. Even Hollowers couldn't account for all that bizarre death, all those missing people. And that, Bennie suspected, had something to do with what Erik hadn't told him. But Bennie was a detective first, and he had been taught to follow the leads he actually had first. He would see to tying up loose ends after.

He didn't see the shambling thing in the road until he was almost too close to stop. The nub of cigarette unlit and forgotten, he flinched, wide-eyed, muttered a curse in Spanish, and slammed the break. The back end of the car fish-tailed a little but the front bumper stopped short of the hairy hide of the beast in the road.

He was pretty sure he hadn't hit it, but it wasn't darting away like the usual local wildlife did, either, high on adrenaline and fear, sensing how close it had come to death. In fact, it wasn't moving at all. Bennie put the car in reverse to put some space between him and the animal and get a better look at it.

He bit back a shout. The thing in the road was unlike any animal he'd ever seen. It had a massive, hairy head with wide, fur-covered plates for cheek and snout bones that fanned out toward the front like an axe blade. The head hung from a thick neck whose jagged vertebrae sprouted from the growth of wiry brown hair all the way down its back in a bony ridge. It had no apparent eyes or ears, but what looked to be a number of noses, deep nostril pits opening and closing as it swung its head in front of the car. Its stout, thick legs upheld a compact, shaggy-haired body that arched up in the back and ended in a bobbed tail. Its paws were massive, front and back. Long black talons scraped at the asphalt. It picked up its head and roared.

Bennie's first instinct was to hit it over and over again with the car. He wanted to; looking at the thing filled him with revulsion. He was afraid its massive head and up-curving bulk would damage the front end, though, and he'd need the car to escape. It looked solid, the kind of animal that killed with pure brute strength. He felt sure, although he had no reason to at the time, that as slow as the thing was now in exploring the front bumper, it could be fast if it wanted to. If it were chasing prey, for example.

He backed the car up a little more, very slowly.

The massive head swung in his direction. The heavy lower jaw dropped and Bennie could see rows of thick ivory teeth. From between them, a long red tongue, barbed on the tip, stretched lazily outward. The many nostrils flared. Then it screamed, high and loud, and charged the front end of his car. The thud jarred loose an immediate headache. It charged again, and this time, the whine of crumpling metal spurred him to action. He slammed on the gas and the car, still in reverse, leaped backward.

The thing swung its massive head from side to side as if shaking off the impact with the car. Bennie took the opportunity to turn the car around, hoping it wouldn't decide to charge him while the car was sideways. It roared again from down the road. He swung the car around so the thing was behind him, threw the car into Drive, and checked in his rear view mirror.

It was galloping after him. For such stumpy legs, it was moving surprisingly fast.

Bennie let out a little choked cry and hit the gas again. The car shot forward.

The back road he was on, like many in Lakehaven, was flanked on both sides by tall and densely packed trees. The road itself wound through the trees and around the small hills and pockets of water connected to the greater lake. He'd been called out plenty of times to scenes where kids had been taking those curves too fast in the dark and had folded the front ends of their cars around nearby trees. Bennie took them now at 55, even 60. The thing behind him, galloping and growling and huffing, never slowed. The road dipped and his car lifted into the air, landing hard and throwing back gravel. He swung around a turn and came within inches of the guard rail. A quick glance in the rear view showed the beast was still following him.

Finally he shot out onto the main road, narrowly avoiding a gray Sedan that honked and swerved around him. He glanced back toward the side road.

The thing was gone.

He slowed down, looked behind him, and looked in the lane to his left, but there was no sign of the thing. Whatever had been there had either turned back to the safety of the backwoods gloom or had simply disappeared.

Erik had warned him that hallucinations were a tactic of the Hollowers. *"Except they aren't hallucinations, exactly,"* he'd said. Others might not be able to see them, but they were real and could do real damage.

He thought he ought to call Anita and check on her when his cell buzzed in his pocket. He reached for it, noted the home number, and pushed "Accept."

"Anita?"

"No," a mingling of voices from the other end said, bordering on hysterical with glee. "She's with us, but we called to talk to you."

Immediate panic seared his stomach. He thought of Cora and Anita corralled by those things, and helplessness burned into anger. "Stay the fuck away from my family. They haven't done anyth—"

"First we're going to wring tears from those swollen orbs in their heads. Then we will crack them open and feed on them. Then, we will come for you."

Before Bennie could respond, the connection went dead.

He cursed, slamming his fist against the steering wheel and picking up speed. If they had hurt Anita and Cora, he'd never forgive himself. He couldn't live without his girls.

He floored it, checking occasionally in the rear view to make sure he wasn't being followed.

***

It had been a tough decision for Anita DeMarco Mendez to decide not to go back to work after maternity leave at the Lakehaven Police Department. Growing up, Anita had never played with baby dolls. She wanted to be a police woman like her father, not a housewife like her mother. It wasn't that she didn't love her mother or respect her for all that she did; she just saw how exhausted her mother seemed to be, cooking and cleaning and picking up, doing the wash and checking her homework. Her father was tired, too, at the end of the day, but Anita didn't see the day-to-day minutiae of his job that got him there. She didn't see the hours of phone records to pour through, the hours of legwork knocking on doors and trying to wrestle kernels of information from reticent witnesses. What she imagined her father exhausting himself doing was fighting crimes, catching bad guys like on TV. And she wanted to be just like him when she grew up.

If either of her parents had discouraged her, it might have been a bumpy road. But her mother beamed with pride that she wanted a career as a police woman—as a detective, like daddy—and her father, never one to extinguish the light in his little girl's eyes if possible, taught her little tips and tricks to help her sharpen her case-solving skills. Both parents watched her draw careful little chalk outlines around her Barbies on the driveway, or around a fallen elephant or floppy dog, and then interrogate a row of stuffed animals. They watched her line up her brother's GI Joes and Star Wars action figures and ask his Million Dollar Man which of the line-up had hit him with their car. As she got older, her father would set up little crime scenes for her, hiding clues throughout the house for her to find that would lead her to the culprit.

Anita had loved being a detective and was good at it. But she had found, somewhat to her surprise, that she enjoyed being a mother as much as she had ever enjoyed being a detective. The pregnancy had been discovered during their second year together as husband and wife; it had been unplanned, but Bennie had been so excited, so proud, that it went a long way in allaying her fears about it. He meant to take care of her and the baby. Although she was not a woman accustomed to or comfortable with the idea of being taken care of by a spouse while she assumed a role of housewife and mother, Bennie could and would assume the role of sole provider if Anita needed him to. Their captain was an old friend and flexible enough that whenever cases allowed, he could give Bennie extra hours or ease up on the work load to accommodate both he and Anita being new parents. And he had unwavering faith that she would be an excellent mother. The same gut instincts, he'd tell her, that made her a good cop would make her a good mom.

And she'd tell him, only half jokingly, that if their infant was a homicidal maniac, then sure, she was ready to rock. But otherwise, she wasn't sure how the two could form a parallel at all.

Bennie would laugh, the soft, warm chuckle he had for intimate moments with her, and tell her their baby would be fine and strong and good, and that the instinct—knowing when to protect, knowing when to follow up, when to check on a detail, a little thing, and when to believe—all those where things parents all over the world wished they had the innate ability to do. Her natural instinct as a cop, that ability to observe, assess, and act accordingly, would make her just as good a mother. And her big heart, her compassion, would bond her to that child and its needs in a way unlike any she had ever experienced. And he had been right.

That Bennie Mendez could be a smart *hombre* when he wanted to be.

Being a mother wasn't about hunting a predator. It wasn't about solving the little threads of mysteries that braided themselves into a larger mystery in an open case to be solved. It might be in ten or fifteen years, or hell, maybe even in four or five before parenting got to be like that. But for now, it was often about observing a little person unable to give information crucial to its survival and well-being, other than by little non-verbal cues. And as she observed this little person and interacted with her, the subtle nuances of those cues—the kind of cry at night or the gurgle during the day—became clues to help her know when to feed the baby, change the baby, make her warm or keep her cool.

Plus, the baby had been breathtakingly beautiful, if she did say so herself.

From before she had ever met Cora, Anita had loved her. Once she was born, Anita fell in love all over again. She loved the little blue eyes, the soft and sweet-smelling wisps of hair, the teeny-tiny fingers and toes, the way she smiled (Anita preferred to think of it as smiling, even at that young age, rather than gas). And the oath to protect and serve had whole new meaning now.

When she did have occasion to miss grown-up conversation, even the bawdy talk of the guys at the department, she could consult. That made the decision to stay on permanent leave a little easier. So did Bennie's unflagging support in whatever she decided. But the final sway was that little Cora had two parents who were cops. That meant the possibility of losing both parents, both of whom had been field detectives. Lakehaven was not a hot seat of crime, but it could certainly be a bed of weird, and in the end, Anita didn't want Cora to ever worry that she could lose them both. She could assure that, barring acts of God, at least one parent would be safe.

She couldn't have accounted for the bloody mess under the sink, and what it meant to their safety inside the home.

She had just gotten Cora down for the night, and the baby monitor on the counter captured and reported the reassuring little snores and coos. As she moved toward the pile of dirty dishes sitting in their foamy pool in the sink, she noticed the mess on the door of the cabinet beneath.

Anita stopped short, frowning.

The oak door had across its front surface what looked like a gaping wound, torn and tender flesh, bloody beneath swollen black and blood-clotted masses of tougher hide. It reminded her a bit of a shotgun wound, if such a wound were to begin festering during the healing process. She crouched down to examine it and was nearly knocked back on her haunches by the putrid smell of rot, a sickish yellow smell, an over-sweet organic smell that triggered sharp gagging in her. She grabbed a dishtowel off the oven door handle and held it to her face, leaning in as close as she could stand.

Her first thought was that she had just changed Cora, who was mostly potty-trained except for overnight, and there had been no wounds on her. And so far as Anita could tell by quickly examining herself, she wasn't hurt, either. Bennie? If he had been hurt enough to leave such a mess on the door, how could she not have noticed? And how could he have not gone to the hospital?

They were natural thoughts, but not particularly practical. They couldn't explain the gore hanging plainly from the door in front of her. The wound on the cabinet door oozed something phlegmy, with thick black strings in it. Tumorous little growths grew, expanded, collapsed, and grew again somewhere else. And with all the movement, blood pumped in little rivulets, pattering onto her kitchen floor. It was a fresh wound, not the aftermath of an injury to someone in the household. And for the same reason—

the movement of the fluids beyond gravity's necessary drip—ruled out some wild animal having broken in and somehow crashed into the door, or having been injured outside, died there.

Maybe something had grown on the door and died or spoiled. Maybe she'd spilled something that had taken root or fed whatever had been growing, and—

That notion sounded ridiculous to Anita. But then, she supposed it was no more far-fetched an explanation than the obvious one staring her in the face—that there was a bloody laceration on her cabinet door, as if the door itself were made of gangrenous flesh and blood instead of wood. And she didn't care how "custom" Country Custom Cabinets were willing to go—she was sure they didn't make cabinet doors that oozed and bled.

She rose slowly, the towel limp in her hand, her gaze fixed on the viscera. She had to call Bennie. She had to—

She heard a knock from the other side of the cabinet door. Another, and another. Three short, controlled knocks, as if a small hand were entreating entrance into the kitchen from the space beneath the sink. That idea seemed less absurd than grotesque and terrible. She hovered there, half-way between her cell phone on the counter and the cabinet door, unsure what to do, when the three short knocks echoed again.

Feeling a touch ridiculous herself, she said, "He-hello?" It was not her cop voice. It was a tiny, unobtrusive thing she barely knew. "Hello?" No other response followed beyond the wound spurting a small arc of blood that pattered a few pattering inches away from the door.

The mother part of her and the cop part of her were in agreement; get Cora, who she still so often thought of as "the baby," go to the neighbor's, and call Bennie. But another part of her, a part she hadn't seen surface in a good five or six years, seemed to have the upper hand. That part brought her down into a crouch again. This time, she used the towel to touch the handle, easing open the cabinet door.

That part of her had to know.

Beneath the sink, the gloom formed itself into familiar shapes—the curving pipe, a box of steel wool pads, an unopened package of sponges, a bottle of drain cleaner. No little hand.

She exhaled a sigh of relief. No little hand. Maybe she hadn't heard the knocking coming from inside the cabinet at all. Maybe it had been some weird acoustical trick, or—

She peered around the cabinet door. Acoustical tricks wouldn't explain the mess on the front of the door.

But that was gone, too. The faint curdled smell of rot still lingered, but that was dissipating, too. She closed the cabinet and stood up, still staring at the unblemished oak. What the hell had just happened?

"Hello, Anita."

The voices from behind made her jump and she whirled around, but her brain knew even before her eyes took them in what she'd find. She recognized those voices—the mix of tones and strands, the insane energy, the chilling hatred that saturated every word.

Three Hollowers stood in the doorway of her kitchen.

The world grew white around the edges and that white threatened to swallow up everything in her view. She dug her fingernails into the palms of her hands until the pain made the world bright and fresh again. Every fiber of her wanted to scream, needed to scream. She didn't. Maternal instinct kept her silent. If Cora woke up, a part of her mind reasoned, they would be able to find and hurt her before Anita could get to her and protect her.

"Get out," she whispered. It was all she could manage.

Their laughter filled the room like a poisonous gas. It was everywhere, inside and outside her head. "We're not going anywhere," the middle one told her.

The right one added, "But you are."

Chapter 6

Bennie tried Anita again on the cell. It went to her voice mail for the fourth time. He tried the house line again, and that, too, went to voice mail.

"Damn it!" He thumbed "End" and dropped the cell into his lap. He hoped it was just that they both were asleep (very unlikely, after his multiple calls) or that Anita was busy settling Cora down (more likely). He looked down at the dashboard clock. Its light green glow printed 8:45 into the darkness. It had been twenty minutes. He didn't know how fast the Hollowers traveled, but he still had another eight minutes before he hit the driveway.

He tried the cell again.

***

Anita considered the possibility of getting around them and making it up the stairs to her daughter. Between the three of them, they were blocking access to both the dining room and the living room. If she ducked out the back door and came around the front and up the stairs, she'd lose time. Furthermore, the front door was locked.

As she considered those things, the Hollower's words finally sank in.

"We're not going anywhere."

"But you are."

"No," she finally answered, more to stall for time than because the import of their suggestion had been fully realized. "No, I'm not going anywhere."

"You can't protect her," the left one told her.

Anita's heart beat faster. She forgot that they knew her thoughts.

"She's already dead," the right one said. The faceless head turned toward the baby monitor.

Anita listened intently, studying the video. There was no movement from the bed, and no sounds.

Tears immediately sprang to her eyes. "Leave my baby alone."

"She stopped breathing," the left one said. "It happens sometimes with little ones—especially those whose mothers are too busy messing around under the kitchen sink to hear the little choking sounds."

"Little ones are so fragile. So...hard to find," the middle one said. "But we found her. Oh yes. With just enough pressure, those little chests cave in. Those little lungs collapse. So fragile."

The baby on the monitor's little video didn't move. No sigh, no stir, nothing.

Rage, fear, and pain so intense that it made her chest ache flung her forward. She screamed then, running to the monitor, shaking it as if she could jar some life loose and back into the baby. She breathed Cora's name, barely audible, over and over.

Hoping to make a break in their line, she threw the baby monitor at them and it crackled and vanished into the air between them. She charged them, intent on pushing past them if need be and running up the stairs to Cora. She could save her. She would save her. She crossed the kitchen in two strides.

And then she, too, crackled in the air between them and disappeared.

***

Bennie reached the driveway, pulled up next to Anita's car, threw his into "Park," and bolted for the front door. His hands were shaking, but he managed to get the keys in the door. He needn't have bothered; the front door swung open easily.

Inside, the house was shrouded in shadow and unearthly quiet.

"Anita?"

"Up here," she called. "In the baby's room."

Relief flooded Bennie. He took the stairs two at a time and ran to Cora's bedroom. He found Anita in the rocking chair next to the bed, her head bowed. She rocked slowly. In her new big-girl bed, Cora cooed in her sleep.

"You and the baby-girl all right, *mami*? Everything okay?"

"Everything's fine," she said without picking up her head.

Bennie went to the bed and looked down. Cora was on her back, her little eyes closed. She shuddered, sighed, rubbed her little nose, and went back to sleep. He put a gentle hand on her to feel her warmth, feel her little chest rising and falling. He stroked her soft, pudgy little arm.

To Anita he said, "I was worried. I tried to call you a bunch of times on your cell and the house phone but you didn't answer."

"Everything's fine," she repeated, but to Bennie, her voice sounded off.

"Annie?"

"Everything's fine," she said again in that same flat, emotionless tone.

"What happened, Annie? Look at me," he asked in a soft voice.

She looked up and had no face.

"Oh Jesus!" Bennie jumped, scooping up Cora from the bed and backing away from the Anita thing in the chair. Cora stirred and issued a sound of discontent before going back to sleep in his arms.

"What did you do to Anita? Where is she?" he barked at the thing in the chair.

"She's in the closet," it told him gleefully.

"She's under the bed," a voice came from behind the window curtains.

"She's gone to where the monsters live," a voice from under the bed said.

"What did you do with her, goddammit?! What did you do?" Real panic rose in his chest, filling his throat. God, oh godohgodohgod....

"She's gone," the thing in the chair told him. "We've given her to...pets."

"You sons of bitches, if you hurt her—"

"*Todo lo que usted amor será arrebatado,*" it cut him off, its voice razor-sharp with hatred.

He turned with Cora and flew back down the stairs, grabbing Anita's keys. As quickly as he could, he put Cora in the baby seat, his gaze constantly checking the upstairs windows, the front door, the property around him for signs that they were coming for the baby, too. There was no sign of them. No sign of Anita, either.

All you love will be taken away.

He would not let that happen. He would find her.

Satisfied Cora was secured into that contraption—he had never been good with working the baby seat—he closed her door and slid into the driver's seat. As he peeled out of the driveway and headed for Erik's house, he thought he could hear faint strands of laughter following him down the street.

***

Lauren didn't tell anyone what had happened with Mrs. Saltzman, but she started seeing things around the hospital the very next night. What she saw was worse than the dreams.

There were about twenty patients on Lauren's floor. After lights-out, she and another night nurse, Mila Robinowicz, split the rounds. Lauren supposed the dreams were taking their toll; when asked if she was okay, she had told Mila she hadn't been sleeping well lately, and that her nerves were frazzled. By the other nurse's expression, Lauren could see that this story didn't sit well, but Mila was not one to ask questions. Mila was a hard-working, efficient woman, full of form and business-like in manner, but she had a narrow streak of compassion that emerged from time to time. They had a good system, she and Mila; Lauren covered for her when she went on break and vice versa. It was when Mila was on break that Lauren had what she was coming to think of as a mini-nervous breakdown regarding Mrs. Saltzman, and by the time Mila got back, Lauren was too shaken to talk about it.

She had always found the breathing, the snoring, even the occasional shouts in one's sleep from the patient rooms soothing in a way, especially when Mila was on break. It reminded her that she wasn't alone in the big stone building in the woods. It served to remind her that the world was right as it should be, and that all that were in those rooms were sleeping patients. Living, human patients making living, human sleep-sounds. It was when those sounds stopped that next night that she felt her muscles tense and her stomach knot, and a cool sweat break out over her.

Mila was fifteen minutes or so into her break and the sudden silence on the floor caused Lauren to look up from the book she was reading. She was startled to find every one of the patients' doors standing wide open.

It was like the dreams. Oh god, it was just like the dreams.

She put down the book, rising slowly. After lights-out, the patients' rooms were kept necessarily locked for their safety and hers. She had a set of keys and so did Mila, and the doors were only unlocked one at a time during their rounds. She had done the last check, and was sure she had locked each of the doors.

Hadn't she? Of course she had. And the doors closed on their own hinges automatically, so even if she hadn't locked them, there was no way she had left them all open.

She crossed around the desk in the nurses' station, paused, went back for a letter opener, and moved around front again. She stopped. *A letter opener—really, Lauren?* she thought to herself. She was a professional. She didn't need a letter opener to investigate...what, silence? She was being silly. The doors all being open...maybe it was some kind of electrical short. Maybe that accounted for the sudden silence, too.

Maybe. Right. Maybe the doormen were messing with the electricity.

She made her way slowly down the hall to 201, aware of how loud her echoing footsteps were as she walked. At the doorway to 201, she peered inside. Mr. Skolnik was sleeping peacefully on his side, snoring a little. Nothing in the room seemed out of the ordinary to her. She eased the door closed and locked it. It was the same situation in 203, with Mr. Fiorelli curled tightly around his pillow. Nothing amiss. She closed the door and locked it.

Room 205 was already closed and locked—the only one, so far as she could tell. Helen Coley's old room, still unoccupied. She considered unlocking it, just to check inside, and decided against it. She moved on. In each case, she found all as it should be, and she closed and locked each one. Satisfied, she turned back toward the nurses' station and stifled a little scream.

Now, the door to room 205 stood wide open.

Electrical short, my ass. Something is wrong here. Her heart sped up in her chest. "Shit," she whispered. She crept down the hall. "Shit. Damn it, Mila, where are you?"

The clock at the nurses' station read 2:50 a.m. Mila had another ten minutes.

Lauren closed her eyes and opened them, bracing herself to look into room 205. She half expected to see some figure, corpse-pale, hollowed-out sockets where the eyes should be, the skin around the mouth blackening with rot. Of course, her mind pointed out with cruel stolidity, if it were the corpse of Mrs. Coley, then the whole of the face, stripped of skin down to raw muscle, would probably be black with rot, crawling with blind, squirming, legless things. Lauren's stomach lurched, and she pushed that thought out of her head.

Mrs. Coley would not be in there. Mrs. Coley had been put in a coffin, hermetically sealed in a tomb, and buried six feet under the earth of the local cemetery roughly six miles away. There was no way she would be standing in that room.

Taking a deep breath, she turned the corner.

It wasn't Mrs. Coley standing in the room, but she hadn't been too far off in expecting a corpse. It was her dead cousin Dustin, still twelve, sitting on what used to be Mrs. Coley's bed. A part of Lauren wanted to run, but she couldn't. Her legs felt heavy, detached from her.

Dustin looked crooked, jarred into the wrong shape. His right shoulder was out of whack and the left side of his ribcage gnawed down to the bones. Looking at his face made her queasy. It wasn't just around his mouth that was decaying, but the whole of the lips rotted off, and most of the bottom jaw was exposed bone. The skin had fallen away on his left wrist, and the cheek and eye socket portion of his skull was crushed on the right side. Over most of his head, what little hair and skin was left slid around with oily ease on his scalp. One of his eyes was missing, but that was not nearly as bad as the other, a ball of clouded white denser than Mrs. Saltzman's cataracts. Most of his nose was gone, too, and each time he inhaled—he seemed to have kept the habit of breathing, even if only for the sake of habit—the air whistled through the hole in his face.

Lauren gagged but willed herself not to throw up, not to get woozy. She took several deep breaths and was repulsed to find the air tasted waxy, unwholesome, polluted by the rotting thing on the bed.

"Lauren, you let me die."

"I didn't," she choked. "You're not—"

"You knew what my dad was doing to me. You could have done something. You could have helped me. Instead, you let me die. Now look at me."

"Dustin, I tried! I tried to tell Aunt Maggie what Uncle Mark was doing, but—"

"You suck!" he shouted, and stuck his tongue out at her. Bugs crawled in and out of the holes in that blackened slab of meat, wriggling underneath its swollen surface. Lauren gagged again.

"I'm going to make you feel what I felt. I'm going to leave you to die. And ain't no one going to help you. You're alone. You're going to die and all the crazy goddamn animals around you in this place—" he gestured, "they're all going to find you and eat you. They're going to pick your bones clean."

Lauren felt the blood rush from her face and neck, and again she had to fight to keep the world from going black. "Leave me alone," she whispered, "whatever the hell you are. Just leave me alone."

She closed her eyes again and opened them, and Dustin was gone. Standing by the window were three figures Lauren could only assume were Mrs. Saltzman's doormen. They wore black clothes, long black trench coats, black hats, just as Mrs. Saltzman described them. None of them had a face. The one on her left tilted its head as if studying her. The one on the right raised a glove and tightened it into a fist.

"Are you...the doormen?" The word "Hollower" came into her head, though she couldn't fathom why.

"We are death," the one in the middle told her in a string of interwoven voices.

"What do you want from me?"

"We thought that was apparent," the one in the middle answered. "We want you to suffer, and then die."

"Why?" Hot tears spilled from her cheeks. She wanted get away, but still, her legs wouldn't move.

"Because," the right one said, opening its fist again, "it sustains us." Immediately there was a moan from the bed. She turned, and then there was the form of Mrs. Coley, pale and naked, trembled uncontrollably on the bed. A torn mess in the stringy flesh where the mouth should have been parted to release another long moan. The figure sat bolt upright in bed, eyeless craters fixed on her.

The jolt was too much; the world dissolved in gray and then black, and as hard as Lauren tried to swim against that tide, it overtook her. She collapsed in a heap in the doorway.

In the other rooms on the second floor of Lakehaven Psychiatric Hospital, the real world resumed. Patients snored and moaned and shuddered in their sleep. In the vacant room of 205, nothing but Lauren's ragged breathing and a strange chorus of faint maniac laughter broke the silence until Mila came and found her on the floor.

***

Ian couldn't go back into the house just yet. He'd spent the night in his car and the better part of that day out, and as a result, his neck and back ached and he wanted a shower and a change of clothes. But he couldn't quite work up the nerve to go into the house, to see his mother's bedroom door and remember what had opened up beside it.

His gaze trailed to the glove compartment.

Once, it had made him proud when people said he had a mind like his mother. She had been so brilliant. Now, he was afraid his mind was more like hers than ever before.

Even his train of thought was similar. He glanced at the glove compartment again.

It wasn't fair. He wanted to be happy. He might never be great with women or the life of a party, but he had a small group of intimates he was happy to call true friends. He'd never be rich, but he loved the classics of literature and enjoyed teaching them to honors students at Bloomwood County College. He had so much life before him, and it didn't seem fair that the one thing that had gotten him by all his life, from talking his way out of getting beaten up by bullies to job interviews to spirited discussions that had solidified his relationships—that one thing, his mind, now seemed to be turning on him. It had begun showing him things that weren't there, giving him ideas he shouldn't have. It wasn't fair.

The gun in the glove compartment had been his father's. It still worked; a month or so before, he'd taken it into the woods and shot a few cans off of rocks just to make sure. He didn't want to go out like his mother had, but he refused to waste away into a blithering idiot, either. When he came right down to it, he'd rather die with the memories and thoughts and knowledge he loved still somewhat intact than live on in a world of confusion and disjointedness.

He opened the glove compartment and took out the gun, turning it in his hand in the scant moonlight that came through the car window. It was amazing how such a small thing could do so much damage to a person. One shot—that was enough to obliterate someone permanently.

Reluctantly, he put the gun back in the glove compartment. He looked at the upstairs windows. No one moved behind the outdated curtains. Nothing in the house seemed to be moving now. He opened the car door and got out, shuffling toward his front door like a man on his last mile to his execution.

He had left the front door unlocked; it swung easily inward and he stepped inside.

So far so good; nothing came to greet him. No laughter. No voices. No slithering, slimy things from deep lightless abysses. Just his front hallway.

He climbed the stairs to the second floor hallway and followed it to his mother's bedroom door.

"Those aliens at the bank—see there, it's right there in the mail—they want this house. They want to take it away from me, baby, but you and I, we won't let them, will we?"

A painful knot formed in his throat as he paused at the door.

He'd read up on schizophrenia and how it caused sense and logic and simple peace and security to deteriorate in a person's mind.

"No! Leave those alone!"

"But ma," he'd told her. *"All these cans and stuff aren't sanitary. You have to—"*

"They keep the men from the other dimensions from getting through. Those, and those." She had pointed to the plaster bones and horns sticking out of the wall in odd arabesques. *"Trust me."*

That had been the problem, hadn't it? He couldn't trust her. She couldn't trust herself. And he had always felt guilty for knowing that, and being frustrated by it—by her.

He'd been angry at her for being crazy. He felt terrible about that now, but it was true. And the night she'd killed herself, that night she'd called and told him about the alien men without faces, the ones spying on her thoughts and eating her feelings, he'd hung up on her.

Now he thought she might very well have been pleading with him to help her with a very real problem. And he hadn't listened. The stack of papers to grade, including the one he thought he was going to have to submit to the dean as possibly plagiarized—that had weighed heavy on his thoughts. His electric bill, which he was about two weeks late in paying had been on his mind as well. His flat tire, the drip in the upstairs bathroom faucet, and Carryna's advances (where they advances, or had it been wishful interpretation?)—those things had all been on his mind. And after an hour of talking to his mother while juggling dinner and hearing her talk about monsters because she had started refusing again to take the "poison pills" the nurses at the Lakehaven Psychiatric Hospital gave her, he got frustrated and angry. And he'd hung up on her.

And so, feeling alone and helpless to fight those things, she'd disfigured herself (so they would find no use in taking her face, her doctor had assumed, based on counseling sessions), and then she'd hanged herself in the basement of the hospital.

He eased open the door and stepped into her bedroom for the first time since the funeral.

The room was as he remembered it, as it had been when she slept there. The white molding and trim had dulled and grayed along the edges. The light blue bedspread and pillows and a rug of blue patterns entwined with cream were faded, stained in irregular patches by God only knew what. The newspapers taped to the windows cast a sepia hue on the room as the sunlight filtered through them. On the wall across from the bed and the walls to either side, elaborate symmetrical symbols in plaster reached out like long white fingers toward the center of the room. They meant nothing to Ian; they were just a part of her fevered delusions, a language of shapes only she understood. Identical sculptures reached down from the wall toward both night tables flanking the bed, where soda can towers strung together with copper wire sat like miniature Mayan temples, collecting a fluffy layer of dust.

He lifted the lid of the small box on her dresser in which she kept her jewelry, thumbed through the pictures of his father home from Nam and his parents at their wedding. The pictures of himself he scooped up and tucked beneath the jewelry box. It bothered him to see pictures from a time of security taken too soon away from him.

The large brown box of her possessions sent to him from the hospital sat on the bed where he had left it, still sealed with packing tape. A velvet-thin layer of dust coated the top.

What he needed, he supposed, might be in there.

That his mother had had schizophrenia was undeniable. That she was a danger to herself and others had been proven fact. That she might not still have been right, in spite of her illness, about her hallucinations of faceless figures spying on her thoughts and eating her feelings, faceless figures he thought he was now seeing himself—well, that bore looking into.

He opened up the box and poked through the contents. He took out her hairbrush, her folded blue terry-cloth robe, her ID and hospital papers, and some underthings and set them aside on the bedspread. There was a small hand mirror which he also set aside on the bedspread. Beneath that were some of her drawings from art therapy, a few newspaper clippings, and a journal.

The art pictures were actually not bad; there was a finger painting of a clown, a watercolor landscape with a red sky, pinkish clouds, and severe-looking distant mountains layered pink and gray like the Grand Canyon, and a pastels rendering of the hospital and grounds which made somewhat surreal use of the white highlights and gray shadows. There was also a pencil drawing of a faceless humanoid figure. On the back was a date, and the word HOLLOWER written in careful block letters.

He studied the figure in the picture. It was exactly like the three he had seen outside—the blank oval of a head, the black fedora hat tipped low, the black featureless clothing. He tried to remember if she had said anything about these—he flipped the paper over again—these Hollowers, anything that might have colored his own hallucinations. He couldn't remember. He didn't think she'd ever used that word before, and he knew he had never seen this picture. But there is was, a tangible illustration that matched what he had seen exactly.

Looking at it captured on paper like that made it real. Neither of them had hallucinated at least that much. The Hollowers were real.

He set aside the drawing for later and looked through the rest of his mother's things.

The newspaper clippings seemed random and mostly innocuous, at least at first glance—an ad for Pantene Shampoo was folded in half and poked through with little holes the size of a sharpened pencil point; a Family Circus comic strip had been partially colored in with colored pencils; and a Hints from Heloise about getting red wine out of silk had exclamation points drawn in the margins and random words underlined, double-underlined, or circled. There were a couple of actual news articles, too—one about a detective's promotion to Detective Lieutenant, although the name (Corimar) was unfamiliar to him, one about the disappearance of another man (Kohlar) who Ian had never heard of some four years ago, but none of those seemed connected, so far as he could to tell, to her experiences with Hollowers. He found an article about a missing little girl from over a decade ago that looked promising; he skimmed it, but it didn't mention anything about the Hollowers. He found some magazine pictures she had clipped and taped together on the back to form a kind of collage. He knew they did a kind of art therapy with newspaper clippings, where they chose pictures at random for their room that helped them express themselves. It showed a clipping of leather-bound books lined up on a shelf, a daisy in the sunlight, a fluffy little puppy. There was another picture of daisies, a bouquet (they had always been her favorite flower), a picture of the Egyptian Pyramids, and one of the Sphinx. Across the bottom of the last two, she had scribbled "Library" and "Knowledge is the drink that quenches the thirst of the soul." There was a picture of a silhouetted couple standing on a moonlit bridge under a canopy of stars and a mother hugging her young son, under which she had printed in round letters: IAN. It made him sad to look at the collage. It was like some part of her knew what a brilliant mind she had once had, and how it and so much more had been taken away because of her illness. On some level, she knew she wasn't right in the head, and that she mourned the life her insanity forced her to leave behind.

He also found one other news article about a house for sale on River Falls Road, on the other side of town. That last one puzzled him the most. He couldn't imagine why she was interested in a property other than her home; her desire to protect her own real estate exceeded the level of obsessive, as do all consuming notions in a schizophrenic's mind, and he'd already had an apartment he was content with, so he doubted she had been looking at houses for him.

Beneath the papers, he also found a roll of tape.

"Get me my supplies! Hurry! Get me my tape."

His mother's wide-eyed rant just before she cut him played back in his head.

"Ian, I need my tape. Hurry. They're coming. They'll get in through the windows. Get my...you're not Ian. Who are you, and what are you doing in my house?"

Ian closed his eyes for several minutes, waiting for the anger to pass. It didn't. He threw the tape across the room and it bounced off the wall below one of her hateful plaster outcroppings.

At daemon, homini quum struit aliquid malum, pervertit illi primitus mentem suam.

Strangely disappointed at the largely fruitless effort so far, he flipped open her journal, hoping to find something in those pages.

He spent the next two hours reading, and when he was done, he set off for Lakehaven Psychiatric Hospital.

Chapter 7

Erik answered the door to Mendez, wild-eyed and disheveled, a cranky toddler bundled and gripped tightly against his left shoulder.

"She's gone," he breathed, and his eyes shined wet with unspilled tears. "They took her." He pushed in past Erik, lightly bouncing Cora in his arms to soothe her. He looked frantic.

"Who?" Erik already knew. He didn't want to hear it, didn't want it to be true, but he knew.

"Anita," Mendez confirmed. "She's gone. Erik, what am I gonna do? I have to get her back."

"Okay, calm down and let's figure this all out. Come this way." Erik led Mendez, by way of the kitchen, where he grabbed a beer for Mendez and a Coke for himself, into the den. They sat down on opposite chairs. "What happened to her?"

"I don't know." Mendez's voice was low and shaky. He took a big gulp of the beer. Cora snored lightly in his other arm.

Erik frowned. "What do you—"

"She's *gone*, Erik. They took her," he repeated. "I don't know where she is."

"But...but they don't—I mean, they can't—"

"They did." Mendez looked down at his daughter. "They were with Cora when I got home. I don't know what I would have done if...." His voice trailed off and for a moment, Erik thought those tears he was holding onto were finally going to fall.

Looking at her, Erik said, "You want to put her down somewhere?"

Mendez considered it for just a second before shaking his head. Instead, he put the beer down on the nearby coffee table. He wrapped both arms around his baby in a protective embrace.

"Anita's tough," Erik said after a moment. "She's strong. She wouldn't have let them trick her. What, exactly, did they say to you?"

"They told me she was 'where the monsters live.' That they had 'given her to pets' or something."

"What the blue fuck does that mean?"

Mendez's voice sounded strained. "Was hoping you could tell me. You're the expert."

Erik ran a hand through his hair and sighed, leaning forward in the chair, his elbows on his knees. "I don't know. Like I said, I can't imagine where they could have brought her. Sally was a different story."

"Sally Kohlar? Your friend Dave's sister? They took her?"

Erik nodded. "We found her at the Feinstein place. I guess when the Hollowers have to retreat somewhere in this dimension, they go to where they opened the rip. The only person I know of them ever actually taking was Sally, and it made sense, I guess, for it to have taken her to that house. That's where it was hiding out. That's where its rip was."

"How do you know? Where their current rip is, I mean?"

Erik shrugged. "We started where the killings started. Two for two, that worked."

Mendez shot up out of his seat, startling Cora in her sleep. "Well, let's go, then! It's got to be the Feinstein house. That's where Jake Dylan and Dorrie Weatherin were found."

At the mention of their names, Erik felt a pang. To Mendez, he said, "Now hold up a minute. We can't just go charging over there."

"Why not?" Mendez's impatient tone echoed his hurried glances toward the door.

"Lots of reasons. First, there's no way you can bring her. No way."

"Maybe Casey could watch her," Mendez cut in.

"Second, we don't even know if Jake's and Dorrie's...deaths...were the first this time around."

"Well, where else? I can't think of anything. I mean, I'm the police. I'd know if there were other deaths connected to this."

"Would you?" Erik asked softly. "If you didn't know to look for a pattern, would you?"

Mendez paused, sinking slowly back to the chair.

"We don't want to waste time going somewhere Anita isn't," Erik continued. "So think about it for a minute. You have any weird cases prior to Jake's and Dorrie's? Anything you put in those—what do you guys call them? The Weird NJ files?"

After a few minutes, he said, "A suicide." His voice was so soft that Erik barely heard it, but it was there. Mendez had something.

Erik prompted him for details. "Whose? Where?"

Mendez looked up at him. He seemed to be remembering something now. "Her face," he finished the thought out loud, and then for Erik's benefit, said, "A fifty-something patient over at Lakehaven Psychiatric Hospital. Collridge...no, Coley. Coley. She mutilated her own face before hanging herself in the basement." Mendez swallowed hard, his tanned cheeks grown pale. "She was a schizophrenic. Her son said she used to claim faceless demons were trying to cross dimensions to get her. God...."

Erik was reminded of that old saying: *Just because you're paranoid, that doesn't mean they aren't out to get you.* Out loud, he said instead, "There will be a lot of red tape at a psychiatric hospital. Can we get in and look around?"

Mendez rocked Cora, who was mumbling tiny unhappy half-words in her sleep. He wondered briefly if toddler-nightmares were enough for the Hollowers to sense. He hoped not.

To Erik he said, "I have the card of the night nurse on duty that night in the file. We can talk to her."

"Good. Stay here the night, then. Get sleep. Tomorrow night, we'll go."

Mendez frowned, the protest all over his features. "Why not tonight? Anita—"

"We need a plan. We need rest. We need a safe place for Cora. Anita would never forgive you—or me—if you went half-cocked without seeing to those things first."

Mendez, still not thoroughly convinced, nodded anyway. "Can we stay here?"

"Wouldn't suggest anything but," Erik said.

***

Lauren was brought back to the world by the sharp odor of ammonia. She opened her eyes to see Mila above her, waving a smelling salt under her nose. She found herself lying on the empty bed of the room in whose doorway she had lost consciousness. She assumed Mila, with the help of one or two of the orderlies, had found her, picked her up off the floor, and put her on the bed. Standing next to Mila, mirroring her look of vague concern, was Dr. Stubin, who was on call that night.

After shining a quick light in her eyes and asking her a few questions, he pronounced her okay and said, "You fainted. Mila found you by the door there. You been sleeping okay?"

"Actually," she said, "I haven't." Her head hurt, she guessed from impact with the floor, and her face hurt—her cheek, just below the left eye. She felt jarred all over. "Why?"

"You mumbled something about nightmares just now. And if you're not sleeping or eating, that could have caused you to pass out."

She sat up, which sent a sharp spike of pain through her head. She winced. "I'm okay. Just some bad dreams, is all."

"Would you like glass of water?" Mila asked in her stilted accent. She was tall, well put together, with hair dyed a coppery red. Her face was pretty but mostly inexpressive. She watched Lauren expectantly.

"No, thank you—I'm fine. Really. I just—"

Just saw monsters in here, and a dead patient, writhing and mutilated, on this bed.

At the memory of the latter, she suddenly found lying down unbearable. She struggled to get up. "I just need to get back to work."

The other two let her aside, their expressions conveying that they didn't quite believe she was fine at all.

"I'm fine," Lauren repeated, ducking her head. As she walked away, she could feel their eyes on her back.

"You're sure you don't want to go home?" Mila touched her arm. Her concern, seemingly lacking in her face and voice, was evident in her touch.

Lauren stopped to consider it; the thought of hours of watching the patients' bedroom doors, hours of waiting for something else to happen, for the hallways to change and for corpses to call to her and monsters to threaten her, almost made her crumple to the floor again. But then she thought of going home alone, of the empty quiet of her apartment, and of Barry's clothes neatly folded and piled with his boxed-up things, and she shook her head.

The rest of the night was quiet, aside from Mr. Turner having a bad dream and Mrs. Meyers complaining the dead people wouldn't stop shouting from over some non-existent suburban fence and were keeping her up and didn't they know what time it was? Lauren wanted to answer that the dead that afflicted the people at LPH had no compunctions about making themselves heard, so keeping up little old ladies wasn't a big concern, but she didn't; when a nurse started holding conversations with patients about their perfectly reasonable delusions involving the noisy dead, it was time to check into a room there herself.

When she left early the next morning, there was a man waiting outside the doors to the main entrance of the hospital, clutching a large spiral-bound notebook. Lauren was aware of him out of the corner of her eye and vaguely recognized him, but her mind was elsewhere. She passed him without a second thought.

"Ms. Seavers?"

Startled, Lauren turned, hesitating. She didn't think it was wise to stop for strange men at such an early hour, but he had a kind face, young enough to look innocent, and a slight build that she assessed she could take on if she had to (provided, that little voice in her mind told her, he didn't have the strength of the hopelessly and criminally insane).

"Do I know you?" Her body tensed as he approached. He seemed to sense that, and stopped a few feet away.

"I'm Ian Coley. I think—I mean, I understand you were one of my mother's nurses when she was a patient here?" This was presented as more of a question than a statement; Mrs. Coley's son had not visited often, and stayed just under an hour on the occasions when he did visit, so it was no surprise to her that he might not know the staff well who had cared for his mother.

"Yes," she told him, trying to keep her voice even. "Yes, I remember your mother. I'm so sorry for your loss. She was a sweet woman."

The young man looked down and away from her. "Thanks. Uh, I was wondering if I could ask you a few questions about her stay here. And about her things—I mean, the things you packed up from her room and sent to me."

Lauren hesitated again, and Ian said, "Not here, I mean. I could follow you to a well-lit and well-populated diner, if that would make you feel better." He offered her a weak smile which faded as he seemed to realize something. "And, I mean, if you're not busy—"

She nodded tightly. "No problem. Follow me."

***

During the lightening, the Triumvirate pulled back to the Convergence to decide on the place called Earth. They did not need so much sustenance as any individual member of the Likekind, their union giving them strength, but they had nonetheless fed in that world. In spite of the noxious physicality of the place and the bombardment of assaults on crude senses, in spite of the appallingly commonplace practice they had of touching each other, the meats of that world made good prey. The Triumvirate understood the Secondary's and the Primary's preference for hunting there—those meats had complex and conflicting sensations and notions wrapped often in their mindsounds, complicated emotions that for a time could keep the twisting and churning inside them at bay. It was necessary to cultivate a number of them at one time, to learn *words*, those foul utterances of sound, in order to dig out sustenance from those awful fleshy shells, but the output was satisfying.

The oddity the meats thought of as "baby" the Triumvirate could not quite understand, other than observing how the implication of harm to it produced greater amounts of Terror and Guilt in two of the meats. It was somehow connected to a range of useless emotions the Triumvirate did not understand and did not care about. They found it difficult to sense "baby," but gathered it was something more important to use as leverage than to destroy. They thought they had used it effectively to that end, and in doing so, had catalyzed their decision regarding the others.

As for the meats who posed a threat to the Likekind, the solution seemed simpler than initially proposed. They could pinch the Convergence as they had done with the one and send those specific meats elsewhere. There were other places where even the meats' meager abilities would not save them, they could feed on them, and then the kinds that inhabited those places would make quick work of them. They could observe and reap the delicious Fear, Insecurity, Anxiety, and Pain for themselves.

There was rarely dissent among the Three, and this decision was no different.

The meats were, during the lightening when they thought they were safe, making plans to find the Triumvirate, to come to them during the next darkening. This was acceptable.

The Triumvirate would wait, and when the meats came, the Vengeance of the Likekind against them would span dimensions.

***

The surreal aspect and events of only a few hours before seemed to lose some of their hold as the sun broke soft over a pink horizon. Lauren and Ian sat across from each other in a booth at the Lakehaven Town Diner, each with a cup of coffee in front of them—Lauren's with milk and sugar, Ian's black. Neither of them had ordered food, having no appetites, Lauren supposed, for their own personal reasons. Ian had made a few attempts at initiating his reasons for wanting to talk to her, but their conversation became hushed with the approaches of the waitress or the passing of other early-morning patrons. Ian's demeanor gave the impression of tightly reigned-in irritability at being interrupted, and so after the first cups of coffee were served, the waitress gave them wide berth.

"It's about my mother," Ian began, almost as if he were picking up where he was in his thoughts. "She was a patient at Lakehaven Psychiatric Hospital for a while."

"Yes," Lauren said, sipping her coffee. "So you mentioned. I remember her. She was a nice lady."

An expression crossed Ian's face that Lauren couldn't quite read. "She was...unwell."

"Most of the people who come to us are," Lauren answered softly.

Ian took a few sips of his coffee before continuing. "What I'm going to say is probably going to sound as...unwell, I guess, as the things she used to say. But it's important for me to establish to you that I'm telling you about something real. I thought I was going crazy, too—I really did. But I've recently begun to believe that it may not just be me. And my mother may have been accurate about some of her perceptions."

Lauren wasn't sure what to say to that. Faced with hereditary insanity, Ian could be trying to justify his own onset of symptoms. Or he might be trying to force a reasonable explanation of his mother's hallucinations and behaviors where reason just didn't fit. But beneath these logical first impressions, Lauren's gut instinct told her she knew where this was going. She didn't know how she knew, but she did.

"My mother," Ian continued, exhaling slowly, "believed a number of paranoid delusions. She thought the people at the bank who collected her mortgage were ravenous creatures made mostly of mouths and fluttering wings but disguised as human beings, who wanted to devour her home and her belongings. She thought the government had put airborne microchips into the heating system for her to inhale that would help them track her. She thought she could keep out cancer-causing rays from alien satellites by pasting newsprint over the windows. And I never once questioned those things because I believed they were clearly delusions. Even as a little kid, hearing those comments she would make that would be just slightly off, just slightly skewed somehow, even then I knew her perceptions were wrong, that the world didn't quite work the way she thought."

He took another long sip of coffee, seeming to collect his thoughts and order them. At last, he seemed to gather enough courage to continue. "Lately, I've had...experiences which I can't explain. Experiences which seem to coincide quite closely with one—only one—of her delusions. Closely enough that I finally went into her room and went through her things. I hadn't been in there, see, since the funeral. And the box LPH sent after she...after her death was still sitting on the bed."

"What experiences were you having?"

The waitress came by and refilled their coffee cups. When she had moved a safe distance away, Ian said, "I've been seeing bad things. Bad people. Well, not really people. I mean, they don't have faces and—"

Her reaction to this must have been obvious, because his face suddenly filled with concern and he reached out to touch her hand. "Are you okay?"

She opted for the glass of water beside her coffee and took several long swigs before nodding. "Please, continue."

Hesitantly, he went on. "I started seeing them after my mother's funeral. I don't know what they are or where they come from, except what I feel about them, which is mostly hate—very cold, very dark hate—and what I read about them in my mother's journal. She called them 'Hollowers.' A lot of what she wrote in that journal was tangential theories—the delusions, blooming into other delusions, decaying into obsessive thought and rebuilding themselves as new ideas. It was hard to follow. But I read the parts about the Hollowers a couple of times each. See, in those passages, there was coherence and consistency. Those passages...well, they made sense.

"In her journal, she described decades' worth of death and disfigurement, complete with seemingly incidental newspaper clippings taped inside. I missed those clippings at first because she'd separated them from the other ones loose in the box and taped them to the back cover of her journal, then marked them. A1, A2, B16, that sort of thing. And throughout the entries regarding the Hollowers, there would be these little inline references: 'Ref. A1.' And A1 would be about a woman discovered dead in her back yard with her face cut up and her neighbors baffled. I mean, she really had a pretty detailed cross-referencing of her information. You'd almost have to believe...."

He sipped his coffee and continued. "And she also referred to individuals, mostly by initials, who she claimed were having the same kinds of experiences with these Hollowers as the people in the articles were. As she was. She was terrified of them. She wrote that they weren't from this world, weren't even fully in it—but that they could act on it in terrible ways. That they knew things, and could show you things. Horrible things. She wrote that they're dangerous, they're ageless, and they're unkillable. I think...I think they killed my mother."

From his body language, it looked like he was bracing himself for scorn and disbelief. Instead, Lauren took a chance and told him the truth. "I've seen them."

Ian looked stunned. "What?"

Lauren, her stomach roiling now with coffee soured by the grave information he had given her, said, "At the hospital. In your mother's old room. They threatened me tonight—I think they were going to kill me."

Ian's eyes narrowed. "Are you humoring me because you think I'm crazy?"

She leaned over her cup to meet his gaze. Her voice was low and level. "There are three of them. Black hats, gloves, and clothes. No faces. Voices like a chorus in hell."

Ian swallowed, nodding slowly.

"What do they want?"

"I don't know," Ian said. "I think they just want to kill us. I think they're just pure evil. I don't know if they have a reason—if they even need one."

"Was there anything in your mother's journal about how to stop them?"

"No," Ian said. "But I sought you out tonight because she wrote that there were others in the hospital who could see them. I thought you might be able to tell me who. And she wrote they passed into and out of this world through 'doors that weren't doors' in her room."

"The doormen," she murmured, and when he asked her to repeat herself, she shook her head. "You're right; at least one patient can see them, besides me. And that was just something she calls them. They don't seem to bother her, but she knows about them. She can see them."

"So...can you get me in tonight to see my mother's room? I'm sure there are answers there. I can't imagine what we would find that you wouldn't have already come across, but...I just need to see for myself. I need to know. If there's some kind of doorway that lets them in, maybe we can shut it and keep them out."

"I can get you in," she said. "Meet me at the front entrance at 10 p.m. That's when I go on break. I can get you past security that way."

Ian breathed a sigh of relief. "Thank you Ms. Seavers —"

"Lauren," she said.

"Lauren. Thank you so much." He smiled at her.

"What would you have done if I didn't believe you? If I had thought you were crazy?"

Ian thought it over a moment and then shrugged. "I don't know how to explain it, but I knew you wouldn't. I knew I could confide in you. I felt it."

"Same here," she said. "I knew...I knew I could trust meeting up with you."

"Maybe," Ian said, "there's something in the universe that protects us from the evils of other universes."

"It's a nice thought," Lauren replied non-commitally.

***

"Don't leave me," Casey whispered into the pillow. It sounded like she wanted to say something else, but didn't.

They were lying in bed, her back against his chest, his arm around her. He could smell her hair, feel the lithe curves of her and her warmth. He never wanted to let her go.

"Baby, I'd never leave you. You're my wife. I love you more than anything in the world."

There was a pause. "You're leaving tomorrow with that detective."

When he began to explain, she cut him off gently. "I know you have to. I know these...things...are back. I just worry that...that they'll take you from me. I just...I finally have you back, after so much. I don't want to lose you. I want to hold you and kiss you and make love to you. I want to share things with you and take care of you. I want to know that you'll come home to me in the evenings. I want to have a family with you...." This last she said hesitantly.

"I want those things, too," he said into her hair.

"Really?"

"Really."

There was a pause and then she said, "I had no idea how much you went through, with those...things."

"It's okay. I'm all right. Everything'll be okay." He wasn't sure what to say to her or what she needed to hear, and he didn't like that. He wanted to make everything better.

"These things really mean to kill. And there's no changing their mind. I...I guess I understand about the baby. I didn't before, but I guess I do now. I...I don't know what I'm trying to say, really, except that I love you, and no matter what you need to do, I support you. I'm just scared. I'm really scared."

Me too, he thought, but out loud he said, "I'm going to make it right—for good this time. I want a good life with you. I don't ever want you to regret marrying me."

"Oh baby, I never would." She snuggled closer to him and he gave her a squeeze and kissed the top of her head.

They were silent for a while and he thought she might have fallen asleep until she said, "Please come back."

He wrapped his arm tighter around her, pulling her close. A hundred fears ran through his head.

He said, "Not even Hell could stop me from coming back to you."

Chapter 8

Bennie lay awake most of the rest of that night. He kept checking on Cora, not just to make sure she was still breathing, but to make sure she was still there. When he did drift off into light and troubled dozing, he had dreams about Anita. In them, the skin of her face was being flayed by demon creatures and she was screaming. Her blood sprayed the walls, the ceiling, the floor, the front of her tank top as she whipped her head back and forth in an attempt to get away from the razored tentacles biting into her skin. Bennie was helpless to rescue her; in the dreams, something had ripped off his arms and legs and propped his bloody stump against a wall. He cursed and wailed in Spanish while an inky cloud ebbed and flowed and lashed solid tentacles against Anita's face, and strips of skin, pieces of nose or lip, and an eyelid were ripped away and tossed to the stone floor below her.

When he awoke, sweat made him damp and cold and his stomach turned over, queasy. When he dozed again, his dreams continued, the high-pitched, tense laughter of many unearthly voices mingling with Anita's screams.

By 6 a.m., he had fed, changed, and dressed Cora, played tea-time with her and her stuffed elephant Officer Trunk, and sat back down on the couch where he had insisted on sleeping, watching the clock with an impatient fidgeting. Cora was talking to herself, immersed in whatever story she was telling herself and Officer Trunk, so he turned on the TV and tried to watch the infomercials until regular morning news programming kicked in. His mind only half-recorded the reports of foreign unrest, domestic policy, and domestic unrest. There was a plane crash and a missing toddler found crushed to death in her step-father's basement; there was a new medical study on the cancer-causing effects of vegetable pesticides and the cancer-preventing effects of additives and preservatives; there was a CFO indicted for embezzlement and a celebrity who had overdosed as a result of doctor-shopping.

None of it mattered to Bennie. He just wanted his wife back.

By 8 a.m., he was itching to call the nurse from the Lakehaven Psychiatric Hospital, but he knew it was early. He thought about Anita, lost in the folds of space, a void of the unknown, and his stomach lurched. Did she have her gun? Was she hurt? Was she conscious? He knew her pretty well, and thought if she had left Cora with those nightmare *monstruos*, she couldn't have been in any capacity to fight.

He glanced at the clock, and noticed the minute hand had creaked its way to the two: 8:10 a.m. He could wait an hour, maybe. An hour before calling.

Erik was downstairs and making coffee for them by 8:30. They went over a tentative plan, and that made Bennie feel a little better. They would call the nurse and tell her they had to see Mrs. Coley's room to finish off the paperwork on the investigation into her suicide. If Anita was somehow there, sandwiched in between this world and another—if there was some way to get to her through that hospital, that room—Benjamin Horatio Mendez would find her.

At 9:30 a.m., Bennie began calling the nurse. He got her voice mail: *Hi, this is Lauren. I'm not home, but leave me a message and I'll get back to you as soon as I can.*

He left a message. He left his cell number. He told her it was urgent. He waited.

After three hours of silence, he called again and left another message. This time he mentioned Mrs. Coley, and the necessity of his stopping by that evening to look around so he could close his case.

Again he waited. When he got out of the shower, he saw he had missed a call and swore in Spanish. He went to the voice mail and thumbed the PLAY MESSAGE button.

"Hello, Detective Mendez. Um, this is Lauren Seavers, returning your call? I—"

***

"—just got your message, and of course you can come around tonight. I'll be there from 7 p.m. on," Lauren said into her phone.

She chewed on her thumbnail. She had just returned home from her coffee talk with Ian Coley to discover a thinly controlled, terse series of messages from Detective Benjamin Mendez regarding the very room and woman who had been the subject of conversation not that long before.

"Please come. Um...yes. Yes, I'll see you then. Bye." She hung up the phone. A policeman there might not be such a bad idea. The thought gave her a small measure of peace about the night to come. She was afraid of whatever she and Ian Coley might find in that room, whatever the godawful monsters haunting and twisting it into a den of pain and death might have planned for them if they knew. It occurred to her that maybe the presence of other people—authority figures like the police—might somehow chase those creatures away. It was a naïve thought and she knew it, but she didn't like the idea of facing down monsters with no plan and only the son of a crazy woman as company. Any measure of security was better than none. She had been taught since childhood to trust policemen like her Uncle Henry. They protected people. They restored order. They made the world a little more real, a little less chaotic. She believed that, with the wholehearted and sincere eagerness of a child. She needed to right then.

And if nothing else, policemen had guns.

Yes, she would most definitely feel better with Detective Mendez there.

***

"—I just got your message, and I know what you're planning. I know what you want to do. And I'll kill you," was the message,

144

just barely audible beneath a wind tunnel's worth of static. "I'll kill the baby. You'll never be able to protect her, just like you couldn't protect your wife. You'll die if you interfere, Detective. You, and all those you love will die." By the end of the message, the words had decayed into a multitude of voices now familiar to him.

It threw him at first, the way the voice he remembered had changed into something else, something inhuman. And it scared him, the hate and hostility, the suggestion that he had failed his family. The latter ate into him worse than the former. He had failed Anita in his mind; he hadn't been there for her when she needed him. When both his girls needed him. And now, he might never find her.

It also worried him that anything he and Erik planned, those *putas* would know. They knew, even when they went to wherever they went when they weren't hurting people here.

They knew he and Erik were coming. Well hell, let them know; let them throw out their threats. Let them open up hell if that's what they wanted. He meant to have his wife back, no matter what.

***

Ian collapsed on the bed, exhausted. His limbs felt like dead weight. His mind was burdened with thoughts of those creatures. The Hollowers, his mother had called them. His heart was heavy with thoughts of his mother. And interspersed with these thoughts in both his heart and his mind were thoughts of Lauren. She was beautiful. To him, she was what music would look like if it had a body, what a season would sound like if it could speak. He'd been easily taken with her, and therefore, now included her under his umbrella of worry. He hoped he'd done the right thing in contacting her, and that he hadn't made things any worse—for him or her.

At that moment, he wanted to stop thinking and stop worrying. He just wanted sleep, a few blessedly peaceful hours of uninterrupted oblivion. And that seemed within his reach, so much so that when he first heard the woman calling his name, he discounted it as being part of a dream.

She kept calling, though, and by the fourth or fifth time, the voice began to pull him back from the edge of sleep.

"Ian...."

"Five more minutes," he told the familiar voice.

"Ian, baby, where are you? I need you to get my supplies."

"Mom, I'm sleeping. It's—"

It's my mother's voice, he thought, and beneath the surface of twilight sleep, an alarm bell went off in his head.

"You've got to get my supplies. I need them—hurry!"

He sat straight up in bed. Both the voice and the urgency behind it had echoed in this house many times before.

"Mom?" His voice sounded small and scared, just as it had those years ago when he realized the person who had spent nearly two decades taking care of him was now completely unable to care for herself.

He had never been afraid to be alone with her until the night the hospital people came to pick her up.

"Get my tape! I need my tape."

He slid off the bed and padded into the living room. It was where he'd found her that night, frantically trying to hold newspaper over the front window with one hand and rummage for tape in the nearby desk drawer with the other hand. Her head had been bleeding over the left eye, her nose was running, her knee looked swollen, and her eyes...when she'd finally looked at him, those glassy eyes saw someone else, someone she hadn't recognized, someone alien and dangerous.

He'd gone to call the hospital under the guise of retrieving her supplies. She'd gone to get a knife out of the wooden block on the kitchen counter under the guise of promising to go take her pills. Honesty between them had long since crumbled; what was there to being honest when reality itself was always such a fluctuating thing?

She had cut his arm and nearly speared his rib cage before he managed to wrestle the knife from her. The hospital staff who'd come to pick her up found a crumpled, middle-aged woman half-dressed and shrieking about her tape and bloodied up kid looking shocked, sad, and terrified. She'd screamed obscenities at him as they took her away, blaming him for letting the government take her for dissection to find the alien pieces they kept putting inside her.

The scene unfolding in his present-day living room was different. She was there in the room, as he had been half-expecting and utterly dreading, but she just sat on the couch, spaced out as she so often looked on her pills, pale, veiny hands folded in her lap. To Ian they looked like two large, dead moths. She leaned slightly to the left. She did not look up when he came in.

He felt his stomach clench at the sight of her. "Mom?"

She didn't stir. Those dead moths didn't flutter.

On some level, a voice in his head screamed against what his eyes were seeing, screamed for him to get out of there, to leave that apparition and get out of the house. The voice told him she was not, and in no way could be, his mother. And yet the thing on the couch looked like her, smelled like her perfume, even breathed like her.

"You left me," it said to him.

"What?" The words were icy and he felt the sting of them.

"You left me there." It looked up at him. "To die."

"No! No, mom, I—"

"Look what they did to me," she slurred. "Look at me."

"Mom, I—"

"How could you? They killed me and you weren't there! You didn't stop them! You left me here and forgot about me!" The skin of her face began peeling around her hairline, and she dragged her nails across it, leaving long bloody furrows.

"Please, mom, you—"

"You wanted me to die! You hoped for it! You probably sent those things after me so you could get rid of me and be free! You felt free when I died, didn't you? Didn't you?!?"

She had never gotten up and yet somehow she was closer to him, up in his face, those dead moths now angry blanched boulders. Flaps of the facial skin she had loosened hung down into her eyes. She tore a them, dropping them in wet little clumps at his feet. The muscle beneath was red, pooling with blood as she worked her jaw and eyes.

"This is your fault! Your fault! Your fault!"

"Stop it!" He couldn't take anymore. He bolted back to the bedroom, slammed the door shut, and locked it, just as he had countless times before. Let her keep the crazy out there with her—and the guilt, and the embarrassment. He didn't want any part of it leaking in toward him.

He closed his eyes. *It's not my fault*, he told himself, then whispered it out loud to try to make it true. "It's not my fault."

He sat up, wide awake, locked in his room until it was time to leave for the Lakehaven Psychiatric Hospital.

***

The Triumvirate watched from an empty chamber inside the structure where they had opened the rip as each of the intended meats arrived in their ground conveyances. First came the female who spent most of the darkenings there, tending to other meats. Next came the intruding one, and the one they recognized as the destroyer of the Secondary and the Primary. Finally came the last one, the spawn of their first prey in this world. This close, the Triumvirate could hear their mindsounds teeming with their noisome *words* for things—so many words, words for everything, words that identified those concrete things in their physical world. In the structure where they waited, they could understand the words "nurse" and "detective" and "teacher" indicated their roles among other meats. There were words for more abstract and broadly defined roles, too: "father," "wife," and "friend." These were more difficult to understand, but in many ways, more significant to their prey.

They could see how the Likekind before them could grow tired of such a world, where to understand so much of the world was to understand its effect on their base senses. The meats were sensitive to words. Words caused these beings Pain, Guilt, and Doubt. They caused Insecurity, Jealousy, and Despair. The act the meats called "lying" could do a great deal in getting them to produce desired sustenance. But the meats had so very many words, and some of them worked against the Triumvirate. Some of them produced an opposite effect. When that began to happen, it was time to move in and decimate.

Still, for as noxious as words could be, they were useful in the hunt. So close to the meats, the Triumvirate had everything they needed to tear into the souls of the meats.

One thing the Triumvirate found interesting was that the meats even had a word for the Likekind. It was understood the word "Hollower" meant one of them. It was a word for which there were many delicious Emotions, primarily Fear. They liked that.

That darkening, they would feed well.

Mary SanGiovanni

Chapter 9

When Erik and Mendez arrived at the nurse's desk on the second floor of Lakehaven Psychiatric Hospital, the nurse he assumed to be Lauren Seavers and another young guy were already there. They'd had no trouble getting in. Mendez had flashed his badge to the night guard on duty and explained he needed to follow up with Ms. Seavers regarding the suicide of patient Helen Coley, and the guard had waved them in without question. Erik supposed the guard had called up to let Ms. Seavers know they were on their way, because the expressions of the nurse and her companion gave away their worry.

Mendez seemed to draw the same conclusion because he put on a smile as warm as he could make it and said, "Ms. Seavers, good to see you again. We won't be long—I'm just following up on the Coley suicide, and need to check a few things."

She shook Mendez's outstretched hand. "Please, call me Lauren," she said with a nervous giggle. Then she turned to Erik. "Are you a detective, too?"

"He's a consultant," Mendez said evenly. "This is Erik McGavin."

Erik noticed the boy behind Lauren blanch a little.

Mendez moved beyond her and introduced himself to the boy.

"I know," the boy muttered. "I'm sorry to hear about your partner."

Mendez looked at him with thinly veiled suspicion. "Did you know him?"

The boy looked queasy. "No, my...my mother did, I suppose. She mentioned him in her journals." It looked as if he was going to say more, but didn't.

After a pause, Mendez said, "Coley, is it? You're Mrs. Coley's son?"

The boy nodded. "Yes—sorry. Yes, I'm Ian."

"Are you okay?" Erik was sure in his bones that the boy knew, or at least suspected, why they were there.

The boy nodded again. "Just a lot of bad memories connected to that room," he said, and looked at the doorway as if not really seeing it. "A lot of bad stuff."

"I can imagine," Mendez said in a soft voice. Erik, who knew him pretty well, could hear the impatient strain beneath the carefully practiced patience. "I assure you, we won't be long."

"I don't know what you'll be able to find," Lauren said. "I mean, they've since cleared out her room."

"I understand," Mendez said with that same practiced patience. "We just need to look around here and in the basement, and then we'll be on our way."

He and Mendez had discussed the basement on the way to LPH, and both were in agreement that it would be as important, if not more so, to check the basement as well, since that was where they found Mrs. Coley's body.

"The basement," Lauren said as if being given the answer to a puzzle. "Of course."

"We appreciate your cooperation," Mendez answered.

Alone inside Mrs. Coley's room, Erik said to Mendez, "They know."

"What?"

Erik looked back at the doorway. "I've seen the look before. Both of them. They've seen the Hollowers. It wouldn't surprise me if they were here tonight to do...well, exactly what we're doing.

"How can you be sure?"

"Experience."

"Should we say something?"

Erik looked away, thinking of Dave. "There's something to be said for strength in numbers. They're safer with us than without us."

"I don't know, Erik. I think—"

"I think Erik's right."

The timid voice that came from the doorway belonged to Ian. He stood there with Lauren behind him, both looking a shade short of terrified. "I'm sorry," he said. "We didn't mean to eavesdrop. It's just that... we—I mean my mother, she—you, and Steve, and Erik, and others, she knew them, wrote about them, wrote about the...the...." He looked flustered. He stopped, took a deep breath, and blurted, "Please, we need help. What are they? And how do we stop them?"

"Stop who?" Mendez asked with a sidelong glance at Erik.

"The Hollowers."

"Whatever you're looking for," Lauren added. "We're going to help. We have to."

***

Erik snorted. "This would be easier with the video."

Ian and Lauren sat on the bed in the room that used to belong to Mrs. Coley, and Mendez sat in the guest chair next to it. Erik, who had been pacing, trying to figure out where to begin his part of the story, leaned up against the windowsill.

Ian had explained that ever since his mother's death, he had been haunted by these three faceless phantoms who seemed hell-bent on making him suffer, and ultimately, trying to kill him. He explained how he had been afraid he was going crazy like his mother, but then he'd found her journals. He told them about how amidst all her delusions, she had written about experiences with beings very much like what he had been seeing. He said she'd mentioned both Mendez and Erik as if she had known them, specifically in connection with her other entries in which she talked about creatures she called "Hollowers."

Lauren had related her own experiences in the hospital, the bad dreams she had, and what Mrs. Saltzman (a name Erik recognized but for the life of him could not remember why) had told him about the "doormen" from another dimension.

Mendez had explained to them that Erik had survived ordeals with two different Hollowers and had managed to kill them both ("With help," Erik had pointed out), and that he knew more than anyone alive about the Hollowers. Something about the wording of that bothered Erik—"more than anyone alive"—but he supposed it was true. And so he felt compelled then to share with them what he knew.

He had no idea where to begin. It really would have been easier with the video.

"Huh?"

Erik explained. "My friend, Dave. When this all first started, he'd gotten a video in the mail from a guy named Max Feinstein who knew more about the Hollowers than any of us. The first of the Hollowers came through a rip in his house, we think. Anyway, he had been fighting it off a long time. He told us what we were up against in the video. He warned us."

"Well, let's go talk to him, right?" Ian looked hopeful.

"We can't." Erik shook his head.

"Why?"

"He's dead," Bennie said. "Suicide by shotgun, right after the video was made."

Ian paled. "Oh."

"What did he say in the video?" Lauren asked. "What the hell *are* we up against?"

Erik had only ever seen the video twice, and still he thought he could recite the better part of what Feinstein had said from memory.

"It feeds on its victims' sense of unreality," Feinstein had said. *"On their surreality, if you will. People's confusions. Their insecurities. The Hollower is sustained by impressions and perceptions and points of view. Its greatest protection is its anonymity and androgyny. How does it find you on such vague terms, you ask? By 'smelling' your most skewed thoughts. By 'smelling' your irrational feelings."* Erik fought an internal shiver, the words of the dead man still echoing in his head.

"Well, he said Hollowers were intangible beings. That where our senses stop, the Hollowers' senses start, and continue way beyond psychic powers. So they don't see you or feel you exactly...they sense you. And he said they feed on our emotions, our fears and insecurities and skewed perceptions. They look to confuse us and heighten those emotions by creating a sense of unreality from the things we want to love and trust. Hollowers can sense whatever you most want to hide from the world, especially if you feel it makes you weaker.

"He also said that since they have no real physical form here, they can collect identities and voices at will and use them against you. They hurt people the way people hurt themselves—by making it so you can't trust the people you know and love, or trust yourself. They make it so you worry that a secret might get out or a weakness, or that an addiction might overpower us. They remind us of the worst we have ever done and ever been. And like Feinstein said, little else shakes our faith in ourselves so much as self-doubt, however off-kilter or misplaced."

"Did he tell you how to kill it?"

Erik looked away. "No. Each time we've had to kill one, it was done differently. I don't know if there is one sure way to kill them. And I don't know if the same way will work twice. They hate physical bodies, and making physical contact with them hurt them, but it hurt us a lot worse. Our best defense, I guess, had always been the strength and self-confidence we found in being together. That seemed to make it harder for the Hollowers to find us. They couldn't 'see' what wasn't distorted and scared. Despairing. Terrified. We could slip under their radar when we could muster up enough courage to fight back." He paused, then added, "But we've never dealt with three of them at once. I didn't even know they hunted in packs."

"I don't think they do," Ian said. They turned to look at him. Ian looked at them almost apologetically. "I mean, my mother didn't, at least so far as she wrote in her journals. She didn't have as much information as what Erik told us, but she did say something about how 'only the Triumvirate can close doorways forever,' and 'only the Triumvirate can see and gather.' I don't know exactly what she meant, but it looked to me like she believed the rare occasion of three Hollowers at once indicated a special situation. In all her other writings about them, it was always singular—'it' came through, 'it' wants to kill her, that sort of thing."

Erik said, "I saw them once before, as three." They watched him, waiting for him to continue. "Now that I think about it, when we killed the first Hollower, the one called a Secondary, it called to them. As it lay dying, it called and a rip opened up and three Hollowers came to take the body. It was one of those three—a Primary—that came for us the second time. I guess maybe it wasn't as strong without the other two."

"So, this group of three—they're all Primaries?" Lauren shifted on the bed. She still glanced at it from time to time like something poisonous lay under the tightly tucked sheets.

"That would be my guess, yeah," Erik said. "And from the sound of it, if Ian's mom was right, they're much stronger as this special group of three than they are alone."

"It would explain the injuries," Mendez said, "to the victims we've found—our friend Steve, and Erik's friends, Jake and Dorrie before that. Their attacks were different, more animal than other Hollower attacks. It was something Ian said before, about only the Triumvirate being able to see and gather. Think about it. They seemed able to sense me, but told me they had no business with me. If they can see—or sense, or whatever—beings from other dimensions even outside the scope of a normal Hollower, then they could have limitless access to any creature of just about any dimension. And if that were true, the fact that they can't touch us doesn't matter. They can call on other worlds' worth of monsters to do the things they can't. To provide a real physical threat as well as a whole bunch of mental ones. They can destroy us inside out, or outside in, whichever is more convenient at the time."

There was a long pause as the group considered this. What they were up against was outside the realm of anyone's experience, even Erik's. He remembered that once the boy who had been with them originally, Sean, had said that everything had a weakness, even monsters, and that it was just a matter of finding it. Erik couldn't imagine, though, what possible weakness they could find in creatures who could push and pull dimensions and the creatures living in them at will.

Finally, Mendez got up. "We can't sit here. They have my wife."

"They have your wife?" Lauren looked horrified.

"Yes. I came home and she was gone. They weren't. I need to find her."

Lauren got off the bed, too, and Ian followed. "We will," she said. "We will. And I suggest we try looking in the basement now." She looked at her watch. "Mila's got a half a night off tonight and I don't have to give the patients their meds for another half hour, so no one should bother us about looking in the basement for a while."

"I think that's a good place to start," Erik agreed.

Lauren led the way. They took the staff elevator at the end of the hall, the only one which went to the basement level. It was there that the Lakehaven Psychiatric Hospital's morgue and assorted storerooms were. It was also there that a lot of the surplus medication was kept. Lauren explained that one needed the passkey and a code to get the elevator to work, which had made it all the more baffling that Mrs. Coley had made it down to the basement. Erik noticed Ian's expression as he eyed the floor buttons and the elevator wall adjacent to them, and felt immediate sympathy. Something in the boy's eyes showed that he had been in this elevator once before—probably after his mother's suicide—and it was bringing back some pretty rough memories now.

The elevator door opened on a rough-hewn concrete cave beneath the hospital, lit with dim bulbs of a sickly yellow and marked throughout with painted signs to KEEP OUT and keep alert. Everything neat, clean, and thoroughly efficient about the hospital above was absent here. Down here, the last of comfort and security crumbled away.

Mendez, Lauren, and Ian had all been in the basement before. They had all been present, evidently, when Mrs. Coley's body had been found. Erik followed them as they made their wordless way to a spot some fifteen feet away from the elevator door, under a thick gray pipe, beneath which the cement flooring had been stained a dark brown.

"I'm sorry," Lauren said, squeezing Ian's shoulder.

Erik assumed she had been talking about the blood stain, but Ian replied, "It wasn't your fault. You can't...you can't always stop people from dying."

"None of us can," Erik said, and his voice was so soft he wasn't sure he'd said it out loud.

"What does a rip look like?" Ian asked.

Glad for the subject change, Erik said, "Well, it looks—"

A low, sharp growl reverberated among the concrete beams, its source impossible to determine. Erik felt his chest grow cold and heavy. He looked around.

The growl came again, this time closer. It was coming from behind the morgue door.

"Jesus." Mendez was looking at the floor. From beneath the door, a small surge of blood was spreading outward toward their feet.

"That can't be possible," Lauren whispered.

The blood formed a pool in the center with four long rivulets reaching ever outward, as well as one shorter one to the side. The formation gave the distinct impression of a hand with long fingers, clawing at them, threatening to draw them back under the door and into the vaults of the dead.

"Oh, no fucking way." Erik looked at Lauren. "Tell me that door is locked, and that you don't have a key."

The heavy steel door grunted open on its own, once, twice, and once more so that the space beyond was enough to let them in.

"Guys, you know, maybe we should have started with my mom's room—"

The door opened again, and a voice from inside said, "Bennie? Is that you out there?"

Mendez's eyes grew big and hopeful. "Anita?" He didn't wait for an answer, but rushed toward the door.

"Mendez, wait—"

Mendez wasn't listening to Erik. He was shouldering the door further open. Erik ran after him, and the others followed. Last inside, Lauren flipped the light switch and blazing fluorescents illumined the room.

"Shit!" Mendez looked deeply pained to find no one else but them were in the room. "You sons of bitches—"

Anita's laughter rained down from the overhead lights. Around them, the cold chambers lined the walls like filing cabinet drawers, all closed. To one wall was a small table with a metal tray of instruments. In the center of the room was an empty gurney with a sheet crumpled up on it. Erik shivered.

Behind them, the door slammed, and they jumped. Ian cried out. Lauren's hand fluttered up to her chest to steady her heart.

"Mendez," Erik said. "I don't like this."

"This room is off," Lauren said. "It's not right. It's not—"

One of the cold chamber doors opened on a squeaking hinge. Inside, the pale and bloated face of Dave Kohlar filled the space.

"Well hi there, Erik! Long time no talk, buddy. How've you been?"

Erik held the face of his dead friend in an even gaze. "You're not Dave."

"And you're no fun. What happened to you? You used to know how to party." The face made a sniffing sound that caused Erik, even after all that time, to blush.

"You're not Dave," he repeated, his voice a little weaker than before.

"And Bennie Mendez! How's Anita? Dismembered by the kind with a thousand mouths? So unfortunate. How about your partner Steve? The same? Well, how about your little girl? Oh, don't answer that. While you all are here, we'll be there to see for ourselves. We'll devour her, and Erik's skinny little piece of ass wife, too." The head jerked to the right. "Lauren Seavers. Well, aren't you some nurse? Helen Coley, dead. Mrs. Saltzman, crazy as a shithouse rat and getting worse. Some caregiver you are. You don't give a damn about them. Just like your poor little cousin Dustin. So young, to want to die."

"It wasn't my fault." Lauren's eyes filled with tears.

"And Ian," Dave's face said, jerking again to get a better look at him. "Your mother says hi. She's right here, where you left her. Where you abandoned her. She's right here with us."

Ian closed his eyes. He looked as if he might be sick.

Lauren charged the cold chamber and slammed its door. The metal *thwang!* echoed even in the small room.

From first one, then all of the cold chambers, there came a sound indistinguishable as laughing or crying, a noise that rose in pitch and volume until it was deafening. Erik thought he might be screaming but couldn't tell.

Suddenly, the space between them and the cold chambers sizzled as a bolt of black lightning cut through the air. The bolt folded in on itself, seeming to indent the very fabric of the reality around them in a jagged, crackling cut. It spread to about six feet from top to bottom and then pulled itself open. Beyond the fluttering edges of the rip, a gaping inkiness yawned. The smell of ozone was cloying.

All sound ceased in an instant.

The four of them stood staring into the illimitable emptiness. Erik said, "That's what a rip looks like."

"Yes," the multi-voice behind them confirmed. They flinched and collectively wheeled around.

The Triumvirate stood between them and the morgue doorway. They looked imposingly tall, crisp with arctic hate, stark with their luminous blank heads and black clothes.

"Found you," the one on the right said, and giggled.

"Where's Anita?" Mendez demanded. "If you hurt her—"

"We warned you not to interfere," the one on the left told him with a placid flick of a glove.

"She's someplace else. We may toss the baby there, too," the middle one said, and with a tilt of the head to Erik, "And your Casey."

"Shame, about the air. The water. So many poisonous things to such fragile bodies." The left said "bodies" as if the word itself caused pain.

"I'll kill you myself if you hurt any of them," Mendez said.

The left one said, "You can't kill us. We won't die. We are not like the others."

"We'll find a way," Erik said.

"You can try," said the leftmost one.

"And fail," added the middle one.

"We will absorb your Despair."

They took a step forward and instinctively, the group took a step back. Behind him, Erik could hear the cosmos churning eternally in the void, and he was acutely aware of how close he stood to the edge.

"What are you?" Lauren screamed.

The middle one tilted its head toward her. "We are the end," it said, "to everything. The end to you."

It raised a glove in a wave, made a fist, then made a gesture like it was throwing seeds to the wind. Erik felt a hard shove against his chest and for just a moment, the thought that he was going to fall straight off the earth eclipsed all others.

Then came the startled cries of his friends and the tug at his back and he was falling backward in lightlessness, neither hot nor cold, neither breathing nor suffocating. Liquid black poured all around him, crackling in his ears. He couldn't see the others but he could feel them falling, too, and before senselessness obscured even that, he wondered for a moment if this was what it had felt like for Dave to die.

Mary SanGiovanni

Chapter 10

When the crackling subsided and the liquid black sluiced away, Erik found himself outside. He checked on the others. Bennie was getting to one knee with a groan. Ian sat up, rubbing his neck. Lauren lay face-down. She wasn't moving.

Panic hit hard and fast; maybe being forced through...whatever they had passed through had killed her. Ian had already seen her and crouched by her side, shaking her shoulder. Erik went to her and turned her over on her back.

"Lauren? Hey, you okay? Lauren?"

She didn't move. Erik lightly tapped her cheeks. "Lauren! Come on, Lauren, wake up!"

Her eyelids fluttered, and when she saw where she was, she jumped and skittered away from Erik and the others. "Oh—oh God. Where are we?"

"Good question," Erik said, looking around.

The landscape before them contained, to varying degrees, elements of physical wrongness somehow. It was hard at first to pinpoint specific examples of that wrongness, but Erik felt it. Wherever they were, Erik felt in his bones that it was not obligated to obey the laws of physics that existed on Earth or its surrounding universe. The world they had been thrust into was alien in ways they could only imagine.

Streaks of heavy crimson and sickly pink arced across a sky which reminded Erik of the underside of something rather than its upper dome. The air was thin and tasted greasy—that was the only way he could think to describe it—and fighting to get the oxygen he needed from it was already giving him a slight headache. They appeared to be on some kind of dirt plain in a valley. Rough pink and gray striated cliffs rose to their left and continued around to and across the distant horizon. They blocked off further view in those directions. The ground beneath his feet was a hard-packed red clay that kicked up in little puffs of dust if he kicked at it with his sneaker. Low-growing white plants with jagged, purple-tipped leaves grew sporadically in little clumps. Even more sporadically and much taller, spiky fractal things reached upward, their thin limbs baring bunches of flat white triangles that jingled in the tepid breeze. Erik would have thought they were trees except that they moved infinitesimally across the landscape. A fairly sizable lake of indigo whose slight tidal movement frothed pink like fermenting grapes, lay to the right. Its surface remained perfectly unbroken by life beneath. If anything swam in its depths, no evidence rippled up and out.

In the distance were geometrically distorted structures that hurt his eyes if he looked at any one part of them too long. He supposed they could be buildings, although he shivered inwardly to imagine what might live or work inside them. They seemed to shift, too, at odd intervals but so slightly, Erik couldn't really be sure.

"What now?" Bennie came up alongside Erik.

Erik shrugged. "I honestly don't know. They've never done something like this before."

"Are we stuck here?" Lauren stepped over one of the small plants, which had shifted just a little too close toward her feet, and joined them. "Wherever 'here' is?"

Erik remembered the carvings on that long-ago cave wall half in and half out of his home universe. There were other places. Other creatures tormented. And other creatures who brought widespread pain and death....

"This isn't anywhere from our universe," Ian said from behind her. "I know that. We all do. We all feel it, I'm sure." He was holding a shiny deep blue stone that was rocking back and forth in his palm and cooing. When an eye opened up on the top surface plane, Ian cried out and dropped the rock. Spider-legs sprouted along two of its sides and spirited it over the cool red clay and away from them.

"Oh, God, what do we do?" Lauren's eyes shone with tears.

"What can we do but look around?" Ian shrugged. "Maybe we can find another rip."

"What if we can't?" Lauren's voice was soft but insistent. "Something's not right here. The air, the ground. Everything here is slightly stale, or...or slightly spoiled, somehow."

Erik thought of Casey, her beautiful eyes, her tea-and-honey hair, the smell of her skin. He thought of the baby she wanted, the one he wouldn't give her because such things as Hollowers existed and were too often poisoning the world. He thought of kissing her good-bye earlier that evening, and how yet again he'd promised to return even though they both knew it was a promise he might not be able to keep.

"Not even Hell could stop me from coming back to you."

He loved her—simply, completely, and unconditionally. He would find a way home to her. He had to.

"We're going to find a way out," he said. His tone indicated there could be no argument about it. The others looked at him. Finally, Bennie scratched his cheek and said, "How?"

Erik nodded toward the buildings. "We start there. The Hollowers' rips always seem to coincide with a building in our world. Maybe it works the same way here."

Bennie nodded. "Let's do it."

***

In the Convergence, the Triumvirate watched and waited. The black holes inside them were nearly unbearable when in sync, their ferocity matching the power of those who sought to contain them, fill them with the Emotions of others.

The meats would not survive that world. To such fragile physical creatures, it was largely inhospitable. There was no sustenance. The air they sucked into those disgusting sacs in their chests they would find unsatisfying and unclean. And there were lesser beasts who would tear them apart as they had torn apart the three other meats when dragged through to the place called Earth.

They hovered near that dimension, content to let those others kill, but close enough to feed off the Fear and Confusion.

The Likekind was unique in its ability to not only survive crossing between dimensions and through the Convergence, but also in its ability to manipulate the environments in those dimensions. Beyond the ordinary abilities of the Likekind, the Triumvirate could use their extra senses to manipulate multiple worlds at once, and draw creatures, even those beyond their scope of perception, toward them and each other across those multiple worlds. These extra senses they employed now to track those from the place called Earth.

If the beasts of this world couldn't destroy them, there were others. There were many. The insane *hinshing* in their world of chaos and wild abandon, or the ancient Ones Without Names from the worlds in starless space. Or the cunning shades from the place the Earth beings called Hell. The Triumvirate were not alarmed. They would feed and they would evaluate—they were, among them, fairly certain that whatever threat the beings from the Earth world posed would be taken care of, here or elsewhere.

There were many.

***

Erik, whose job naturally required a need to be in relatively good shape, found himself winded as they made their way across the relatively flat landscape. The air had grown even thinner, and had taken on a waxy, sour smell in addition to the greasiness it left in his nose and throat as he breathed. They hadn't come across anything else living yet—no animal life, big or small—and for that, Erik was glad. He couldn't get those carvings of others worlds out of his head. There they were on another planet in another universe entirely, the kind of thing that even wild dreams couldn't hold up to. And while that initial awe lingered, it was undercut by a sense of impatient unease, as if their time was limited, and that time would prove to be difficult and unpleasant at best, deadly at the worst.

He kept waiting, in a sense, for the other shoe to drop, for something right out of a Godzilla movie to come crashing across the arid landscape in frenzied clouds of red dust, or careening through the crime-scene sky with its blood-streak clouds, hell-bent on cutting him down and devouring him in easy pieces.

No animal life yet—but he figured it was only a matter of time before they did come across living inhabitants of this place. The longer they could avoid it, the better. They had no weapons, exertion in this thin air might possibly prove toxic over time, and just moving in this environment felt a little like moving through water. Fighting monsters on the front lawn of a suburban home or in the dark tunnels beneath an assisted living facility, even if they were halfway in and halfway out of familiar reality, were one thing; they had had something of the home field advantage. But here, they were mightily screwed, by Erik's estimation.

"I keep thinking of her." Mendez's voice, soft, was suddenly by his side. He was breathing a little harder, too, but keeping up with Erik. "Keep hoping if she's anywhere, we can find her here."

It was the first time he'd mentioned Anita since the night she'd disappeared. Erik knew he had to be going crazy with worry; he would have been if it had been Casey. Mendez looked like he hadn't slept in a while. Erik knew the feeling.

"We'll find her, Mendez."

Mendez didn't answer right away. His gaze alternated between the alien landscape underfoot and the structures, now looming with proximity, on the horizon. As they drew closer, they could see the buildings were indeed rotating, and shuffling an inch or so from time to time across the land on which they were grouped. Finally, Mendez said, "Don't know what I'd ever tell Cora."

Erik glanced at him. The dark bags under his eyes made him look unusually pale. More than that, he was beginning to take on that haunted, shadowed look in his eyes that he was sure he, as well as Dave and Steve and all the others, had carried around since their first experiences. He told the detective, "You'll tell her all about how you traveled to exotic locations and rescued her mother from dragons and evil wizards."

Mendez returned a small smile. "That's not too far from the truth."

"Exactly. All great stories work that way."

They reached an area where irregular brownish stones set in the clay formed geometric patterns. Erik thought it looked like some kind of courtyard. He saw a jumble of larger stones forming a crumbling wall corner at the far back of the set stones and wondered how, having let that wall around them fall apart, the beings who owned these structures kept them from wandering off. The moving buildings shuffled a half inch or so in random directions every few minutes. There were, by Erik's estimation, about ten of them, grouped in no discernible way. Most of the buildings looked like long inverted pyramids, balanced and occasionally rotating on smaller rectangular bases with the groan of grinding rock. Some looked to be just the bases now; maybe their buildings had gone spinning and shuffling off into the dust. He didn't think they were made of any recognizable version of metal or stone, but seemed to have qualities of both, varying shades of matte grays and browns with spidery black and red veins like marble. The way the buildings leaned and bowed, though, whatever they were made of had to be flexible. Also, there were no divisions of individual bricks. There were no windows that Erik could see and no doors, nor were there any adornments or embellishments of any kind except on one building, the largest. On that one, symbols, both carved and in bas-relief, wrapped around it from the point on the bottom toward the wide, flat base. Erik recognized some of the symbols from that long-ago cave wall, and found he couldn't look at them for long without feeling cold all over.

"Hot damn," Ian said. Erik saw recognition in his eyes as well, and wondered what his mother had somehow seen and replicated in that bedroom.

The building nearest to them leaned toward them as if eavesdropping, then leaned away. Erik heard the faint sound like laughter, boisterous at its source but eerily tinny; it reminded Erik of the recordings they played at the local summer firemen's carnival fun house.

"So which one?" Lauren shivered, wrapping her arms around herself. She gazed up at the laughing building with wariness.

"Not sure," Erik said. He frankly didn't relish the thought of entering any of those buildings, especially ones that laughed at him.

"How about that one?" Mendez pointed to one just off center of the group. It was the one that had gotten Erik's attention as well, the largest one, with the symbols spiraling up its sides. "Seems to me that one might be important. Question is, how do we get in?"

No one answered. They stood huddled together, their breathing ragged, their faces thoughtful. Finally, Ian spoke what Erik had been thinking.

"What if they aren't buildings? What if we try to get inside one of them and it swallows us up?"

As if the structures had heard them, they stopped moving completely. Above them, the skies bellowed distant thunder. The structure that Mendez pointed out seemed to solidify. Its exterior darkened, grew pock-marked and cracked like aged stone. A diamond-shaped hole opened in between the spiral of symbols like an irregular mouth, receding into a dark interior. From their distance, Erik thought he could see the base of a stone staircase.

"Is that an invitation?" Ian chuckled, but the sound was small and humorless in the silence around them.

"It's a door, I think," Lauren said. "Do we go in?"

He didn't like being the one to make the group's decisions, the default "expert" on the Hollowers and the horrors they twisted around people like personal nooses. He realized Dave must have felt much the same way, trying to navigate the Hollowers' mind games while keeping them all alive. Erik understood the weight of being responsible for these other lives, these trusting lives, and the fear of failing them. It made him acutely aware of the potential consequences of each decision.

Erik and Mendez exchanged glances. Mendez gave him a slight nod, and he was glad for it; he needed the encouragement. It made him feel less alone in shouldering the responsibility of the others' lives.

"It's worth exploring," Erik said. He led them forward.

As they moved across the stone courtyard, the other buildings inched out of their way, one or the other of them occasionally rotating just once on its base, drawing out a groan, then stopping.

Erik could hear echoed sounds, high and excited like children's voices, from the interiors of the flanking structures, though he couldn't make out individual words.

The structure with the door stood still. It didn't twitch. No sound came from its dim interior.

When he reached the doorway, Erik turned back to look at the group behind him. He saw wide-eyed, expectant expressions on the faces of Ian and Lauren. Mendez held onto a stoic kind of calm. He had clicked the safety off his gun and his right hand rested on it, waiting too—not for Erik's decision, but for anything to spring itself on them that might impede that decision. That gave Erik another much-needed boost of courage. He exhaled, nodded affirmatively, and plunged through the opening in the building.

What Erik had initially thought to be the base of a staircase turned out to be a series of stone-like blocks so white that they gave off a kind of luminescence of their own. They created a kind of central altar, a rough ring inside of which were a number of small rectangular objects wrapped in a smooth kind of cloth, half rotted now. What the rectangles were beneath the cloth, Erik couldn't begin to guess, but they were lined up neatly in stacked rings around the interior of the rock altar like books on a shelf. They gave off a phosphorescence that ate into the gloom of the chamber. In fact, from their soft glow, Erik could see the room's cavernous interior fairly well, with shelves at periodic and varying heights. On these shelves were irregular and transparent objects which could have been anything from vases and jars to organs of some kind. The air smelled musty, like dust and rotting paper, and the way it curled around his arms and the back of his neck made him shiver. He felt touched by something unpleasantly foreign, something he didn't think he'd be able to get off his skin.

"It's cold in here," Lauren said, and her voice, magnified by the alien air, echoed up above their heads among the strange trinkets.

"What is this place? Some kind of a museum?" Ian reached for a pale blue decanter on a nearby low shelf, seemed to think better of it, and pulled his hand back.

"Who knows?" Mendez gave a twinkling clear bauble a wary glance. "I wouldn't touch anything you don't have to, though. We don't know what anything here is made of. The air is wrong. The ground is wrong. This place is *una locura de una mala manera.* Crazy-bad."

"Not that I can be sure, but uh, I don't see anything inside here that looks like a portal, or...or the makings of a portal. Do you guys?" Lauren leaned against the altar, peering into its center for herself.

"Not me," Erik said. "What do you think these things are?"

"They look a little like canopic jars," Ian said.

"What?"

"Canopic jars. The, uh, ancient Egyptians used them during the, uh, burial process. They kept the important organs, the ones they believed would be needed by the deceased in the afterlife, in the jars. The rest of the body was then carefully preserved as well."

"So...you think these jars have...like, alien organs in them?"

"God, I hope not," Erik said.

"All the more reason not to touch them." Mendez stepped toward the rock altar in the center of the room. "So what's this?"

"Not sure," Erik said, "but this glow is coming from those things on the shelves under there."

"This might be a stupid question, but, could this be a portal? I mean, they don't all have to look like the ones the Hollowers do on Earth, right?"

Erik heaved himself up onto the altar ring's edge, then dropped to the center inside. He waited a moment, but nothing happened.

Mendez shrugged. "Maybe it needs to be activated somehow?"

"Like, with these glowing packages?"

"Maybe." Mendez peered over the side. "No way to know."

Erik crouched down to get a better look at the glowing parcels. Up close, he could see that what he mistook for cloth was more like a kind of skin, not quite as dry as leather, but possessed of an organic smoothness and infinitesimal movement lines. The glow seemed to come from those lines, and the nearly invisible pores, though whether that was a natural property of the skin or part of the treatment process, he didn't know. What he did know was that he wanted even less to do with whatever was inside those packages, and he was not too keen on touching them, even if it meant juicing up a portal home.

He glanced up at the objects on the shelves. Canopic jars. If this was a museum, it had some pretty grisly objects on display. A burial chamber then, where the body had been neatly divided into glowing parcels and pretty jars? Or was it a flat-out butcher shop?

"So what do you think?" Mendez asked, leaning casually on the stone edge above him.

He stood up. "Well, I don't see...." Erik's voice trailed off. Behind Ian, the wall was breathing. That's what it looked like to Erik, that the wall was expanding and receding, stretching and shrinking. Erik hopped out of the altar's center, moving quickly toward Ian. The wall behind him twisted in on itself in the center and then shot outward. Erik grabbed Ian's arm and yanked him out of the way.

"What the—?" Ian yelped, and when Erik lifted a chin toward the hardening spike of wall that had occupied the space where Ian had just been, the kid paled. "Whoa. Thanks."

"No problem. Now, let's get the fuck out of here, huh?"

Erik moved toward the doorway but it shot upward, the substance of the walls filling in the space where the doorway had been, while the space leading to the outside reopened fifteen feet or so above their heads.

"*Mierde*," Mendez muttered. He went to a shelf about knee-height, paused, then quickly took the green tube on it and moved it to the floor, wiping the hand that had touched it on his pants. He hoisted a leg onto the shelf and bounced a little on it, testing its strength. To Erik, he said, "Maybe we can climb—" before the wall opened up and swallowed him. Erik dove to try and grab at him and his arm sank into the wall up to the elbow. Panic flared in his chest as an icy pain shot from his fingertips up to his shoulder. Ian and Lauren were immediately at his sides, pulling on him, trying to free his arm. Erik cried out as the wall bit into his skin, holding him, surging up toward his shoulder.

"Get out!" he shouted. "Get out of here!"

"We're not leaving you!" Lauren shouted back. She renewed her tugging efforts.

"I can't—" The wall swelled up and around his shoulder and yanked him through and sealed up behind him.

The two left behind stood stunned, staring at the spot. In the pale glow of the room, tears glistened in Lauren's eyes. Ian held the scrap of his shirt the wall had cut off.

Erik, like Mendez, was gone.

Mary SanGiovanni

Chapter 11

After several moments, Ian looked at Lauren and said, "We've got to get out of here."

She nodded slowly, turning around. Behind them, the room had changed again.

"Oh shit," she muttered.

The glow had gone from a soft teal to a harsh red, and it was no longer coming from the stone altar in the center of the room. It was coming from the walls themselves, little flashing beacons of light as if they were in a can punched through with holes to let in the light of a terrible red giant star. All over the walls took heaving breaths, which rocked the shelves like small boats on an ocean gathering a storm. The various containers still sat on the shelves, but those shelves were in different places and formed I-shapes. The containers themselves were filled to varying degrees with dark red fluid.

She had time to think *Blood. Oh God, those things are filled with blood* before the jars started to tremble, then shake violently. The fluids inside splashed out and splattered the rocking shelves and the walls around the objects. The contrast of light and darkness through the blood was ghastly; it made the blood patterns appear to move on their own. Lauren bit back a scream. She felt Ian's hand on her arm, tugging her.

"Come on!" he shouted. "The place is melting!" He was pointing toward the opening, the bottom corner of which was sagging like a glob of spit down toward them. The shelves began to lose shape, too, bending and dripping their substance onto the floor. The walls pulled down rivulets of the splattered blood and mixed with it. The air inside the room had grown stuffy and unbearable, thick with the unsavory scent of cooking blood. The sudden explosion of glass to their right startled Lauren into a scream, followed by a short succession of others as tiny slivers of glass slid painfully under the skin of her arm and cheek. Ian pulled her out of the way as several of the splintering objects popped and their bigger pieces fell off the melting shelves. Ian reached up toward the opening to the outside world, the edge of which had now dropped low enough to reach, and tugged down. The opening stretched further toward them. Lauren reached up too. The substance of the melting wall was hot beneath her hands and rough, like sand under the summer sun all day. She winced, but tugged hard. Between the two of them, they managed to pull the bottom edge of the opening down to waist-level.

Behind them, the stone structure in the middle began to crumble.

"Come on," he shouted over the din of the melting, toppling room. "I'll give you a boost!"

She hesitated a moment, flinched as something crashed behind her, and nodded. He locked his fingers at about knee height, the palms of his hands turned upward. Balancing herself with a hand on his shoulder, she stepped up onto his palm, then reached for the opening. She didn't look out to what she was dropping onto; she felt him heave her over the edge and then she was falling. A jarring thud as she hit ground sent a shock wave of pain through her frame. There was another thud, and Ian landed next to her with a little groan.

She sat up. "You okay?" Her left arm hurt at the elbow, and the side of her knee throbbed.

Laying on his back, he coughed once and said, "Yeah, I think so. You?"

"I'm okay." She got to her feet and helped him up, then looked around. They were back in the courtyard. The other buildings rotated occasionally and shifted an inch or so as if doing some gratingly slow dance. They seemed utterly unphased by the return of the humans or the melting of their fellow building. That, Lauren noticed, was because the building they had been in, the one with the symbols, was gone.

She took in a breath of sour, waxy air and still felt better than taking the horrible stink of that melting room into her lungs. A part of her wanted to cry or scream, but she was surprised to find that was a very small part of her. Some survival instinct inside had switched on, and she felt that to scream was to lose whatever tenuous hold she had left on her self-control. She couldn't have that.

Instead, she forced more of that stale air in and out of her lungs and asked, "So what now? Where do you think Erik and Mendez are?"

"I don't know," Ian said. He threw up his hands. He looked closer to the edge of hysterical, and she felt for him—wanted to hug him, even stroke his hair, she realized. He looked lost. "I really have no idea."

***

For a moment, all sense and thought was swallowed by white, and then a musty smell filled Erik's nose. The white cleared like dissipating smoke and he saw Mendez sitting on hard ground, leaning against a rock wall, rubbing his forehead. To either side of them, the rock stretched overhead and down into darkness. They were in a tunnel. Erik recognized the tunnel, or thought he did. He felt sick in his stomach.

"Where are we?" Mendez looked around.

"Inside the Hollowers' heads," Erik muttered. He had been half-kidding, but it actually made sense. The Hollowers could manipulate his world; it wasn't so far a stretch that they could manipulate other worlds, too. Where logic and reason and self-assurance might set his world right again, he had no frame of reference for "right" in this world. Here, they were really and truly lost.

"What do you mean?"

"I mean that they're probably doing to us in this dimension what they do to us in our own. Think about it—they thrive on confusion. They feed on fear and insecurity. They...." His voice trailed off, as his eye caught something horrible carved into the wall nearby, and from the low whistle at the outside edge of his hearing, he sensed that Mendez's gaze had alighted on the same thing his had.

About ten feet down, carved into a smooth spot in the rough rock, was a mural crudely painted and framed in symbols. Before the drugs he'd been nuts about National Geographic, and a lot of the symbols were somewhat reminiscent of ancient languages— Aztec, Mayan, ancient Egyptian. But he was pretty sure these symbols weren't from any kind of Earth language. They looked like a kind of cuneiform—not, he thought, that he'd know cuneiform from Colorforms, but that was what came to mind. A cuneiform of an alien race.

The pictures the ancient symbol-language framed were of a more modern cast. The mural was fairly complex and detailed, a contrast to the garish paint applied haphazardly to the surface. The figure on the left side was a Confederate soldier corpse astride a skeleton horse rearing on its hind legs. It was the same figure his father had tattooed on his arm, the same figure he had spent countless beatings memorizing the details of while spittle and sour beer breath hung like a dark cloud over his head. He had hated that tattoo, and the man it belonged to, for a very long time. Nowadays, he was more numb to the memories of the latter. The former, he was dismayed to discover, still inspired a kind of dread that had not diminished even in all those years since his father's death.

In the mural, there was a figure being trampled beneath the corpse soldier's horse. That figure reminded him an awful lot of himself.

There was more. The mural background, a sparse forest of dead trees, extended from behind the dead soldier toward a number of inverted pyramids like the one that had swallowed them up and secreted them into the tunnel. The pyramids were painted in shades of blue, with Saturn-like rings around them and bases painted with ornate designs. Snaking tendrils writhed in and out of and in between the pyramid buildings. Erik thought again of the animals that possibly constituted the wildlife of the dimension, and hoped that Ian and Lauren were okay.

The branches of a tree behind one of the pyramid buildings reached up into a night sky, the black paint slathered around little sparking bits in the rock itself. That sky stretched into a new scene, one that looked painted by a child, albeit a very disturbed child; large, unblinking eyes, their pupils grossly out of proportion, floated over the heads of stick figures whose round heads were split wide open by actual cracks in the rocks. Red paint dribbled from the corners of those eyes and onto the heads of the stick figures. The blood—Erik knew it to represent blood—spilled along the ground into another scene. In that one, there was a long table, and on it were lined up the naked human bodies of two men and two women, their arms crossed like dead pharaohs on their chests. The men and one woman looked young, the body of the woman on the other end slightly larger and sagging in places. The leftmost man's large forearm had a Chinese dragon tattoo Erik recognized. In fact, he thought he knew who each of those figures were meant to represent, and it sent a pang of pain through his chest. The figures had no faces; the rough rock was scored and chipped where the faces should have been and painted over in splashes of red. Still, he knew. And somehow seeing their bodies, pale and naked and otherwise untouched in contrast to the indicated mess of their faces, made the injuries more horrible.

"Holy mother of God," Mendez said, getting to his feet. He went to the portion of the mural with the dead figures of Steve, Jake, Dorrie, and Mrs. Coley and touched it gingerly. Red dust came off on his fingertips. "What is this? What the hell is this, Erik?"

His fingertips followed further along the mural until he came upon something that set loose a string of Spanish which, by its tone, could only have been curses. Erik got up and went over to see what he had found. Mendez had gone so far as to pull his gun on the offending carving as if he could threaten it into receding. He paced, waving his gun at it. When Erik saw it, he understood why.

It was a figure of a woman torn wide open, a small woman with frizzy hair nearly obliterated by whatever had scratched away her face. From the gaping wound in her mid-section, there was a smaller figure—a small child—whose dismembered limbs were black with decay.

"What did they do to her? Oh God, what did they do?"

"Walk away, man. They're just fucking with you. Come on, just walk away." Erik grabbed Mendez's arm and pulled him away from the mural altogether, tugging him down through the tunnel. The darkness receded at their approach, the feeble light always focused on wherever they were but swallowed up before and behind them.

"I've got to find her, man. I've got to find her."

"We will," Erik told him. "We will."

"How?" Mendez re-holstered the gun. He didn't state the obvious, that they were in a world inside a world outside the limits of anything in the known universe, that they were trapped and at the mercy of monsters who wanted them dead, who'd bleed them dry of emotions and then toss their husks to beasts from the places beyond the insides of closets and underside of beds. He didn't state it because it hung there between them on the tail of his question, a kind of despair more complete and engulfing than any Erik had ever felt. He fought it with everything he had.

Erik didn't know how they would find Anita, or Ian and Lauren, or a way out. But he'd be damned if he'd let despair swallow him up. When his father had tried to beat the soul out of him, he had turned to coke, and the despair had nearly killed him. He'd sworn never to let that happen again—not when the first or the second Hollower threatened to take away everything, and not now. He'd breathe, he'd count to a thousand or a million if he had to, and he'd keep moving until his legs wouldn't hold him up if that's what it took. Maybe it was a form of resistance to authority, or a super-sharpened sense of self-preservation. Maybe it was Casey. Likely, it was Casey—she was the best thing he had to live for. All he knew was that he'd be damned if he let those faceless fucking devils win without a fight.

"We will find her." Erik said each word with deliberate clarity and authority. His tone left no room for question or argument. "You and I will get out of here, and we will find her."

Mendez searched his face, seemed to find what he was looking for, and moved forward with renewed determination.

When they reached a fork in the tunnel, it was Mendez who said, "This way."

"How do you know?"

Mendez almost smiled. "Breeze. There's a breeze from this direction. Feel it? Nothing from that direction."

Erik could feel it. It was the same stagnant air of the foreign dimension, but to Erik, it was a good sign. If it was a trick, he was okay just then with letting it be.

They walked a long time in the direction that Mendez chose, and Erik was just about to voice his first rumbling of doubt when he saw a small oval of light beyond the darkness in front of them.

"Look!" he pointed, and the two started running. The oval of light grew larger, and the breeze of stagnant air from the outside stronger. They were so intent on reaching the outside before the Hollowers sealed up the tunnel and plunged them into blackness that Erik didn't see the bony, jointed appendage snaking down from the mouth of the cave until it had grabbed a hold of Mendez's neck and tossed him clear onto the red ground. He landed with an "oof" and rolled over on his back. A trickle of blood ran from beneath his right ear and another from the corner of his mouth. The wind had been knocked out of him and he was gasping for air. It sounded like he was trying to say Erik's name. He looked above the mouth of the cave at something and his eyes grew wide. He dived to the right as a lance of bone shot into the ground where he had just been.

"Mendez!" Erik shouted, and came running out of the tunnel. He stumbled once and nearly tumbled to the ground beside Mendez, but caught his balance and turned in time to see another long spike of bone cleaving the air toward him. He dodged and that time, he did lose his balance, rolling out of the way in a kicked-up cloud of red dust.

"Shit!" Erik scrambled to his feet. In seconds, Mendez was beside him. The cave had formed an opening in that long range of cliffs they had seen when they first got to this world. Shelves of rock jutted out and up for miles. Erik guessed they had ended up at least a few miles down the length of the range. There was no sign of the inverted pyramids and no sign of the courtyard stones.

What Erik did see—what both of them were drawn to stare at in horror—was the thing perched on the mouth of the cave.

The center of it was a swirling black mass like a dense cloud about twenty feet in circumference. From it, faces emerged and receded. Sometimes these faces were alien, and only identifiable as faces at all because of the inclusion of eyes and mouths. Some of the faces were human, but mask-like, frozen in the glazed-eyed, slack-jawed expression of the dead. At times, those human faces suggested familiarity, taking on Casey's features for a moment or Anita's, Dave's or Steve's. There was a terrible noise rising from that swirling center and those dead gaping mouths, the scream of a storm gaining momentum, the whine of wind and its rending powers of destruction. Erik thought he heard human screaming as well, and realized it was him.

The creature had several long, barbed, multi-pronged appendages that lashed at the air above its center. Erik supposed it was one of those lashing things that had flung Mendez from the cave. From either side of its center, spanning the length of the beast beneath those wildly whipping appendages, jointed spider legs arced up and out. Wisps of the black center swirled and spiraled around the legs, occasionally separating themselves and solidifying into bony spikes.

With one of those whips, it tore a forming bone-spike from the shin of one leg and hurled it at them. It landed between them. They both screamed.

Mendez raised his gun at the thing and fired. He hit one of the spider legs and black ichor exploded out and behind it. It roared, wobbling a little on the injured leg. Then the black of its center floated up to the wound and filled it in like clay. Mendez fired off a couple more rounds into the center of the thing, but succeeded only in hitting a face that resembled his own. He shoved the gun back into its holster again.

The thing rose on its spider legs to an imposing height. It roared again, and then leaped off the mouth of the cave.

The two stumbled backward in terror, then took off at a run along the cliff wall. Behind them, they could hear a rapid scrabbling, like a hundred feet clamoring over the red, rocky soil. It screamed, and Erik thought the faces inside it might be screaming, too. The air cracked above their heads and Erik thought he caught a whiff of ozone. He was afraid to look back, to slow his stride even so much as a little, but suspected that the whips of the thing had cut the air above them and changed it somehow.

A cold, stale wind blew against their faces. Thunder echoed through clouds that looked like smears of blood across a menacing sky. Erik wasn't sure if it was the storm of charged air around the creature pursuing them, or if another separate storm was brewing ahead of them, but neither boded well for them. Beneath the thoughts of immediate death, of being torn apart by the swirling monstrosity behind them, he found himself wondering about acid rain and lightning in this place.

His chest hurt from the pace. The air his body necessarily sucked into his lungs tasted like exhaust and made his chest hurt even worse. His legs burned from the exertion of running through the thick atmosphere. It was nightmare-running, where one's legs just couldn't move him fast enough to get away. They wouldn't be able to keep up a sufficient pace to outrun the thing for long. His eyes darted along the length of rock for some haven they could dive into before the beast behind them overtook them. *Please oh please oh pleaseohpleaseohplease....*

Then, there it was—a small fissure in the rock that was just narrow enough for them to slip through but too narrow, Erik thought, for those barbed whips.

Mendez was keeping up beside him but panting and coughing. He tugged Mendez toward the fissure and they both ducked through, clearing the entrance by a few feet before stopping to catch their breaths. Beyond the pocket of boulders where they stood was a small valley that continued along the length of the cliffs but was canopied by outcroppings of rock formations. As they considered where to go next, there was a thunderous crash as one of the tails slammed against the narrow rock arch. The creature bellowed in frustration, and another booming sound echoed through the valley as it pounded the arch again. It was trying to break through. They couldn't stay where they were. Erik looked uneasily above him, where a faint sound of creaking rock echoed down beneath the cacophony. He hoped that the Higher Power N.A. had been so fond of invoking, whatever it was and wherever it was, could span universes too, and if so, keep an avalanche from crushing them to death against the extrinsic stone.

They made their way as quickly and carefully as they could tight along the cliff face beneath the rock canopy where the beast couldn't reach them. After what seemed to Erik like an eternity, the frustrated bellows of the creature behind them receded to angry rumbles. Occasionally the creaking above them drew their eyes up to scan for signs of loose rock about to fall. The uneven terrain beneath them offered nothing safer; it threatened to twist limbs and break bones with a misstep. It was rough work and took what felt like hours of sweating and puffing before the canopy of rock above them pulled back and a familiar vista opened up. Half a mile or so ahead were the shifting, rotating bases of the inverted pyramids.

It was all they could do not to run—until they heard the scream.

Chapter 12

Ian had never considered himself a take-charge kind of guy. He had an IQ of 152 and a photographic memory and could pick up the basics of a language with only limited exposure to it, but these skills had never been the kind that, in his mind, made a leader. Leaders were strong, brave, resourceful, athletic, quick, and bold. Ian was none of those things.

However, seeing the way Lauren had crumpled to the ground, seeing the fear in her eyes, he felt he needed to do something, or at least to say something that would let her know everything was going to be all right. Lauren was smart; he could tell that just from talking to her. She was brave and strong—she had to be, to work with the kind of patients she did, though he doubted she saw it that way. He suspected that when Lauren needed to, she could take charge quite effectively. But this situation seemed to be beyond her ability to think through at the moment. He didn't want her to feel helpless. If Erik was right, then that would only leave her more vulnerable to the Hollowers' attacks. And he had no doubt that just because they had shoved clear of anything in his own known universe, that didn't mean that the Hollowers weren't watching and waiting, somewhere in the periphery.

"Lauren," he began. She looked up at him from where she sat on the ground. Her eyes—they were really very beautiful eyes—were wet with tears.

"Lauren, we're going to get out of here."

She sighed. "I don't see how."

He looked around at the structures, still shuffling infinitesimally and rotating from time to time on their bases. "I think," he said, "that Erik had the right idea. Wrong building maybe, but the right idea." He crouched down beside her. "See, the one we picked had markings inside. Hieroglyphics and symbols from even older languages. Earth languages, mostly. This is a whole other universe. Those languages could only be known if there were, at some point, some crossing of worlds. It's possible this whole grouping of buildings or whatever they are may have little pieces we need to get out of here."

She looked from him to the buildings, then back to him. "What about Erik and Detective Mendez?"

"Well," he answered softly, "we won't find them sitting here. Come on." They rose and faced the buildings.

After a moment, Lauren said, "I think we should try that one." The building she was looking at was smaller than the others, and leaning to the left.

He smiled, glad she had recovered from her shock quickly and enough to want to contribute. "Why that one?"

She pointed to a symbol carved into the front-most face that hadn't been visible from that angle before its most recent rotation.

"I don't know what that actual symbol means in any language, but to me, it looks like caduceus, with the staff part there and those coiling things like snakes around it. If I'm even close, that would be some kind of medical building. The Hollowers came through to our world via a medical building. Maybe there has to be something corresponding on the other side."

Ian squeezed her shoulder and noticed she blushed a little. "Good thinking. Let's go."

They moved with caution toward the building Lauren had indicated. It wasn't so much a conscious thought in Ian's mind that it would be dangerous to startle the structures, but the sentiment was there all the same. Whatever these structures had been created for, they were more than just shells, more than just buildings.

The structure which had the caduceus carved into it leaned over them as they approached, bulging about halfway toward the top of the flat base. The bulge grew defined in shape—a rectangle—and from beneath it, another rectangle flipped outward on an angle and then another until a crude detached staircase had formed in a spiral around the whole pyramid. At the top of the stairs, the stony substance puckered and fell away like sand, sinking to form an opening about six feet in height.

"Should we...?"

Lauren took his hand, squeezed it, and started up the stairs. He followed close behind her. They made their way up with slow and careful steps, a hand on the wall to steady them. Beneath his palm, the surface of the structure felt cool and slightly grainy, like a fine-grade sandpaper. Occasionally, it rippled beneath his fingers, particularly if he pressed it harder for balance.

When they reached the top, they peered together into the building's interior beyond the opening. It was unlighted inside, but from the top step, they could see an impossibly long hallway. Lauren squeezed his hand again, and together, they went inside.

The hallway reverberated a hollow echo as he and Lauren crept along. From what he could make out in the dim light, white cobblestones ran the length of floor beneath him, and smooth white stone comprised the walls and ceiling.

The faint strain of a child's laugh—or a cry; it was hard to be sure—made its way back to them. In the dark, he could feel Lauren squeeze his hand again. Just then the tunnel opened up, and they found themselves in a large, domed room, Victorian in style and entirely white with light blue trim, wainscoting, and breadboard. The ceiling dome was painted a light blue like the sky, and someone had painted clouds that suggested faces overlaid. Whether they were faces of angels or gods or even demons, Lauren couldn't say. There was no furniture in the room except for a single wing-back easy chair slightly off-center. The chair's blue paisley cushions had long slashes in them as if from knives or claws.

"Where are—" Before Lauren could finish the question, the chair scraped across the floor.

A young boy was sitting in it. His feet barley brushed the floor. He was pale, hollow-eyed and dark-haired. His head was bowed so that his chin touched the top of his bony little chest.

The boy's bones looked to be all broken and disjointed, and his flesh was rotting away. Something—his eye, Ian thought— hung limp and drying from a socket.

A rush of dizziness seemed to come over her, and he caught her and held her up as she fought it.

"Dustin?"

The boy looked up. His right eye swung from its socket.

"Dustin?" Her voice cracked.

"That's not your cousin," Ian told her. He touched her arm. "Come on."

"You let him hurt me." The voice from the thing that looked like Lauren's cousin was scratchy, a smoker's voice, an old man's voice. *No*, he thought. *A mangled voice. The voice of a crushed windpipe.*

"I tried to help you."

"Ignore it," Ian told her. "You know that's not your cousin. Ignore whatever it says to you."

The child-thing ran a fingernail beneath a protruding shard of rib, following the curve still encased in his thin skin, and drew blood. He peeled back the pale flap of flesh and it sloughed off easily into his hand.

"I'm sorry. I tried." Lauren's voice was losing steam, losing volume and strength. The memory, Ian supposed, was a very powerful one.

"You didn't! You didn't try!" It rose from the chair.

"Please," she whispered, begging with it. "Please."

Ian looked around the room for something he could throw at it, something he could puncture the illusion with. There was debris in the corners, suggesting a room long relegated to locked doors and disuse—part of a cardboard box, some papers, broken pieces of the crown molding and wainscoting He spied a lone table leg and lifted it to hurl it at the thing in the chair. When he turned to it, however, it was his mother. Leather straps around her wrists and ankles bound her to an uncomfortable-looking wooden chair. She looked worn and pale. Her hair hung limp and colorless around her face.

"You're a rotten son," it said in that same terrible, choked voice. "You let them kill me."

"You. Are. Not. My. Mother!" he screamed, and threw the table leg as hard as he could. It hit the thing just above the right eyebrow, and the head burst open like a pinata. From inside, blue light poured forth, lighting the corners that gloom had obscured. In those corners, corpses slumped in chairs, their bony wrists strapped down. There were a dozen of them, maybe more.

In a far corner of the room was a doorway, and Ian tugged Lauren through the blue light toward it. Lauren's hip bumped one of the chairs and the head of the corpse sitting in it rolled down the chest and onto the floor in a puff of dust. From the neck, hundreds of shiny black bugs began to pore out, chirping and creaking and scrabbling on thousands of tiny legs. Lauren gagged and ran to catch up with Ian, who was waiting for her in the doorway. The two pitched through and sailed down a long flight of stone steps that spiraled round and round and round until Ian felt seasick.

Finally, the stairs emptied out onto a stone landing and into another room.

"Where the hell are we now?" Frustration and anger were beginning to weigh on him. They weren't getting anywhere except deeper in trouble.

The room they were in was also made of a kind of stone, but sand-colored. Whereas the room upstairs had been most definitively human in style, this room was alien in its strange asymmetrical angles and odd slopes. The impossible geometries and physics of the larger structures outside were, in smaller scale, present in this room as well. Looking too long at any one aspect of the architecture made Ian feel sick.

"I don't know." Lauren's own frustration colored her expression as well.

There was nothing in the room except for a long, jade-green slab irregularly cut but polished to a shine. On this slab were large oval stones. Ian walked up to them and looked down.

At first, the symbols carved in the stones were unfamiliar, a language he had never seen before. Then the symbols swam in his vision and reformed themselves into words he recognized. His mother had taught them to him just as she had taught him Latin and Greek, Egyptian and Phoenician. His major in Ancient Languages had touched on it, too. Nothing in the room may have been human, but the language on those stones now was. It was ancient Aramaic.

"I can read this," he said.

"What?" Lauren looked at him, surprised.

"Yeah, languages—that's sort of my specialty. Ancient Languages. This is Aramaic. It's an Afroasiatic language believed to be at least 3000—" He felt the blush in his cheeks, knowing how obscure and probably unsexy all that sounded.

But she startled him by saying, "Wow, that's really cool. I've never met anyone who knew ancient languages. That's really amazing."

He studied her face to see if she was being sarcastic, but both her tone and the look in her eyes were sincere.

"Well, thanks." He returned her smile.

"So what does it say?"

"Oh, right. Let's see...." He studied the symbols carefully. "This here is talking about the mind and the soul...about...soul eaters." He frowned. "It's talking about how the soul eaters swim through the...I'm not sure what that is, but I think it's empty space. How they swim through the empty space looking for souls and that whatever they devour becomes lost forever. It says nothing can contain them except their...."

"Their what?" Lauren asked when he paused.

"The black hole of their home."

She frowned. "What does that mean?"

"It...it almost sounds like it's talking about the Hollowers. They are soul eaters, in a way."

"That last part...if we send them home...?"

"I—"

Just then, a loud siren wail filled the room. Ian covered his ears. The stones trembled and broke into pieces. The jade slab beneath cracked in half and fell down into the pit beneath.

"What the—"

Then something pushed him and he was falling forward, falling down, down that long pit. He heard Lauren screaming and knew she was falling too. Part of him wanted to just keep falling, to avoid whatever was at the bottom and whatever the Hollowers wanted to throw at them next. He couldn't imagine how Erik could have kept picking himself up and dusting himself off, over and over. As he fell toward the unknown, a part of him just wanted to give up. He closed his eyes.

He landed hard enough to bite his tongue. He heard a hard thump next to him, and Lauren coughing. He opened his eyes. They were outside again in the courtyard.

"This is getting old," Ian said, sitting up. He got up and helped Lauren to her feet.

The buildings had all cleared to the side of the courtyard. In the center, hovering a few feet above the stones, was a mass of whirring black wings. That was all Ian could see at first, just a mass of black wings moving so quickly they blurred. Then some of the wings stopped moving and Ian could make out three mouths in a triangle shape, thin black lips bared to show sharp yellow teeth.

"Oh! Oh shit!" Lauren grabbed Ian's arm.

The wings started up again and the monster lunged toward them. Lauren screamed.

A moment later there was the pounding of feet and Ian turned to see Erik and Mendez running from between the rocks of the cliffs across from them. Relief, even in the face of the thing in front of them, washed over him. He grabbed Lauren's hand and tugged her away from the monster and toward the guys.

The whir of wings behind them reminded Ian of an electric knife. As he and Lauren reached Erik and Detective Mendez, that buzzing sliced the air by his ear. He felt a cold graze of pain over his shoulder blade and down his back. The shock more than the pain drove him down on one knee and the buzzing sailed above him. He tried to stand but the pain in his back was immense. Already, the left side of his back was growing cold and tacky with the blood seeping through his torn shirt.

"Ian!" Lauren skidded in the dirt and turned back to him, a look of concern on her face. She didn't even see the claws descend and dig into her shoulders, scraping to gain purchase around her arms, and he didn't have time to get to her before the thing lifted her up off the ground. Lauren screamed again, struggling and evidently discovering this made things worse. She whimpered, her hands scratching at the claws, trying to pry them loose. Blood bloomed at her shoulders and spread down the front of her top.

"Help me! Detective Mendez, please! Ian! Erik! Somebody—ow!"

Mendez pulled his gun and aimed at the beast, but hesitated in firing.

"Do something!" Ian shouted, rising to his feet with a painful groan.

"I can't!" Mendez said, keeping the gun trained on the monster. "I'll hit her!"

The beast lurched upward and Lauren cried out in pain. She closed her eyes as the wings whirred faster and the creature lifted her again.

Then the monster jerked mid-air with a bellow of pain and anger, and then dropped Lauren clumsily to the ground. It landed with a heavy thump on the ground next to her. She began to shake all over, crying and kicking between the thing's wings while simultaneously crab-scuttling away from it. Ian ran to Lauren and held her as she cried. He peered over the bulk of the thing to see what had taken it down.

A small woman with frizzy brown hair, clothes torn and face smudged with red dirt, both hands gripping the sharpened stick that now protruded from the center of the beast's mouths, muttered, "Fucker," and spit at the thing.

"Anita!" Mendez ran to her scooping up her little frame in his arms and crushing her to him, pelting the top of her head with kisses. *"Dios mio*, I thought I'd never see you again." When he pulled her back, her eyes were red and wet with tears.

"Cora?" she whispered.

"She's fine. Alive and well and cute as ever."

"Oh thank God." Anita's voice, scratchy with grit and choked with emotion, broke into sobs of relief. Mendez pulled her tightly to him again. Muffled into his chest, she said, "Thank God. They told me...." She seemed unable to finish.

"They lied. The baby is fine."

Erik, Lauren, and Ian let her cry out her relief, let Mendez hold her until he felt secure in her realness, in his having found her. When the two finally pulled apart, Erik said, "Let's get the hell out of here, huh?"

The Triumvirate

Chapter 13

Ian helped Lauren and Mendez helped Anita as they followed Erik toward the rocky valley where he and Mendez had made their way back to the courtyard. They needed to rest, to regroup someplace where nothing could hurt them. So far, the valley, even with its ever-present threat of falling rock, was still the safest and most reliable place they had been in that world.

Ian helped Lauren onto a nearby flat rock and sat down next to her. Anita and Mendez sank onto an adjacent rock, and Erik leaned against another. For a long time, no one spoke. Finally, Erik said, "I'm sorry."

The rest of them looked at him.

"For what?" Mendez asked.

"For...not being Dave. Not being able to keep us together, or get us out of this mess. I'm sorry. I just...I don't know what to do next."

He noticed others exchanging glances of sympathy. Anita got up and came over to him, putting her thin arm around his shoulders. "Listen, sugar," she said, "you have always been willing to do whatever it took to protect the people you love. You've risked your life for others, and you've survived something that has the kind of odds of being in not one, but three plane crashes. And you've come out okay. We've all come out okay. This situation is nothing like any experience any of us has ever had, and there's no way to prepare for it. We're holding on and doing what we can to survive and get home. No one—not even Dave—could do more."

The others nodded in agreement and offered their own affirmatives. Anita went on. "I'll tell you what I told Dave, when all was said and done. I told him that from time to time, we accept roles as caretakers of others. Sometimes as a parent, a spouse, a sibling, whatever that role is, we feel it's our responsibility to take care of someone else. But there aren't any guidelines to it. You do the best you can. That's all anyone in your care, to whatever degree, can possibly ask of you."

"Erik," Lauren added, "we're all still here. In fact, we found Mrs. Mendez, so I'd say we're ahead of the game."

Anita smiled. "See, you found me. Mission accomplished." She winked at her husband and returned to the rock next to him.

Erik smiled a little at her. "Highlight of my day."

"Look, man, we've got your back. We're going home. You told me that."

Erik ran a hand through his hair and sighed. "We still have to find a way out of here."

"We could try that way." Ian gestured at a rock pathway leading in a different direction from where Erik and Mendez had come. This path looked deliberate, the stone arch along its length overhead even and smooth. At the far end, a couple hundred feet down, Erik could just make out some kind of stone block or pillar.

"Why that way?" Mendez asked.

"Because I think...I think that might be a door."

The others rose to look, and Erik thought the kid might be right. It could be a door down there; that was as viable an option as anything else here. There were no guidelines, as Anita had said. They'd just have to go on instinct. They'd just have to...well, trust themselves, he supposed.

"Let's try it," he said, and he and Ian led the way down the path.

The pathway opened to a small courtyard of bleached stone. A white stone ring stood upright, framing a thin rectangular stone slab. Two larger vaults lay on the ground, any writing having long worn away to indecipherable grooves. Erik moved around the vaults, ran a hand along the edge of the ring, and looked behind the slab. If it was a door, it didn't seem to go anywhere. If it had to be activated somehow, the mechanism was hidden.

Mendez voiced the thought on Erik's mind. "So how do we make it work?"

"Not sure," Ian said, unperturbed. He examined the ring, searching its flat surface carefully. He ran a hand over the slab they had taken to be a door. Then he turned to the vaults. Brushing some red dust off the surface of one, he said, "I think...." He blinked, rubbing his eyes. "I think this is the same kind of writing as what Lauren and I found back in one of those pyramids. It...see, it changes. It's like it automatically translates for the species reading it. Although, given that it's ancient Aramaic, my guess is that whoever developed this kind of Rosetta Stone-like feature of writing did it back, well...before the Rosetta Stone. Still, I think I can make some of it out...."

The others crowded around him.

"What are you, some kind of linguist?" Mendez asked.

Ian flushed red. "I...yes, I suppose you could say that. My mother—well, when she was sane...and you know, still alive—she taught me ancient languages. I had an ear for them, so that's what I went to school for."

"I think it's really cool," Lauren said, and squeezed his arm. He smiled at her.

"Actually," Mendez said, "that is pretty impressive. And very lucky—for all of us. What does this say?"

"Well," Ian said, running a finger in the grooves to try to clear them of further dust. "This part's nearly all worn away. This...is something about gods...something about the ancient Ones Without Names, who amuse themselves with the chaosium of galaxies, who existed before time and who created universes from the voids. Not much help there.... And this part's too faded." His finger traced down a few lines, then he skipped to the next vault. A line or two down, he continued. "This talks about... uh...the end. Of these people. They saw it coming. They knew the soul-eaters had come with pieces of their dying world inside them. The soul-eaters brought...others. In the end, they brought others with them and... oh God."

"What does it say?" Lauren touched his arm.

"They tried to open up their own rip...at least, I think that's what they mean. They call it a mouth of worlds right here...." He pointed as he looked up at them, judged from their expressions that they had no idea what he was pointing at, and went back to translating. "They tried to open up a rip to the Hollowers' home world. The Triumvirate—here they call them a...like, a committee, a triumvirate—found out beforehand and brought the...can't read that but it looks from the sentence after like the Hollowers brought in gods from other universes. Fierce predator gods."

"Does it say how they did it?" Erik asked. "I mean, how these people or whatever they were opened up a rip to the Hollowers' own dimension?"

Ian scanned the faded carvings for a moment and said, "Only contextually. It looks like they made some kind of artifact, but had no time to activate it. The Hollowers and these predator gods got to them first, and the artifact was...sent away. Not sure what that means. It ends here with this inscription: 'We are echoes in the wind. Our last words are scars on the skin of time.' It looks like after that, there are symbols. Designs, maybe. Nothing I can identify as words."

The others were quiet for a time. Lauren broke the silence with a little choked sob. "They wiped out an entire race. They destroyed...oh God." Ian put his arm around her and hugged her. They looked to Erik like survivors of a terrible war, their clothes ripped and bloody, their faces smudged with red dirt.

"So...this artifact, this thing they used to open the rip. It was...sent away?" Mendez eyed the ring and the slab.

"My guess," Ian said, "would be they sent it someplace the Hollowers wouldn't find it."

"I'm a little surprised the Hollowers haven't tried to come down on this party. Why would they let us find—or even send us to a dimension where we could find—suggestions on how to defeat them?"

The others looked at Ian, who, realizing they were awaiting an answer, shrugged and blushed again. "Well, I don't really know. I'm just throwing out a theory here, but the Hollowers seem to borrow other languages in order to interact with their prey. My guess is that they don't have a language of their own—a written language, at least. Although they seem able to sense and understand whatever they need once they're in a dimension, they didn't sense this. So it's my guess that whatever advanced technology could create writing that translates itself could also create writing that is encoded somehow so the destroyers of their race couldn't read it even if they wanted to."

"I'd buy that," Anita said. "But all this doesn't put that artifact in our hands, or get us home. There's nothing in that writing that tells us where they sent it, or how they got it there?"

Ian shook his head apologetically.

"I say we see what's in these vaults," Lauren said. "I mean, everything Ian translated for us is on the covers of these vaults. So maybe whatever we need to activate this door or find this artifact, whatever it is, is inside."

Erik sized up the cover of the vault nearest to him, running a finger along its lower edge. "It's pretty solid. Probably pretty heavy."

"Can we lift it, the three of us?" Mendez indicated himself, Erik, and Ian.

"Doubt it, but you might be able to lift it with the five of us." Anita raised an eyebrow at her husband and he laughed.

"You're right, my dear. How about you and Lauren come around to my side, and Erik and Ian can take the other side?"

They moved around the vault to the positions Mendez had suggested.

"Okay," Mendez said, "on the count of three, we'll pick it up and move it down that way. Ready? One, two, three!"

With a series of effortful grunts and the grating of stone against stone, they managed to first loosen, then slide the cover of one vault along its edge and clumsily topple it to the ground. They stood back, panting from the effort, and took a look inside.

"Oh my God," Anita said, blessing herself in old Roman Catholic tradition.

The vault was bottomless, a well looking down on deep space full of stars and distant nebulae. Comets shot across the scope of their visible field, and Erik thought he saw a planet out there, wreathed by rings of shining dust. There was no sound, no sense of cold or warmth, no pull toward that planet and those stars. It was a portion of space neatly contained, a portal to the rest of that dimension's celestial universe.

"How...what.... Damn." Erik looked up at Mendez. "We need to open the other one."

The five of them lined up in the same positions around the second vault. Mendez counted off again and they heaved the cover off and onto the ground.

Inside the second vault's deep space had a different configuration of stars, a system of small, rocky planets encircled by even smaller moons. Far off, galaxies swirled, bright and twinkling with the suns of countless solar systems.

From the canyon around them, the rocks began to hum. That was the only way Erik could think to describe it; the rock structures—the ring and the slab, the vaults—began to vibrate slightly and emit a low hum. The parcels of space inside the vaults drew from deep within their silence a rushing sound like crashing waves.

Behind them, layers of the stone slab's surface crumbled and chipped away and Erik could see the galaxy inside it exposed beneath. Whole chunks of pale stone fell away, and Erik and the others found themselves standing in the center of a triangle of exposed outer space. They were struck dumb with awe, unable to move until that hum reached its peak and both the vaults and the slab took on a dark purple glow. Slowly, Erik backed away, he and Mendez shepherding the others out from the middle of the configuration.

The glow of each space formed beams which shot out, meeting in the middle. As they poured into each other, the purple glow slid, almost like a liquid on glass, down the length of air beneath it, growing darker and darker. The tangy smell of ozone permeated the canyon.

"It's making a rip!" Ian called out.

Erik thought he might be right. The dark spill of light from the intersecting beams folded in, pinching the air and finally puncturing it. Like the unzipping of a tent flap, a rip flared open, its edges rippling from the force of the purple beams above it.

It was then that the canyon began to crumble. Shards and boulders thundered above them, sliding out of place. Erik felt the ground beneath him shake, the cliffs above echoing the sounds of moving rock.

"What's going on?" Lauren asked. Rocks tumbled down the side of the cliff. A large boulder fully the size of a man crashed down onto the archway over the path they had come down.

"The canyon—it's crumbling! It's gonna landslide." Erik looked at Mendez, then the rip, then back at Mendez, who nodded.

"Let's go," he said to the others.

"Where?" Anita asked.

"Anywhere but here, my dear," Mendez answered, and tugged his wife after Erik. Lauren and Ian followed suit.

At the edge of the rip, Erik peered in. Beyond it was another night sky, but beneath it was a beautiful city containing strange buildings of sleek, dark stone and soft glowing lights. Erik didn't give it much thought beyond that. He jumped, and the liquid black which swallowed him muted the sounds of falling rock behind him.

***

In the dimension to which the Triumvirate had sent the meats, there had been many, many lightenings and darkenings since a lifekind had existed which had the capability of producing the complex emotions on which the Likekind fed. All that remained of life on that world were savage physical beings who engaged in the repulsive acts of sustaining and recreating physical life, and nothing else. The Triumvirate, however, found many of the kinds to be easily manipulated, both in their world and in others. Though the beings' physicality rapidly deteriorated in the Earth world, they still retained enough instinct and cohesion long enough to destroy Earth beings, which was all the Triumvirate needed them for, anyway.

Like so many beings in so many worlds, the continuation of a being's essence was connected to the physical shell which contained it. The Likekind had learned long ago that to threaten that shell with damage or destruction was often sufficient to heighten the production of Emotions, and to ultimately crack that shell yielded much to quell the tearing, churning emptinesses that drove the Likekind to feed.

The Triumvirate had also learned that many beings in many worlds fed instead on the shells of other, usually lesser, beings. While they could not fathom something so meaningless and revolting, they recognized that it often worked in their favor, in such instances as the Earth meats in the world a sentient lifekind once called Cayuad-bthl.

That sentient lifekind had known its distinction was imminent. It had tried to stop it, to stop the Triumvirate Who Had Come Before. It had failed. None were left. The world belonged to the lesser lifekinds now.

But that lifekind had left a message in those motionprints called "writing." They had used that rare ability they and very few others seemed to have of crafting the motionprints so that the decipherer would "see" them in a language of their own world. It was, from what the Triumvirate had gathered, a technique they had used to record their most important knowledge, for the benefit of any who might come after.

And the Triumvirate had been unable to detect it. They had been unable, from either the Convergence or from Cayuad-bthl, to sense and comprehend the message.

That had been another sly skill of the extinct lifekind in the art of motionprints.

The Triumvirate were angry that a dead lifekind had given the meats secrets. They were frustrated that the meats had figured out a way to access that dead lifekind's means of conveyance. It made their own Hate strong enough to stir the inside into black holes inside into motion again. They had been tempted to seal up that world of bestial life with the Earth meats in it, but they had found some sort of rift created by the dead ones before their annihilation. The meats had activated it and it had moved them into a space outside the realm of known dimensions. The Triumvirate could not sense the meats at first. This did not alarm so much as frustrate them. It would take focus among them, but the meats would be found.

Still, the meats were proving to be more resourceful and thus, more dangerous than at first perceived. The Likekind were right in wanting to see them terminated. Their numbers were not as they were during the Ages of Origin. There were so few of the Likekind left, and so many meats in the place called Earth. That such an inferior lifekind could, even in comparatively small numbers, end the energies of any one of the Likekind was both a surprise and a threat to the Likekind as a whole. The Triumvirate, to whom all information flowed, and from whom all retribution was dealt, felt that such a situation could not be allowed to continue.

It took quite a while for the Triumvirate to locate them in the new world, a place beyond even the Likekind's notice. Perhaps that had been intentional. It was no matter. They had found the meats once again, and the Triumvirate were in agreement that it was time for the meats to die.

Chapter 14

Erik opened his eyes to what his mind told him were the sounds of summer nights—tree frogs and crickets. The air was stale but mild, and Erik found it a little easier to breathe. For a moment, he thought maybe they had slipped through a rip that had landed them right back on Earth somehow. But then he rose painfully and limped to the low, moonlight-streaked stone wall that surrounded the small city, fully taking in the buildings in front of him. It was obvious this was no place anywhere on his own home world.

All the buildings as far as Erik could see were made of the same shiny stone, polished dark gray tinged with veins of bright blues and greens. The soft glow of blue and green lights was visible through keystone-shaped fixtures in crisscrossing gold holders hung at the gates, at the bases of staircases, adorning archways, and flanking doorways all throughout the city. None of the buildings had signs or symbols identifying their type, nor could Erik see any windows or doors. Erik approximated the center of the city from the placement of the tallest of the buildings, an imposing obelisk leaning impossibly both to the left and, further up, to the right, with a spiral twist at the top. It didn't appear to have windows, but several long silver streamers lay against the walls in the usual places windows would appear in an office building. Occasionally, the breeze coaxed them into dancing for a moment and then let them go, and they'd clink against the surface of the polished stone. Several of the other smaller buildings imitated the oddly angled architecture by starting as obelisks and topping off with curving or leaning geometric feats and flourishes that seemed to defy gravity. A few bullet-shaped buildings surrounded the larger obelisks, with bony arcs, round blades, and fin-like structures embedded in the soft points of their peaks. The roads between buildings had been paved with shiny black stones in kidney shapes, more or less interlocking.

Closer to him were the first signs of wildlife. Strange lush bushes grew along the length of the outer city wall, the tips and edges of their leaves glowing a light blue. The red flowers nestled into those bushes nipped and snapped and yawned at the tiny glowing particles that darted near and around them. Erik crouched down and reached a tentative finger toward a brilliant crimson bloom. It pulled back its center petals to reveal tiny, sharp-looking teeth and lunged at him. He pulled his finger back, awed.

Remembering the others, he looked around and saw them nearby, groaning and standing and taking in the city as he had. Behind them, a night so thick that no light penetrated it, including the subdued glow of the moon over the city.

"Wow." Lauren joined him at the outer wall, her eyes wide and shining as she gazed at the city. In the moonlight, the blood on her top looked black. She scratched at the claw-mark on her arm absently. "It's kind of beautiful, isn't it?"

"It's wild," Erik said, a little breathlessly.

"*A Dios mio*," Mendez said behind him.

"Do you think there are people here?" Lauren asked.

"Possibly," Ian said, coming up beside her. "There are lights. Could be a sign the sentient species is still running the place."

"I think we should look around," Anita said. "That other race from the other world had their escape hatch or whatever it was open here for a reason. Maybe whoever wrote those words or made that artifact to send the Hollowers back to their own dimension escaped here. Or at the very least, maybe the artifact itself is here."

Erik looked doubtfully at the black behind her. "How do we know it's not out there?"

"We don't," she answered, then smiled playfully. "I don't know about you, Erik, but I'd rather start in a lit city first, huh?"

"Can't argue there," he said, returning her smile with effort. "Let's go."

They approached the gates to the city, two panels of elaborate metal scroll work parted just enough to let something of human size through.

Behind them, the pitch black rumbled. Erik couldn't tell if it was thunder, machinery, or the sinister growl of something angry at their intrusion, and decided he really didn't want to find out. "We better move," he said, eying the black, and slipped through the parted gates. Mendez and Anita slipped in after, followed by Lauren and finally, Ian.

"Should we pull the gate closed?" Ian's hand rest on one of the metal curls in the scroll work

"I don't think so," Erik said. "We may need to get the hell out of here in a hurry."

"Good point," Ian said, and let go of the gate. "So, where to start?"

"Why don't we just walk a bit through the streets, get a feel for the place? We've been striking out with buildings so far."

They moved as a group, quiet and close to each other, each step careful, each gaze still tinged with awe. Their footsteps made clipped echoes that sounded stale somehow in Erik's ears, as if the place had long forgotten how to process the sound of living things moving through it. They passed silent monuments of smooth stone, soaring arches and grand staircases leading to terraces above the main level of the city. No living beings that they could see looked down from the carved stone railings or stared from the shadowed corners of alleys and overhangs. There wasn't anything Erik could identify as a street sign or marker, and the buildings, on closer inspection, upheld his initial impression of being largely similar, so he tried to fix landmarks in his head. He was starting to think of the city as a graveyard, with stone monuments to the long-gone architects who had built them. But there were no real signs of decay from disuse, and there were the lights. So where were the people?

He turned the word "people" over in his head. Were they people? Were they anything like his concept of people at all?

A bridge loomed over them, linking terrace to terrace, and the curved underside glowed a faint violet that teased and twisted the darkness beneath into shapes, but as they drew closer, passing under, passing through, nothing made a move to touch them.

In the distance, Erik heard another rumble like before, from beyond the gates of the city. It sounded closer.

"That doesn't sound good," Anita said.

"No," Erik agreed. "It doesn't."

There was a groaning of metal and another sound, and this time, it sounded clearer; not a machine and not thunder, but something mobile and very large, something recently emerged from the darkness beyond the gates of the city. Something animal and alien, most definitely not Erik's idea of "people" at all.

"Oh my God," Ian breathed, and they all turned to see what he was looking at.

They could only see part of the beast outside the gate over the tops of the buildings, but that meant it was big, easily three stories. It was a soapstone kind of greenish-gray, veined with black. It had a grouping of pupilless black eyes set high in a massive head. A row of talon-like teeth, thick and curved, ringed a series of hanging stalks grouped beneath the eyes that swung like thick vines with its movements. It didn't look like it had a bottom jaw; rather, a thick neck supported the head somehow underneath that curtain of stalks. Erik could see a set of leathery wings drawn close to its curved back. The rest of its body was obscured by the buildings. The gates rattled and groaned, and it roared again, swung its massive head, grumbled, and shook those stalks vigorously. It amazed Erik that the thing could shake so big a head so fast.

"I hope to God that's not one of the city's inhabitants," Lauren said in a low voice.

"I don't think it can get in. At least, I hope it can't." Ian took a step forward. "It's huge."

Erik looked around and, spying a terrace overhang completely in shadow, he said, "Let's move out of its way. Here, under here." The group moved together into the shadow. Erik backed up until he felt cool stone against his back. From their hiding place they could no longer see the beast, but they heard it rattle the gate again and utter a halfhearted roar. After what felt like an hour or so of waiting in silence, the rumbling receded. There were no sounds of footsteps or even of the flapping of wings. However it managed to move its great bulk, it was silent except for its low thunder-rumble.

Erik was just about to suggest they move on when they heard a kittenish mewling from the street. Its source, too, was beyond their sight line.

"Well, we know at least something is alive in this city," Anita said.

"Whatever that was," Mendez's voice floated to him, "it sounds like it's a hell of a lot easier to handle than that Goliath outside the gate."

A tiny shadow stained the moonlit stones of the pavement. It was hard to make out a distinct shape, but it appeared to have at least four short legs. It mewled again, but the sound distorted as it drew out. It sounded strangled, crushed inside the throat making it. A moment later, whatever it was darted away.

Minutes ticked off as they waited to see if it, or anything else, would come back. Nothing did.

Erik felt a hand clap him on the shoulder in the darkness.

"I think it's safe to move now," Mendez said.

Erik watched him and Anita emerge as silhouettes at the edge of the overhang, joined a moment after by Ian and then Lauren.

The hand still clasped his shoulder.

He gave a shout and whirled around, squinting, trying to force his eyes to see what was in the heavy shadow behind him. There was nothing there.

"Erik, what's wrong, man? You okay?" Mendez took a few steps toward him, but he waved that he was fine.

"Everything's, uh...yeah, let's go."

He joined the others at the edge of the overhang, casting several glances over his shoulder to make sure nothing was coming up behind them. Outside in the moonlight, he examined his shoulder. Coppery smudges formed a distinct hand print on his jacket where he'd felt the hand. The fingers, he saw, were very long. There was a slight tear in the jacket fabric about where the fingernails would have been. He shuddered. Mendez, who had been watching him, touched the rip and muttered something to himself in Spanish that Erik didn't quite catch.

"What happened back there?" Anita eyed his shoulder.

"Don't know. Something touched me."

Mendez looked at the overhang's unbroken, silent shadow, and said, "Maybe it was a ghost."

"Seriously?" Erik cast him a curious, side-long glance.

Mendez met his skepticism with a look that said he was most definitely serious. "Sure, why not? If ghosts are trapped souls and souls are energy, it is not so far-fetched to believe that when creatures in other worlds and on other planets die, their energy might sometimes get trapped, too."

Erik considered it for a moment. The idea made his mind reel. How were they supposed to handle entities which were both alien and ghost, functioning in a world where the laws of physics and metaphysics might not apply as they did back home? What, in God's name (or maybe, far outside of it) were they dealing with?

"Detective Mendez has a point," Ian said after a while. "I mean, it really isn't any crazier than anything else we've seen." From the tightness beneath his words, Erik got a brief sense of the toll all this was taking on him, the strain to the sanity he was so afraid of losing. "This could be a graveyard world. Or for all we know, this could be the Heaven—or Hell—for an alien race, another dimension."

Erik ran a hand through his hair and sighed. The massive implications made his head hurt. "I suppose it's possible. Geez, alien ghosts. And that thing out there—I can't even begin to...." He shook his head. He could hear the tension in his own voice, the weariness, and tried his best to keep it from creeping into irritation. "Okay, look, let's keep looking around. My brain has just about reached its processing limit. I think you guys are probably dead on about this place, but I don't want any part of some alternate Heaven or Hell. If those aliens or whatever sent their artifact here, let's find it and find a way out of here."

"Agreed," Mendez said. The others nodded.

As they walked, Erik could feel the others' eyes on his back. He thought Mendez may have told them to give him a little space. They were all tired, sore, beaten up, scared, hungry, and thirsty. They had all been through a lot. But Erik thought they recognized that he had shouldered the responsibility for them on top of all that, despite their protests. And that responsibility was monumental in a world so unlike anything they had ever seen. They hadn't found water yet, nor could they be sure that any plant there wouldn't cause them to die outright of poisoning or explode on the spot or something. There was no way home except by accident or the will of the Hollowers who had sent them away to begin with. They were looking for an artifact they had never seen before, on the off chance that it might still work after, what? Centuries? Millenia? And if they should find that particular needle in a haystack, they'd still need to draw the Hollowers out of wherever they were and time it so that they could use the thing before the Hollowers opened up portals to only God knew where. He had promised

Casey that even Hell wouldn't keep him from getting home to her. And it was a promise he had every intention of keeping if he could. He was just starting to run out of faith that he could, in the face of what they were up against. This wasn't like the other times.

It was like closing one's eyes and spitting, and hoping to hit that face on Mars.

He remembered a conversation he and Dave had had once about the odd coincidence of their having found each other. Dave had thought it was a lucky accident, but at the time, Erik believed that it might have been more. He thought then that whatever quality that had drawn the Hollowers to them maybe had drawn them to each other. He hadn't thought of it so much as a guiding force like angels or even fate, really. It was just some quality, some extra sense that maybe even humans had to some degree that had helped them find each other. Maybe it had been some kind of cosmic yin to a yang.

But having seen other dimensions, whole other worlds not just outside his solar system but his whole known universe, he wondered. Maybe it was more than even an extra sense. Maybe there was some force as intertwined with the Hollowers as they were, and that somehow, maybe in visiting these worlds, they had become as intertwined with that force as they were with each other. Maybe, like Feinstein, that force wanted to be able to pass on help and knowledge, even in death.

That concept made him feel less lost, less hopeless.

Behind him, snippets of conversation made their way between his thoughts.

"...that only happens in horror movies...."

"Ghosts can't do that. Besides, I think that's only if you believe, or something...."

"...at least it's quiet. We're not being smacked around by tentacles and...."

"...haven't found us yet...."

"...angels or demons, or maybe carrion-eaters. Who knows?"

"...tombstones for one crazy-big head. Can only imagine what the mausoleums are like."

Erik noticed the soft gray wisps of mist just then, swirling around him and ahead of him. At times, the formations looked to him like faces before stretching or shifting out of shape. The mist felt cool and damp where it brushed against his skin. He looked down at his arms and noticed tiny pearlescent beads were left behind it the wake of the mist's sweep. He brushed them off and they floated away and pulled apart.

The mist swirled in front of him again, whirling up in a mini-cyclone, then shaping itself into something vaguely humanoid. Impressions mimicked the features of a face: two half-dollar-sized indents for eyes, a small rise for a nose, a curve of a mouth.

Erik stopped. He ran a hand through his hair, and the mist figure simulated the action. He tilted his head, and the figure did the same.

He heard the others stop short behind him.

"What the—?"

The mist figure looked up at Mendez's voice and the vague face of it changed. The round impressions of eyes shrank to slits, the bump of a nose and curve of mouth elongating into a snout. Its bottom draw dropped and stretched, and it unearthed a growl that blew the hair back off Erik's forehead. They screamed, and were about to run when the mist figure fell apart and blew away.

"Okay, seriously, what the fuck was that?" Mendez was breathing hard, one protective arm around his wife's shoulders.

"Ghost," Erik said in between pants.

"No shit," Mendez said. "Maybe it's time to get off the streets."

They backed toward a nearby staircase and made their way up two and three at a time. The staircase wound around the massive sides of an obelisk building, climbing higher than suggested from the street. Erik supposed it was the skewed physics of the place, that things found space to be where there didn't appear to be any.

They reached a landing that turned out to be three stories up, looking out over the city wall to the landscape beyond. Erik could see the foliage-fringed edge of a dense jungle in the sand before that impenetrable darkness swallowed it in obscurity. Watching a low frond like a palm rustle in the sliver of moonlight, Erik thought it wasn't such a dead world after all. That was, unless the only things living here fed on the dead. Remembering the plant outside the city and the beast from the lightless desert beyond it, that theory seemed entirely possible.

"I think I found a door," Lauren said, pulling Erik out of his thoughts. He turned to see her standing by a slab of stone with a rounded top and an ornate x-shaped handle of silver where a doorknob would have been. It was free-floating somewhat close to the side of the building but not embedded in it. Erik looked around at the other terraces and saw from his new vantage point that many of them had such similar slabs near various buildings.

He went over to it, checked behind it, and ran a hand across its surface. It floated a couple of feet off the ground, but the handle was within reach. He wrapped a hand around it but hesitated.

"Go ahead," Mendez said. "Open it."

Erik glanced back at him and the others in turn. They were all nodding encouragement.

"Okay, here goes." He yanked on the handle, and all hell broke free.

Chapter 15

The moment Erik pulled on the handle, the stone door swung easily open, and hell came pouring out.

A rush of mist, streams of silver air like he'd seen in the street below, came streaming out of the doorway space. It knocked Erik onto his back and pushed the others up against the railing wall. The mist emitted a high wail like the shearing of metal, and as it got free of the doorway, it began to split off into individual entities that tore frantically around the sky, circling each other. They gained definition, taking on the long-dead skeletal shapes of winged and horned things, of beasts with massive heads overlong muzzles lined with teeth, of things that reminded Erik of the pictures of angler fish he'd seen. There were things that looked to him like masses of eyes and masses of snaking, squirming appendages, there were fish-like things and things vaguely reminiscent of velociraptors. All of them surged and swam and darted across the sky, a smog of them blotting out the moon.

Then the banshee-screaming forms began tearing at each other, ripping into misty flanks with misty mouths, clawing misty underbellies, and the tattered shreds rained down on the terrified group of huddled humans beneath.

"Oh my God," Erik breathed. "Oh my God."

He felt Mendez's hands beneath his arms, pulling him out from under the carnage. Then he was up and they were running down the steps, taking two at a time, gliding down the last few and pounding the black stones of the pavement as they ran back toward the gate. The screeching forms above had noticed them and were following them.

A slicing dagger of pain opened up between his shoulder blades, but Erik kept running. Another opened up along his bicep, and the scream so close to his ear urged him on. He heard cries of pain and surprise from the others as well.

"This way!" Mendez shouted, and veered off to the right. Erik and the others followed him up another wide stone staircase, this one leading first to the right, then banking sharply to the left. The terrace at the top of the staircase had a narrow arch and beyond it, an open veranda at the end of which floated another door.

"Quick!" he shouted. "Get behind it!" The others dove for cover between the gray building and the slab of stone. Erik skidded to a halt alongside Mendez.

"What are you doing?" he shouted.

"I'm gonna open it!"

"What? Are you crazy? What if there's something worse behind—"

One of the wraiths dug a long furrow down his back, sailed up into the night, and circled for a second attack. Another flew right into the building above the heads of the others and broke apart into wisps.

Mendez tugged on the handle and the door flew open. There was a slight sucking sound as the ghosts dived for the open doorway. Screams echoed across the city as the phantoms all zeroed in on that terrace and funneled neatly into the space beyond the doorway. The momentum of their flow through the doorway pulled the heavy stone door shut behind them. Instantly, the empty skies were silent over the dead city.

"How...how did you...?"

"I didn't," Mendez told Erik, breathless. "Know, I mean. It was...just a gut feeling. If something else was in there, it would attack the ghosts. And if not, the emptiness would corral them again."

Erik looked at him skeptically.

"I don't understand it myself. I'm sorry; it was a pretty strong feeling, but I guess it was a pretty stupid thing to try."

Erik punched him lightly in the shoulder. "Risky, maybe. But what hasn't been a risk here? And stupid? Hell no. You saved our lives, *amigo. Muchas gracias.*"

Mendez grinned at him. "*De nada.*"

The others, breathing hard and shaking, rejoined them.

"I really, really want to go home," Lauren whispered. Ian held her close.

"We will," Erik told her. "We will."

***

It took them almost half an hour to find the terrace from which they had released the ghosts. All around the city, the misty shreds lazed up from the street like smoke, dissipating in the breeze. Smears of tiny little pearlescent bubbles dried and popped against the sides of buildings and on arches and railings. They climbed the steps, exhausted, and trudged back to the open doorway.

What they found was a yellow rectangle of open space and light, its edges thin and hard. Beyond it, Erik could see a room. It looked like a vault. Several marbled pedestals rose up from the ground, and on each of them was an object. An easy ten-foot drop from the edge of the doorway to the floor of the room looked promising. Erik climbed over the edge and dropped down into the room.

"Erik, what are you doing?" Lauren asked, nearly hysterical.

"I think...ow! I think we found something," he called up to them.

Mendez dropped beside him, and Ian followed, with Anita helping Lauren over the side, then dropping down herself.

"So what are we looking at here?"

"I think I know," Ian said, looking around with fascination. "I think the rooms—I think they change, depending on which door is opened, and when."

"How's that?" Mendez asked.

"When we opened this door, it was like we'd opened the pen and let out a bunch of animals so crazed and so hungry they cannibalized each other. If you had to contain something like that, you might choose a vault...a mausoleum, maybe. Some kind of containment unit. But not an artifact room. Not someplace like this. And when Detective Mendez opened the other door, they flocked to it like it was inexorable. Whether because of the material of the place or the sense of familiarity and security, they had to return to a room. Therefore, whatever was behind the second door we opened, it was displaced and moved here.

"And here," Anita said slowly, "is an artifact chamber?"

Ian jerked a thumb at a metal ball encased in glowing wires, with a thick twisted wire handle forming a question mark around its circumference. "Looks like. Artifacts from...well, anywhere, possibly. Anywhere at all."

"Do you think the one we want is here? How will we recognize it?" Lauren asked, excited. "Should we take them all?"

"Ever see *Indiana Jones and the Holy Grail*?"

"Huh?"

Erik explained. "We don't know what will happen in here if we pick the wrong one. For all we know, we 'choose poorly' like in the movie, and we wither and turn to dust. I think we should let Ian pick."

"Wait, what? Me?"

"Sure," Mendez said. "You're the only one who can recognize the language the race from the other world used. You know more about ancient languages than any of us, and probably more about their culture, too. If anyone could make an educated guess about which artifact to take, it would be you."

Lauren took his hand and squeezed it. "You can do it. We all believe in you." Softly, she added, "I believe in you."

Ian looked flustered but pleased. "Well, okay, if...if you really think...."

"Go get 'em, tiger," Anita said with a wink.

Ian walked amid the pedestals, studying each of the objects on them carefully. One held a crystal v-shaped object with a tiny teardrop of light dangling between the prongs. Another looked to be an asterisk shape made of some kind of cloth and bound with bright red string. There was something that looked to be made of bone, carved into a double helix shape. Another, surprisingly, held a crucifix. Yet another displayed a glass wand-shaped item with fibrous prongs on either end. There were statuettes and figurines of alien shapes—probably gods—and one framed glass box inside of which swirled a miniature galaxy. But Ian paused the longest at one far off in the corner, checked a few others, and bee-lined right back to it. He seemed to be reading something on it, and he looked excited.

"Uh, guys? I think I found what we're looking for. This one here."

"Go on," Erik encouraged gently. "Pick it up.

Lauren gave him a thumbs up and a bright smile.

He took a deep breath, exhaled, muttered something to himself, and picked up the figure.

For a moment, no one spoke. Glances darted around the room, waiting for a reaction. There was none. It appeared, at least for the moment, that Ian had chosen wisely. They crowded around him to get a look at the thing.

Ian held in his hand a figure of metal, fairly flat and completely symmetrical. It was vaguely cross-shaped, with a diamond shape encasing a tiny blue gem at the head and embellishments to either side that spread up around the head and out like wings. It reminded Erik a little of the tops of colonial archways. The body had a tribal design aspect to it, bars of metal flowing in and out of contact, intersecting and drawing apart, swirling and scrolling, until they eventually met and tapered to a point at the end. In the center of the piece was a metal triangle framing another tiny glittering gem, this one red.

"It's quite a piece of work," Mendez said. "But how did you know to choose that one? What makes that the artifact we're looking for?"

Ian turned it over and showed them tiny marks carved into the back of the piece. The marks swam out of focus for a moment, then reshaped themselves into other symbols—the ones like those on the vault covers that Ian said were ancient Aramaic.

"It was face-down, so this side was up. See, it's an incantation of some kind," Ian said. "A prayer, I guess. A spell. It calls on powers whose names can't be spoken, but whose reach spans the multiverse. The incantation calls this a key. I think it's what opens the portal to the Hollowers' home world."

"You did it! You found it," Lauren said, excited. She threw her arms around him and hugged him. Over her shoulder, Erik could see Ian blushing, and it made him smile. It reminded him of watching Jake and Dorrie when they first got together.

"Good job, kid," Mendez said. Ian gave him a grateful grin.

"So now, the question is: how do we get out of this place?"

Erik nodded toward the doorway with a small smirk. "Plenty of doors to try."

"Not a bad idea," Ian said.

"Hey, man, I was just kidding."

"Yeah, but think about it. It can't hurt to see if there are any inscriptions on the doors. Maybe one could lead us home—or closer to it."

"I don't think I want to open up any more of those doors. Who knows what will fly out next?" Lauren hugged herself, looking worried.

"I've got to agree with the guys here," Anita said. "It's that or strike out into that black desert. And frankly kids, I don't have it in me to do that."

The others looked at Lauren.

"Come on, what do you say?" Ian said to her with a warm smile.

She melted a little. "Okay. Let's find us a way home."

"How about Mendez and I get up there first, so we can help the rest of you? Ian, would you mind helping the ladies from down here?"

"No problem," Ian answered, putting the artifact into one of his deep pants pockets. "Think you guys can get back up there okay?"

"I think so." Mendez gauged the height, looked around, spied the pedestal on which the artifact had rested, and dragged it, with care not to knock into the other pedestals, over to the doorway. It looked heavy, but Mendez managed to maneuver it carefully across the room and into position.

Mendez held onto it while Erik boosted himself up onto it and back up to the doorway. Ian did the same for Mendez. From the terrace, where the air had grown cool, the two men helped Lauren and then Anita, taking their arms and hoisting them up from the pedestal as Ian held it still below. Then Ian pulled himself up on it. It wiggled once and he froze, trying to redistribute his weight and regain balance. After a moment, the pedestal stopped rocking, and he exhaled a sigh of relief. Mendez and Erik reached it and quickly hauled him out.

Once they were all safely back on the terrace, they looked out over the city. Erik imagined that at one time, it was probably very beautiful, but now, the emptiness of it made it more haunting than magnificent. Again he looked out on a number of slab doors like the ones they had opened. He hadn't noticed any kind of writing on any of them before and didn't see any now. But, he reasoned to himself, this world had a strange way of changing once a guy thought he knew what was what, so maybe some kind of writing, either on a door or wall or sign or *something*, might make itself known yet.

To the others he said, "If Ian is right about the contents of rooms switching, then maybe we should close this door before opening another one, so we don't have to keep backtracking to the last door's location. What do you think?"

"Sounds good to me," Ian replied, and the others nodded agreement. He and Erik got on the far side of the door while Mendez waited near the doorway to see if it would need to be pulled as well. With a light push, the door swung closed without a sound.

No words, not on this door, at least. It was again one of many free-floating slabs of stone, its handle only a strange and random adornment.

"Where do we start? Should we just go to the next closest one and work our way around?" Anita indicated the door on the terrace across from them with a lift of the chin. "That one?"

Erik looked at Ian. "What do you think?"

Ian looked out over the street to the door Anita had pointed out. "I think it's as good a plan as any. Just so long as we don't open the one with all the ghosts...."

"That's down the street away," Mendez said. "It was pretty hectic, but I think I'll remember it if I see it. If I'd thought of it then, I would have tried to mark it somehow."

"Wait! I think I have an idea," Lauren said, feeling her earlobes. One showed nothing but a tiny hole, but the other had a diamond stud in it. She removed it and held it up. "Gift from an old boyfriend. He said they were real diamonds. Let's see about that."

She went over to the door and dragged the diamond side of the earring down hard against its surface. It left a long scratch. She smiled in triumph. "At least Barry was good for something," she said. She made a simple star shape out of the scratch.

"Great! On to the next one." Erik smiled at her.

They descended the staircase, joking with each other and laughing for the first time. It felt really good to Erik. It felt secure. It reminded him of the bond he'd shared with Dave and Cheryl, as if they had known each other for years. He wondered again if that was coincidence or some aspect of the situation they were all in, and found he didn't care. Sometimes, he thought, you just have to take something for what it is and enjoy it while you have it. And what it was, for Erik, was a break from worrying, regardless of their strange surroundings, regardless of the uncertainty of the future. They were dirty, bloody, tired, and hungry, but they were laughing, and damn, it felt good.

They circled around one of the bullet-shaped buildings whose large roof-fin blocked out a fan of moonlight, ducked under a low arch, and found the base of the staircase leading up to the terrace. This staircase had a silver railing which caught the muted blues and greens of the city lights and twirled them into little slips along its length. The wide stairs had been gilded with the same silver along the edges. They reached the top and saw the slab-door floating above stones laid out in fan patterns and hemmed by a silver railing like the one on the stairs.

The Triumvirate stood on the terrace next to the door.

The laughter stopped. Erik felt a sheath of icy panic coat his chest and stomach.

"No. Oh no, come on. No, no no," Ian said. Behind him, Lauren paled. Mendez clutched Anita in a tight grip.

In this world, as on Earth, the Hollowers looked somehow superimposed, as if their lines and contours didn't quite fit or flow against the backdrop behind them.

"Found you," the left one said.

Chapter 16

Before Erik and the others could run, the Triumvirate and the door were a mere couple of feet away. The three in unison turned their heads toward the door and it swung open. At first, Erik could see nothing but white through the doorway, but he smelled the faint odor of ozone which lately turned his stomach. Something amorphous was moving inside the white, swimming, rising, falling, turning in circles as it drew closer.

"Please don't," Lauren said. She sounded small and scared, Erik thought, and exhausted.

A wind had picked up behind them, carrying strands of their hair and flaps of their clothing toward the doorway. Erik tried to turn but found the wind made it difficult to move his head. He tried to lift an arm and found it pushed forward. The wind was growing more insistent; Erik's sneakers skidded on the fan of terrace stones as he was pushed forward.

"Hey," Ian said, stumbling toward the door, then bracing his legs against the force behind them.

"Jesus!" Mendez reached for the staircase railing, but the force of the wind yanked his hand back and he, with his arm still around his wife, tumbled forward. It was then that Erik realized the wind wasn't pushing from behind them but pulling from in front—

the doorway was exerting a kind of suction force which he imagined was similar to the force that had sucked those vicious, cannibalistic ghost-things back into their vault. Erik hoped to God the Hollowers weren't sucking them into some death vault, for their bodies to die and decompose while their hungry spirits, trapped for eons, waited restless and angry for someone to let them out. That would be a fate worse than death—nothing short of hell.

He didn't have long to think about it, though, because the Triumvirate said something in a language he couldn't understand and the pull on them grew stronger. Lauren screamed as she was lifted off the ground, and a second later she flew through the doorway into the limitless white.

"Lauren!" Ian cried, and his reach for her, however futile, was enough to lift him up into the air too. He sailed head-first past them and through the doorway. Mendez reached again for the staircase railing and lost his footing; he and Anita stumbled backward and were sucked in as well.

The Hollowers stood watching him with their sightless, eyeless heads, their hate an unpleasant taste in the sucking air between them, a painful prickle across the skin. Erik, afraid to move, tensed his leg muscles and ducked his head, bracing himself against the pull toward oblivion.

"You," the left one said. "You are anathema. And you will die first."

The middle one repeated the words in the language Erik didn't understand, accompanying them with gestures of a black glove, and Erik was shoved hard from behind and lifted off his feet. He tried grabbing the edge of the doorway as he hurtled into the white but missed. Behind him, he heard a swift thud of moving stone, and then all was blurred to colorlessness.

***

About a minute passed where there was no sense or feeling, and Erik couldn't immediately tell if he had been conscious or not. When the white cleared away, there was no jarring thump, no disorientation. He, Mendez, Anita, Ian, and Lauren were all standing in Mrs. Coley's room at Lakehaven Psychiatric Hospital. Each of them wore the same confusion in their faces that Erik felt. With the confusion came suspicion that dampened hope. They appeared to be back on Earth. Damn, he wanted to be back on Earth. But the experience of crossing back through the dimensions to get back was so different than the other times that Erik couldn't help but wonder if it was a trick. Were the Hollowers playing mind games with them again? Were they really back, or was this yet another world, twisted out of shape to look like home? To give them a taste of home and then yank it away again?

For several seconds, no one spoke. Mendez went into the room's small bathroom and turned on the water faucet. At the sound of the lightly rush of water, the others crowded in the doorway.

"Well," Mendez said, running his hand under the water, "the water works." He cupped his hand beneath the stream and drank from it, then backed away so the others could do the same.

"God, that tastes good," Ian said, splashing the water on his face and neck.

After Lauren had washed out her arm wounds, she said, "I'll be right back with some pain reliever and bandages. You guys wash out your cuts and scrapes."

"I'll go with you," Ian said, and when she smiled at him, he added with a blush, "I don't think you should go alone, not until we figure out what's going on." The two went out and down the hall to the supply cabinet.

"You know," Anita said, drying the water off her face, " it is kind of weird, us being sent back here, just like that. Why did they send us home?"

"Maybe they aren't done with us yet," Erik answered, but at that moment, he didn't really want to think about it. The cold water from the sink felt good. It tasted good. Even the sterile, antiseptic hospital air tasted good. What he really wanted was a long, hot shower, followed by a big steak and a cold Diet Coke. Or a warm bed, with Casey in his arms. His body was tired and sore, but his mind was exhausted.

"It just doesn't make sense," she said. "They could have just killed us in the other world. Why bring us home?"

"Are you sure we *are* home, sweetheart?" Mendez asked from the doorway.

Before she could answer, Lauren and Ian were back with the pain relievers, which she gave two of to each of them, and bandages, which she set to work wrapping on Ian first, then Erik.

"You always took the brunt of all this rough-housing," Anita said to Erik with a sad little smile as Lauren wrapped his arm. He returned the same smile, remembering a backyard of razor blade grass and the pounding a Hollower could give when angry, hurt, and forced into solid form.

As Lauren administered to Anita's and Mendez's less serious injuries with Hydrogen Peroxide, Ian reiterated Anita's concern.

"What I don't understand is why they'd just let us go. Why send us home again?"

The pain relievers kicking in, Erik found he could focus again. He said, "They've done this kind of thing before. They give you this false sense of security, let you put your guard down. Then *bam*! They're back to messing with you. I think they do it to make you give up in despair." He sat on the bed, looking out the window. It was still dark out, but the inkiness was fading to blue. The sun would be up in another hour or so. Erik couldn't believe all that had happened had taken only a few hours. Time, he supposed, worked differently in other dimensions. He thought about the situation for a moment and then added, "My guess is, they don't plan on just killing us."

"What do you mean?" Lauren asked.

Erik turned to look at her. "Well, it was something they said before they sent me through. They told me, 'You are anathema.' I don't think they meant just me. I think they meant us—all of us, as a race. See, the last time we fought a Hollower, we were in these catacombs, these tunnels underground. We got separated. They do that—try to make you feel weak because you're alone. So I found myself in this tunnel with all these carvings—kind of like what we saw, remember, Mendez?"

Mendez nodded.

"Those carvings have stuck with me ever since. I tried to forget, to push them down, but...well...." Erik paused. Those carvings had seemed intimate, a message meant specially for him. It made him feel naked somehow to be talking about them now. "Anyway, these carvings showed alien races—maybe even the races whose worlds we saw tonight. I don't know. And these races were slaughtered. Completely wiped out. And...it wasn't just Hollowers doing the slaughtering, either. There were others. Other monsters."

"What are you saying, Erik?" Anita asked softly.

"I'm saying those extinct beings on that red world might not be the only race the Hollowers and others like them have wiped out. And the Hollowers might not be the only beings that can come here. If we're an anathema—that's like a poison, right?—if that's the way the Hollowers see us, then...maybe we're next."

The others exchanged worried, thoughtful looks. He could tell in their eyes that the thought had crossed their minds, but that his saying it out loud brought it home, so to speak. It made very real a possibility they had hoped to leave on a distant world in an entirely alternate universe.

Erik continued. "They aren't done with us. Already there are little signs."

"Like what?" Mendez asked.

"Like, shouldn't there be another night nurse? A doctor, maybe? A noisy patient? Where is everybody? They aren't here, because here is...home, but it isn't. Not quite. It's like River Falls Road, or Oak Hill Assisted Living. We're in an underlayer, or an overlayer, I don't know which. We're here, but not entirely here. There's the Hollowers' influence between us and home." He looked out the window. The sky was still the same eerie blue. It should have begun to lighten already. He listened, and there were no sounds whatsoever in the hospital wing except those made by the others in the room with him. "Hear that? Nothing. No sound. No footsteps, no snoring, no creaking of beds, no machines. Not even the hum of the lights. Nothing."

"I don't know if I can take much more," Lauren said. She shook her head slowly. "If we don't get rid of them, they'll never leave us alone, will they?"

"They'll drive you into the ground," Erik said. "If they don't first turn this world into a playground for every nightmare imaginable—and probably a bunch of unimaginable ones, too."

"Then let's go find them," Mendez said.

"How?" Lauren asked. "Are they here somewhere in the hospital?"

"I suspect they'll find us," Anita said. "They always do. But I say we go meet them head on."

"And then what?"

"We send those fuckers home," Ian said, patting his pocket. "For good."

***

The group moved into the hall. Lauren was aware of how thunderously loud their footsteps were in the still hallway. They backtracked to room 201, where Mr. Skolnik should have been sleeping peacefully on his side, snoring a little. The bed was empty. Mr. Fiorelli was missing from 203, as well. There was no Mr. Idelmann in 202 and no Mrs. Espinoza in 204. They weren't surprised. Empty rooms were a sign of the general wrongness, but not an immediate cause for concern; she was fairly sure that wherever those sleeping patients really were, they were a hell of a lot safer than she was right now. Empty rooms were a go to keep moving. It would be occupancy, in whatever form it took, that would signal danger.

They continued down the hall: no Mr. Turner in room 206; Mr. Ketelburgh missing from 207, check; Mrs. Giamatta missing from 208, check; no Mr. Woo in 209 and no Mrs. Meyers in 210. The beds were empty, made neatly, pillows fluffed. Personal effects of the room were untouched and unremarkable. So far, so good.

As soon as they got to 211, Lauren saw there would be trouble. The room wasn't empty; a silhouetted figure, its back to them, loomed and shrank with breaths of sleep in the bed. It was hard to tell with the blankets and pillows whether it was Mrs. Saltzman. Shadow-figures sat in the guest chairs around her bed, but none of the chests rose or fell. No limbs shifted. Their heads were bent as if dozing. They all wore fedora hats.

"Are they sleeping?" Ian whispered.

"I don't think they sleep," Anita whispered back.

The suddenness with which the Hollowers appeared in the doorway caught them off guard. With startled shouts, they stumbled away from the three, further down the hallway.

Lauren looked to Ian to get out the artifact, but didn't have a chance to speak. The heads of the Hollowers snapped in unison toward room 212, where Mendez and Anita were standing in the doorway. As if shoved by unseen hands, the couple jerked backward into the room and the door slammed. Lauren could hear them banging on the door, jiggling the knob to try and get out.

The heads snapped to 213, and a long arm, the flesh black and flaking, grabbed Erik's shoulder and yanked him inside. The door closed on him, too.

Lauren backed into Ian's arms as the Hollowers turned their attention to them.

"What do you think is the worst way to die, Lauren?" the middle one asked, its voice including a distinct strain that sounded like Dustin, sandwiched amidst its multi-voices. A line of fire sprung up between them and the Hollowers. The intense heat hurt her cheeks, and she turned her head away. She and Ian backed up as the fire flowed in little rivulets across the tiled floor toward them. They had just crossed over the threshold of room 214 when the door slammed shut. In the hallway, Lauren could hear them moaning in ecstatic glee, and it was more awful to her than the siren noises or their laughter. They were feeding one more time, and it was terrible.

***

Erik struggled to shake free of the charred arm and found it gone—no trace of it dangling from above the doorway, and no fingers dug deep into the meat of his shoulder to pull him in. But the situation did not sit well with him; the next two things Erik noticed after the hospital room door slammed shut were that he was no longer in a hospital room, and he wasn't alone.

He recognized the basement of St. Anne's Roman Catholic Church on Byram Avenue. He recognized the cheap folding chairs that creaked every time a body shifted weight. He knew the folding table with the paper table cloth where the coffee machine and foam cups were. He knew the gray tiled floor, the white popcorn ceiling and stucco walls, and the periodic placement of pictures displaying the smiling faces of volunteers juxtaposed with lions and lambs, crosses, and saints. He recognized the faint smell of incense and paper and the faintly metallic smell of holy water blessed and cupped in coppery bowls on the floor above.

He did not recognize the people sitting motionless in the folding chairs with their heads bowed. They had a distinct smell, too—one of spoiled meat, left out in the sun.

It had been a long time since he'd felt the temptation to get high; it wasn't a part of his life anymore and he was glad for that. But he'd taken being a sponsor to Jake very seriously. Jake, who had trusted him. Jake, who had needed him.

He scanned the bowed heads for anyone resembling Jake, but no one stood out. It was a group of boys like any N.A. meeting. Some were there because they wanted to see for themselves the degrees of addiction beyond their experience, so they could convince themselves they didn't really have a problem because it wasn't as bad as the others'. Some were there because the courts had made them; it was either N.A. or jail. Some were there because they had lost too much, and they wanted something to go right and have something good to hold onto for once. Erik had been in that third category, but that hadn't made it much easier to stay clean.

As he really looked at the unmoving forms in the chairs, he noticed what was wrong with them. His stomach curled in on itself and he felt light-headed and panicky.

One guy had a needle still hanging out of his arm. His skin puckered and had turned black around the needle. The rest of his skin looked freezer-burned; pink overlayed by white and blue dead tissue. Another guy had white powder on his fingers, but the whole front of his shirt was soaked in blood, and blood from his nose covered the bottom half of his face. It had started to clot and coagulate, congealing in rubbery strings running from his nostrils to his lap. A boy in the back had a festering, gangrenous patch of rotting skin near the crook of his arm. It oozed, and the thick greenish-yellow fluid slid in gobs down his arm. One after the other, all around the room, the bodies were the same—one holding a handful of his own bloody teeth, one with black, rotting open sores along both his arms, guys with skeletal bodies, lesions, gouges. If they were to pick up their heads, Erik knew he'd see swollen or sunken eyes, black and rotten teeth, lines and wrinkles and that dead-eyed, empty-hearted look so many never quite recovered from.

Erik stood before a folding chair at the head of the group, where the person who ran the meetings usually sat. It occurred to him that maybe the Hollowers really had opened the door to Hell, because this was as close to it as Erik could imagine.

He was afraid to move. He didn't want to wake the motionless forms. He didn't want to see their faces or watch those limbs, beaten to damn near useless by their substance of choice, shaking blood back into circulation. In a way, this was worse than when the Hollowers tried to tempt him, cover him, drown him in coke, because these people here were what he could have been. He had learned to say no to coke. He was still working on saying no to the guilt, to the part of him that demanded he never forgive himself for wasting so much of himself, his life, and his time away. He had almost lost Casey because of coke. He had lost friends. He had lost money. Mostly, he had lost self-respect. He had managed not only to salvage but better his life with his girl, and the rest had come as a matter of due time and hard work. But the part of him that mourned the lost time and the lost him couldn't bear to look at the weak, half-human things that filled the folding chairs.

Erik glanced around the room. There was a door on the far side, beyond the semi-circles of chairs. If he was careful, he could probably back out of the circle and around the outside of the group to the door and maybe those things wouldn't even stir.

He glanced behind him then back to the circle and frowned. There were more guys in more folding chairs, widening the circumference of the circle. It was a small basement area, and with that many chairs, he wasn't sure it would be any easier to go around the circle than right through it. He glanced down to make sure he wouldn't trip over the chair as he inched around it and when he looked up again, he was sure. There were more bodies in more chairs, essentially filling the basement with concentric rings.

He cursed inside his head. He'd have to step over people to get around them now. The only clear spot on the whole floor was dead in the center of the circle, and even that area had shrunken with the sudden, silent influx of recovering dead.

Erik assessed the situation for several minutes and decided it was inevitable. The only way to get to that door was to go straight through the assembly. The thought made his skin crawl. He'd have to keep his eyes on the door, was all. Just keep his eyes on the door. He could make it.

He took a cautious step toward the circle's center. His footsteps made a muted scuff, but no one in the chairs stirred. He took another step and another, his gaze fixed on the door.

He was in the center of the circle. The dead men around him didn't move.

He took a deep breath, let it out as quietly as he could, and moved forward again. At the edge of bodies, he recoiled. The stench of rot and of unwashed hair, clothes, and bodies was overpowering. He would have to pass in between them.

Eyes on the door. Four, maybe five rows of chairs and then the door. Eyes on the door.

He inched carefully between two of the bodies, aware in an almost physical way of their proximity to him. He shuffled to the left and moved between two more bodies. Turning sideways, he crept around one whose bony legs were sprawled out and whose scarecrow arms dangled to either side. He took great care not to trip over the leg nearest him, but had a moment of horror and revulsion as one of the dirty-nailed fingertips brushed beneath the hem of his jacket. He waited, his heart pounding in his chest, for the body to move. It didn't. By degrees, fear released its death-clutch on his chest and he inched along.

He was one row away from the door when the tinkling of a bunch of tiny things falling and bouncing off the tiled floor made him nearly jump out of his skin. He turned to look and saw teeth rolling along the floor.

As if responding to the cue, the bodies in the rows closest to the center of the circle started twitching. It spread like germs to the rows behind until all the bodies were spasming violently in their chairs, bony arms and legs flailing, heads lolling on weakened necks.

Erik turned and bolted for the door. He thought he felt dirty, sharp-tipped fingers tugging at his jacket, but he ripped free, yanked open the door, and dove through.

The hallway on the other side creaked when he stepped into it. Gouged tiles on the floor left irregular holes that fell away to nothing. The paint on the walls peeled like badly burned and blistered skin. The gloom engulfing the end of the hallway drew back like a curtain, and at the far end he could see a door. As he walked down the hall toward it, he wondered if something in his brain chemistry, some embedded code that dreams read and functioned on, told on him as having a fear of never achieving a goal. He had read somewhere that tunnels and hallways symbolized that. It sure captured how he felt about then, tired of working toward the goal of surviving. It had never been an easy goal, long before the Hollowers came. It was damn near impossible now.

He felt watched as he entered the shadowed area of the hallway, and he supposed he was—supposed he had been the whole time. It wasn't just the Hollowers he felt, though. It was tough to get his mind around, but it felt like the walls themselves were watching, that something in and through them was watching. It made him feel cold and damp with anxious sweat across the back of his neck and under his arms.

He was tired of being watched. Tired of being swung at and growled at and tossed through doors and dropped on hard ground. He was tired of feeling nauseous and sore and scared and guilty. He had worked hard to reclaim a normal life, a secure life. He wanted all those things she'd said she wanted—to be held, to make love to her, to hold her hair when she was sick, to count himself lucky every time she took his breath away in a beautiful dress or in sweats, to celebrate their joys and console each other in their sorrows. He wanted a life with her. A family with her. He was tired of fighting and tired of running.

He was very, very tired.

He reached the door and a kind of calm settled over him that he had never felt before. One way or another, this was going to end. If he couldn't have all those things he wanted with her, then he wanted to make sure she had a chance, at least, to have all those things for herself, without ever having to worry about the Hollowers taking it all away again.

Whatever was on the other side of the door, he was ready.

Then he heard the scream.

Chapter 17

Mendez and Anita gave up pounding on the door. Anita swore. They turned to find themselves in a hospital nursery. All around them were little clear cribs, occupied by sleeping bundles. The name on the identification tag of each crib was the same: *MENDEZ, Baby Girl.*

"Bennie...?" Anita said, looking around.

"It's okay," he told her, giving her hand a squeeze. "We just have to ride this out. It'll be okay."

They looked back to the door and Mendez was not surprised to find a flat wall where it had been. Instead, a door stood on the far wall of the room, at the end of a long row of hospital glass through which Mendez could see a dilapidated hallway of broken floor tiles and graffiti-covered walls.

Inside the nursery room itself, peeling paint left irregular patches of wall tinted by steak-juice-colored rust stains. What little paint was left had gone from a sterile white to an unwholesome kind of yellow, scored with gray scuff marks. The ceiling above peeled as well, and occasionally, flecks fell like autumn leaves around the cribs.

None of that was so horrible, though, as what they saw lying in the cribs. Oily stains and splatters of dried brown blood covered the better parts of tiny ducky blankets, soft knit caps of pink and blue, and fleecy white undersheets. Looking at that made Mendez's chest ache, but seeing the little bundles beneath the blankets, wearing the knit caps made him feel sick.

The majority of the tiny bodies had a blue cast to the skin, especially the lips and around the eyes. The tiny chests didn't move. The tiny legs and arms lay limp. The miniscule eyelids did not flutter. Some little bodies were worse off. The blanket cast aside, those chests were opened up, and it looked to Mendez like something had reached in and grabbed hold of the delicate newborn lungs and crushed them. They hung deflated, smashed, even smeared inside the little chest cavities. Mendez fought back the rising gorge in his throat and looked away.

He pulled Anita to him, murmuring, "Don't look. Don't look, *mami*," into her hair, but she had already seen. Her face was wet with tears, her chest hitching, her voice mumbling broken non-words into his chest. He knew she was thinking about Cora, about how they had almost lost her, about how even now, every night, sometimes more than once, she would slip out of bed to check on Cora, to listen for sounds of her breathing or feel her chest, even in her big-girl bed, to make sure she was still breathing. The near brush with Sudden Infant Death Syndrome had made her compulsive, probably obsessive on that one point, and more often than not, Mendez let her go, watching in silence, waiting for her to come back. He supposed he needed to see her return with a relaxed expression, satisfied their daughter was okay.

He honestly didn't know what she would do if the little dead babies in the room began crying all at once.

He couldn't help looking again, taking them in. They didn't look like real people at all like that, but more like dolls designed in extremely poor taste. Babies, he had found, were so full of new life, so full of unspoiled and somehow purer and more intense energy, that to see the little shells devoid of that life and energy looked so much more unnatural than the countless dead adult bodies he had seen in his line of work. Both he and Anita had been given cases where the victims were children, sometimes even young children, and they were horrible, every open minute of them. That was the toughest part of the job. But brand new babies were a different thing entirely. A whole nursery full of them stripped whatever capability for detachment he had and replaced it with horror and revulsion.

"We have to get out of here," she said.

"I know, *mami*. I know."

He took her hand and led her between the tiny cribs. Just before Mendez could reach the door, a figure appeared at the outside of the glass. It slapped the glass with one gray palm and left a greasy smear as it dragged its fingers away. Mendez stopped short.

The gray-skinned woman outside in the hallway wore a traditional nurse's uniform and cap. What little hair remained on her head had been pulled into a tight bun at the base of her bony neck. Her exposed arms, face, and neck collected moisture in the

Mary SanGiovanni

deep crevasses spidering across their surfaces. She reminded Mendez of a weathered rock, a golem watching over the silent forms of the dead.

It turned its head to look at them. The cracks in the liver-colored lips filled with blood. From the nose, then the ears and eventually the corners of the clouded eyes, tiny black tendrils poked and prodded the air, sensing things.

Mendez stepped toward the door with Anita in tow, and the nurse mirrored his action. He clicked the safety off his gun and drew it from the holster. Then he eased open the door.

The nurse watched them pass into the hallway before unhinging her bottom jaw and screaming. Dead things fell out of that gaping maw—shiny bugs, small, furry rodents half-digested, things with far too many legs, surfing on the waves of upheaved ichor that splashed onto the floor between them and carried the dead things along. Baby-doll parts tumbled out, too—at least, Mendez hoped they were only doll-parts. From where he stood, it was hard to tell, and he didn't want to get closer.

"Kill it." Anita's voice in his ear was broken and uncharacteristically cold. He didn't take the time to over-think it, though. He raised the gun and fired a shot into its chest and another into its head. The skull broke apart like a pinata, raining down its prize of tiny bones onto the ground muck.

"Let's go," he said, and led Anita around the mess and down the hall.

After a silence broken only by the sounds of their footsteps, Anita said, "I hope she's okay."

"She's fine," Mendez soothed. "She's with Erik's wife."

"What's to stop them from getting her there?"

"Us. They're too busy with us right now."

Anita sighed. "I'm really scared."

"Yeah," Mendez said. "I am, too."

The hallway turned sharply to the left. As they rounded the corner, they saw further degradation of the halls and floor, which had taken on a slight cant to the right.

"Promise me we'll get home to her."

"We will," he said.

"Promise me." She looked at him. "Even if you don't know if you can keep it."

He squeezed her hand, but he couldn't look at her. "I promise. And I don't break my promises, *mami*."

Far off, they heard a faint scream that broke the moment.

"That way," he said, and tugged her forward.

***

Lauren and Ian found themselves in a large, mostly empty room, its apparent age and disuse stripping anything compassionate or calming away. It was a room of harsh angles and unforgiving concrete. Cold, sharp metal instruments lined a tray against the back wall, and a slab of table laid bare in the center of the room.

"Are we still in the hospital?" Ian looked around.

"A hospital, but not LPH," Lauren said, eying the instruments. She crossed the room to them and picked one up. She remembered from her history of medicine classes in nursing school that it was called a leucotome. The instrument next to it, the one that looked like an ice pick, was called an orbitoclast. Neither had been used in the treatment of psychiatric patients in a good thirty or forty years.

"What are those?" Ian asked, joining her by the tray. She could hear his trepidation.

"Tools for performing lobotomies," she said flatly, putting down the leucotome. Next to her, Ian shivered.

There was a pause, then, and Ian asked almost timidly, "Did my mother...um, did she...?"

"Receive psychosurgery? No." Lauren tried a smile, but found it felt wrong.

"Did she ever get violent?"

Lauren considered this for a minute. "You didn't see her much, once they committed her, did you?" It wasn't an accusation, and she hoped it didn't come off like one. She meant it sympathetically.

He seemed to understand. "Not really." He brushed his hands against his pants and turned toward the table. "She...the night I called the hospital to come pick her up, she tried to stab me."

"Oh, God. Really?" Lauren touched his arm.

"Yeah. She didn't recognize me, I guess. She had been trying to wallpaper the windows with some old newspapers, and she couldn't find her tape—her 'supplies,' as she called it, were a roll of tape, a box of empty soda cans, some plaster, a lighter, a water bottle, and a pen. Oh, and a mirror. I was never sure what the mirror was for, other than her telling me once I'd know what to do with it when the time came."

"So what happened?"

"Honestly, I really don't know." He leaned against the table, the spotlight from somewhere on the ceiling shining bright enough on him that Lauren could make out the little details of his face. She liked his face, she decided.

"See, she was calling me, yelling about her supplies, but when I came into the room, she looked as if she had never seen me before. She was all beat up, had done God only knows what, and something had set her off. But it was in her eyes—I could tell in her eyes that reason and reality had shriveled, maybe died completely in there, and that whoever I had just become, she didn't know and didn't trust.

"I tricked her. I admit it. I told her if she went to take those vitamins the good doctors had given her—that's what I called her pills: her vitamins—that I would go find her box of supplies. She agreed. I went to call the hospital to come get her, and she went to get a knife and stab me before my 'kind could take root and overrun the Earth.' At least, that's what she told her doctor later, when she was medicated and lucid again.

"Did she hurt you badly?"

Ian shrugged, but there was pain in his eyes. "Not really, no. It was just a scratch on my arm. No big deal. I got the knife away from her before the hospital folks arrived." He looked down at his fidgeting hands. "I guess maybe you knew her differently."

"I don't hold it against you for not visiting her, if that's what you're getting at."

He smiled, grateful, and gave a nod.

"She was a nice lady, but under our care, she had therapy and treatments and medication. No psychosurgery, but we kept a pretty close eye on her. We know our patients differently, but only because we know what they can be if not made to be different." Impulsively, she reached out and grabbed his hand, giving it a squeeze. "You did the best you could."

There was what Lauren had always thought of as a "movie moment," where they looked into each other's eyes and found desire there, and their heads inched infinitesimally closer for a kiss.

The clatter of the tools falling to the floor made them jump, snapping the moment.

They turned to find the tools still jittering on the floor, pulling together and moving apart. Lauren realized they were forming letters. The couple backed against the cool edge of the table, watching words form.

LOOK
BEHIND

YOU

They spun around. Lauren thought she was worn out of screams, but the sight before her ripped a hoarse cry from her throat. The two dived away from the table, kicking tools and sending them skittering across the floor.

They saw a tangle of spiny vertebrae ending in long, tapered appendages sheathed in a kind of sausage skin; patches were slick with a rapidly drying and crumbling fluid, and beneath they saw mottled black and pink. The appendages were rooted in a round mass about the size of a loveseat, perched on the operating table. The central mass opened and closed a series of gaping holes that sometimes cupped frenzied shark eyes, all black, and at other times, contained rows of thin, needle-like teeth. It smelled moldy and damp and made terrible gurgling noises in between iron groans.

It snapped one of its spiny appendages like a whip just inches from their faces, and Lauren cringed back. Then it vomited a black fluid onto the floor that smoked as it burned into it.

Lauren didn't see a door anywhere in the room. There was no way out! The range of the thing on the table kept them where they were. From its central location, it could slap those tentacles down on already tender flesh if they got too close. Lauren eyed the lobotomy tools, now within the domain of the thing's reach. If she could get to the orbitoclast, she could stab that awful mass in the middle, shove it up under one of those volcanic glassy orbs. Maybe lobotomize it.

Ian had evidently been thinking the same thing. One moment, he stood next to her, and in the next, he dove for the tool. Just as his fingers closed around it, a tentacle lashed out and wrapped around his neck.

"Ian!" she shouted. His eyes bulged in surprise, and in the sudden obstruction of his air flow. The creature wrapped another tentacle beneath his ribs and hauled him up off the ground, then tossed him overhead and across the room. Ian landed with a frame-jarring thud and rolled toward the far wall, groaning. It was difficult, given the rise and fall of the creature's eyes, to gauge where its attention lay, but for the moment, it seemed to be on Ian. It snapped a tentacle and she heard Ian cry out in pain.

She inched her way closer to the tools and a tentacle snapped back in her direction, licking her cheekbone. Lauren felt the skin open up and wet pain trickle down her cheek. It brought tears to her eyes which she blinked away. She brought a hand up to her face and her fingertips came away with blood.

Ian, who had managed to pull himself up on one knee, roared at the thing. He was out of words, but she thought she knew what he was doing; if he got its attention and distracted it, Lauren could go for the tool and plunge it in.

The thing roared back at him.

She went for the tool again and this time she felt the cold steel in her hand before a tentacle sliced into her right eyebrow, knocking her off her feet. Brilliant, blazing pain filled her eye and then the whole side of her head, but she scrabbled quickly away from a follow-up blow.

"Laur— Damn!" Ian shouted.

She scrambled to her feet and saw him pacing frantically, his lip split open, a long tear in the shin of his pants already stained with blood from the wound beneath.

"You okay?" she asked over the bulk of the thing.

"Yup. You?"

She held up the tool and he smiled. "Atta girl," he said.

He looked around for something to throw at the thing, to distract it, but none of the displaced tools had made it to his side of the room. He bent over and yanked off his sneaker, then hurled it with all his strength. It went high and wide—no baseball player, he—but it got the monster's attention.

She lost no moments in lifting the lobotomy tool high above her head and bringing it down with all the force she could muster, right into one of those gelatinous black eyes.

The beast screamed like a kettle on the boil, the tentacles whipping wildly, and it sucked the eye back inside itself, replacing the socket with a mouth so quickly that it had bitten down on the tool and had it clamped between teeth before it had a chance to fall free of the removed eye.

It twisted a number of tentacles into a thick rope and backhanded her hard. The force of it sent her stumbling back, her head swimming among bright stars of pain. Her head connected hard with the wall behind her, and for a moment, fuzzy white threatened to close in on her vision. She sank against the wall, blinking until the scene before her came back into focus.

"What do we do?" Ian shouted.

She was about to shout back when she saw the door. She was sure it hadn't been there before, but it was there now, not three feet from where Ian stood.

"Look! There's a door!"

Ian turned to where she was pointing, then looked back at her, excited. "Come on!"

She shook her head. "I don't think I can make it across! You go. Go on." Between them, the thing bellowed, retching up more smoking black acid onto the table and floor below it.

"Not without you," he said, and his tone indicated he had neither the time nor inclination to argue. "Now come over here, or I'll come over there and get you."

"No," she called back, using the wall to help her rise. "I'll come to you." It would be dangerous for her to try to get across for sure, but it was foolish and even more dangerous for him to risk coming to get her.

He held a hand out in her direction, and the look on his face gave her strength. "I'll be here. I'm not leaving without you."

The monster roared again, alternately swiping at her and at Ian. Lauren noticed the slime that had covered it was nearly dry now, and whether it was a direct result or not, the tentacles were moving noticeably stiffer and more slowly.

Nevertheless, she kept her back to the wall, moving with slow, deliberate steps sideways, just inches out of reach. She covered the back wall and rounded the corner and the room shook with another of its roars, this one more like a chorus from its multitude of mouths. As she inched her way up the side wall, she saw a tail like that of a lobster unshelled, that greasy, mottled skin making it look naked and somehow that made it more repulsive to her. A number of thin, jointed insect legs slid its bulk toward her and she cringed as another tentacle clumsily sought her face and missed. She moved more quickly down the length of that wall and as soon as she could, broke into a run. Ian caught her up in his arms and hugged her tight.

They were within arm's length of the door when Lauren felt a hundred tiny bites in a band around her arm, yanking her away from Ian. She tumbled in a heap in the middle of the room.

"Shit!"

The tentacle released her arm and smacked at both her ankles, opening up furrows of overturned flesh. Enormous pain filled those furrows, and the blood soaked her sneakers. A tentacle lashed out again and flayed a strip of skin off her thigh. She screamed, and the beast above her screamed with her.

"Lauren!" Ian called helplessly.

That was when the door behind Ian opened.

Chapter 18

Erik emerged through the door, his eyes growing wide as they took in the thing on the operating table.

"Help me," Lauren cried. There was a long, bloody wound on her thigh and slashes around her ankles, as well as a nasty cut across her cheek. A band of hickey-like bruises encircled her upper arm.

"Fuck," Erik muttered, joining Ian against the far wall. Ian slid off his other shoe and threw it at the beast. It bounced off a tentacle and rolled to a stop near Lauren.

"Distract it," Ian said. "I'll grab her."

Erik nodded. As Ian prepared to make a run for her, Erik shouted at it.

"Hey! Hey, over here!" He jogged sideways along the wall away from Ian and Lauren, hoping he was out of reach. The beast shifted its bulk on the table and uncoiled a tentacle in his direction. He tilted his head back and the tentacle whisked past his hair, narrowly avoiding his face.

Ian, meanwhile, had skidded to a crouch beside Lauren and, with his arms under hers, had hoisted her to her feet. The monster started to turn its attention to them, but Erik shouted again.

"Come on, motherfucker, over here! Over here!" He flipped it the bird—it wouldn't understand, but he didn't care. It was a little act of rebellion and it felt good.

Ian and Lauren ducked and ran back to the wall, out of reach while the monster lashed out at Erik. This time, it connected with Erik's chest, splitting open his shirt and the skin beneath in a diagonal line of beading blood. A flare of pain across his chest set his heart pounding. He staggered back toward the wall.

A moment later, Mendez and Anita appeared at the little door, taking in the monster with the same repulsive fascination as the others. Anita rushed to Lauren, shouldering her under the arm as Ian had in order to help her walk. Erik tried to rejoin them but the beast snaked out a tentacle to block his way.

Mendez, who Erik figured by now had come to the same conclusion he had, looked at the monster with abject hate. Without the Hollowers to force it to focus its rage on just the face, it was attacking at will. It, or one like it, had killed Steve. It or one like it had killed Jake and Dorrie. The knowledge for Mendez might have been based on forensics, matching the wounds he remembered to the murder weapons flailing wildly around the room. But Erik suspected Mendez knew for the same reason he did; it was one of those invasive thoughts that was not their own but just as real, like dream knowledge of things that are certain but for no easily traceable reason. The knowledge that a beast like this had killed Steve, Jake, and Dorrie had been shoved into their heads the same way they had been shoved from dimension to dimension. The Triumvirate *wanted* them to know.

Mendez drew his gun on it and emptied the rest of his clip into the writhing thing on the table. It roared and screamed at the first two shots, but then it stopped moving, other than where the impact of the bullets made its flesh dance in tiny explosions.

He and Erik approached it with cautious steps, watching for signs of life. So far as Erik could tell, no part of it breathed. Nothing moved. The openings of the central mass had all settled on half-formed slits through which a random eye or point of a tooth was visible. The dark curves of the eyes had begun to lose shine and shrink to hard little knots of dark gray. Along the tentacles, the last of the slime that had, Erik guessed, kept the skin lubricated had dried away, and the mottled skin looked like tiny sheaths of torn up paper tacked on to the spiny bones beneath. The little spikes that lined the undersides of these tentacles, visible now with proximity and the limbs stilled, looked like loose teeth, sagging in their sockets and occasionally landing on the operating table with tiny metallic pings. It reminded Erik, wildly, of the pine needles falling off Christmas trees after Christmas.

Mendez nudged it with his gun and more spikes fell off. He nudged it again to be sure, and that seemed to catalyze the decomposition. The mass in the middle collapsed in a papery heap and puff of swampy odor, the tentacles and spidery legs folding in toward the middle. Layers of skin blew off, landing on their clothes and in their hair. They recoiled, trying to brush it off. It smeared like ash, but felt oily on their fingers. Within minutes, the whole of the beast was a fluffy white lump, a giant lint ball with the occasional bone poking through. They backed away from it. Erik had a strong urge to kick the table over, to send the foul thing crashing to the floor to break into dust, but he resisted. It was dead. That was enough.

They trudged back to the little door and opened it, piling out into the hallway.

The door swung softly shut behind them, and then everything began to change. A sharp crack like lightning, followed by a boom of thunder, preceded a violent trembling of the hall. The vibrations were strong enough to make the group stumble around to keep balance. Erik and Mendez led the group forward, stopping short when a tearing sound signaled the fall of a huge chunk of ceiling.

"Whoa! Shit!" Erik looked back at Mendez, motioning for him to get the others to back up a little.

"What the hell is that?" Lauren's voice was high and hysterical. She pointed to the space where the ceiling chunk had been. Beyond it was an ocean, upside-down. The waves crashed against some inverted shore beyond their field of vision, and water sprayed down on their upturned faces.

Beneath them, the floor tiles cracked, and little pieces fell away, down into a blue sky smeared with clouds.

"I can't do this anymore," Erik muttered, but no one heard him. Beneath his feet, chunks of floor tile were falling down into the sky. He jumped when he felt a rumble beneath his feet, moving out of the way just as the floor space beneath him broke in half and tumbled out of sight.

Anita cried out and he turned around. Mendez had caught her arm, but her leg had sunk with the tile below into the hole up to her thigh. Erik ran to her side and took her other arm, and the men hoisted her out of the hole. Just then Mendez tumbled back. Anita and Erik grabbed his arms and kept him from pitching backward into a patch of cloudless sky.

"Thanks," he said to them.

"No, thank you," Anita said back, and kissed him quickly.

A crack opened up at the far side of the hallway, beyond the door they had come through, and jittered toward the center above their heads. The roar of waves above it was deafening.

Erik noticed that the center of the hallway had remained more or less in tact, so he tugged Anita and Mendez toward it. "This way," he said to Ian and Lauren. "Stay in the middle. It seems pretty sturdy."

A piece of ceiling to the left of the crack crashed down and, with a creak, fell through the floor. A wave smashed against the hole left in the ceiling, pouring murky water through the room and out the hole in the floor. Erik could see the sky changing to an uneasy, undecided storm color.

Then the walls started to pull apart. Explosions of plaster and paint sent chunks of wall flying outward toward the flipped horizon line. Exposed support beams creaked and splintered under the pressure. More of the floor fell away, leaving only a jagged strip of tiles over a graying sky. High tide above their heads sent foamy water splashing down all around them, soaking their clothes and hair. The water smelled swampy, like the monster they had killed, and Erik wondered if they were twisted up in the Hollowers' half-way place on Earth, or someplace else. Another chunk of ceiling fell, and then the water began pouring in, coating the remaining tiles, pouring off their uneven sides into a sky that had knitted together angry brows of storm clouds.

There was another flash of lightning below them and a clap of thunder, and the ocean pouring down in front of them washed the ceiling chunk right off the side of the tiles. With the obstruction gone, Erik saw that the hallway continued indefinitely in front of them. No Emerald City at the end of *that* road, he thought grimly.

He turned back to Mendez, who was clutching his wife. "We should move!" he shouted over the din. The water in front of them was pouring in faster, washing toward them.

"Which way? The water's coming down too hard!"

"If we wait any longer, it'll get worse! It'll wash us right off this thing!"

Mendez considered it a moment, then nodded. "Everybody, grab hands!" he shouted back to the other two.

Ian took Lauren's hand, who took Mendez's. Mendez had Anita's and Anita reached for Erik's. Again, Erik was leading the way. He put thoughts of slipping off the side out of his mind, and instead put one foot in front of the other, one at a time, nice and easy. There was a roar above his head and he froze. A rush of water poured down in front of him, and every muscle in his body tensed. He could feel Anita's grip tensing, too. Erik closed his eyes until the rush of water stopped, then moved forward again, hoping, begging, praying to the Higher Power that another spout of water didn't crash down on the middle of his chain of people. He considered picking up speed, but decided against it. They couldn't afford a misstep, literally. Slow and easy.

About two hundred feet or so ahead, he noticed the ceiling stopped, but the tile pathway kept going. The water dribbled and drooled off the edge onto the pathway with the rhythm of the waves, but it didn't look like it came down too hard. A light curtain of waterfall, that was all. They could manage that. He noticed, too, that the sky at that point ran 360 degrees around, a vista of grays and blues, cloudless and clear. No sandy shore to fall and bury them alive, which was good. If they could make it that far, they might be able to pick up the pace unhindered.

A scream from the back of the chain froze his heart. He stopped, bracing his legs, looked back, and did a quick headcount. Anita, Mendez, Lauren, Ian, check. It was Lauren, he assumed, who had screamed. A spout of water had poured down behind them, drenching Ian, and had deposited with it an odd fishy creature easily as large as an ottoman. The thing had a long body covered in iridescent silver scales and tiny black eyes. Its mouth, which worked open and closed silently, featured row after row of shark teeth. Black spindles and smaller spikes ran along its back bone and the tapered edges of its fins and tail. It flopped and the back end of the chain flinched. Ian gave it a good kick and sent it sliding off the water-slick path.

"Everyone okay?" he called back.

Ian looked anything but okay, eyes haunted, blond hair plastered to his pale face, but he gave Erik a nod and a thumbs-up.

Erik turned his focus back to the path ahead. Slow and easy. He moved forward again. They were approaching the edge of the ceiling. He fought the urge to tug the chain of them into a run. He kept moving forward until he got to the curtain of water, then plunged through. He felt a muscle in his back strain from the tension of waiting; he thought the water would rush down at any minute, washing the whole lot of them into a Hollower-created oblivion. He emerged on the other side, soaking wet, his nerves strung tight, but okay. He kept moving forward, listening for the little puff of breath or sigh that indicated each of them made it through.

"Clear!" Ian yelled from behind, and Erik's body released some of that tension.

Cleared of ocean splashes, he felt more sure of his footing on the tiles, and picked up the pace a little. He didn't want to move too fast. It was likely they could be surprised yet by something trying to catch them off guard, and it was still a fairly narrow path. He refused to look down. He'd never really considered himself afraid of heights, but it seemed prudent not to get distracted, if possible. Slow and easy, keep following the path. He imagined

Casey was waiting at the end of it for him, and he didn't want anything to keep him from getting to her.

A light breeze blew across him as he put more and more distance between the chain of people and the remains of the hallway. It felt good, cooled the tension sweat on his skin. He couldn't help but notice from his periphery that the blue of the sky all around them was deepening. The path ahead was harder to see, swathed in shades of purple inkiness. However, it looked to him like far up ahead was an archway. Beyond that, he couldn't make anything out. Still, the Hollowers were big on heralding change with landmarks, and he found himself bracing for it.

"Archway up ahead!" he shouted back, and Anita squeezed his hand in acknowledgment.

The breeze picked up, a chuffing sound in his ears, and this time it made him shiver. He kept on, picking up his pace when another gust of air, chilly this time, blew across his face and made his eyes water.

The archway drew a little closer. The path over nowhere seemed to be widening a little as well, and he chanced moving still a bit faster—not quite a jog but almost a power-walk. The others kept pace with him.

A big gust of wind brought him almost to a stop. It was powerful, that wind—strong enough to tug him toward the edge while his foot was raised. He knew that ideally, he should lower his center of gravity, but it would be difficult. He couldn't bend into the wind, either, since it was blowing from the side. He'd just have to keep on, hoping the wind wouldn't pick up tornado momentum. He moved with wide, deliberate steps down the path, focusing on the archway, turning his trunk when he could to offer the wind as few bodily surfaces to push against as possible.

The arch came into view, and now he could see it, and what lay beyond it draped in dusk, more clearly. The arch itself looked like two bent bars of metal. Weaved between them was thin wire from which dangled severed fingers on little snips of ribbon. This struck him as one of the most disturbing things he had seen yet, simple and awful, the trophies of a grisly, efficient trio of killing machines. Beyond the arch was a broad plane of what looked to Erik like fiberglass, over which was painted a lattice of glowing purple. The dusk below them showed through the clear diamonds in the lattice. Beyond the plane, there was nothing—no door, no random floating window, no mouth of a tunnel. There was just dusk, deepening to endless, starless night. He didn't need to worry about falling off the pathway into oblivion; they were already there.

He led them under the arch and onto the lattice before letting go of Anita's hand.

"Where the hell are we now?" Ian asked, exasperated.

"Nowhere," Erik said. "Literally. I think we're actually nowhere."

Ian slumped a little where he stood. "Why?"

Erik gazed at the illimitable gulfs of emptiness all around them. "When the Primary came, it sent us all over the place. Every time we thought we'd conquered one place, we'd end up someplace else. It's a tactic they have for trying to break us. Like I said, they want to push us to the point of giving up."

"Well, guys, I think I'm just about there."

"Me too," Lauren said, her voice hoarse. "I just don't know if I can take any more of this."

Anita and Mendez kept silent. They all looked at Erik.

"I can't," he said softly. "I can't give up."

"I don't know if we have much of a choice, brother," Ian said. "Look around us. We've literally reached the end. Of everything."

Erik felt a pang of hurt in his chest. The kid was right. They really were at the end of everything, and yet Erik still couldn't let go. He couldn't just close his eyes and pitch back into that comfortable nothingness and let it all go.

To the others, he said, "Look, I know how you feel. Believe me." he took a deep breath, exhaling slowly before continuing. "When I was a kid, my dad used to drink. Case of beer every night, sometimes hard liquor. And he was a mean drunk. He was a mean son of a bitch sober, but drunk, he was even worse. And when he'd hit me, I'd just give up. Let my mind go blank, shut down. Then, I discovered coke, and at first, it was like I'd found a way to wake up again, to feel alive again. But it wasn't. It was only another way of giving up, of not caring."

The others said nothing. They looked at him with empathy, maybe with pity. He wasn't sure. Only Mendez looked at him differently. His was an expression Erik couldn't quite make out, but it was the only one that didn't make Erik feel weak and unequal; that was the best way Erik could describe it, that Mendez's expression didn't make him feel less like a man. He didn't fault the others for their sympathy or even pity, if that's what it was; he appreciated it, but didn't want it. Still, he continued.

"I'm not telling you this to guilt you into keeping on, or even to get you to feel sorry for me. I'm trying to make a point, and it's this. When I met Casey, my wife, she gave me a reason to want to fight—my addiction, the world, everything. Fight to keep her. Fight for a better life. I quit drugs for myself, to be a better man. But I wanted to be a better man for her."

He looked down at his shoes, puddled in the gloom between the crosshatches of purple. "I made a promise to my wife before we left for the hospital that not even hell could keep me from her. So you see, I can't give up. I can't let down the person who taught me not to give up on me. I just can't do that. I'm going to get home to her, or I'm gonna die trying."

"We've got your back, man," Mendez said, and held out a fist.

Erik bumped it with his own fist. "Thank you. Seriously. Thank you."

Lauren went over to him with shining eyes and gave him a hug. Ian clapped his shoulder—lightly, as if unsure if it was okay.

"We're behind you," Ian said. "We'll see you home to your wife." He turned to Mendez and Anita. "And you both to your little girl."

"I appreciate it, man, I really do," Erik said.

In the growing dark, it was harder to read expressions, but when he looked at Mendez, he thought he saw approval there.

"Okay," Erik said. "Let's look around—but be careful. And we should stay together."

In the center of the latticework plane, there was a metallic post like an old street lamp. Erik frowned. He was sure that hadn't been there a few minutes before. He walked toward it and the others followed. A gleaming orb perched on top of the post caught the colors of the lattice and distorted them. As they approached it, both the post and the orb above it loomed much larger than they had from several feet away.

Affixed at about eye-height on the post itself was a simple black light switch and surrounding plate.

Erik looked at the others. Their hair and clothes were wet. Although the blood had washed off, scratches and bruises dotted and lined their face, arms, and bodies. They looked scared and tired. They had been through so much.

And yet each of them nodded at him. They understood. He nodded back, and flipped the switch.

Plates in the plane of the floor dropped out and they were falling, falling into the black at the end of the universe.

Chapter 19

Mendez opened his eyes and a sharp bolt of pain seared through his head. It occurred to him that all this exposure to and traveling between different dimensions and layers of his own dimension might very likely wreak untold havoc on the human body. He blinked and pinched the bridge of his nose, trying to see through the haze of pain. After a moment, it subsided a little, and he looked around. Anita lay next to him, her eyes fluttering. She groaned. They were in a rough-hewn concrete cave, lit with dim bulbs of a sickly yellow and marked throughout with painted signs to KEEP OUT and keep alert. Near where Ian and Lauren lay sprawled on the floor was a dark brown stain in the concrete flooring, and a thick gray pipe ran above their heads. A thick rope tied in a noose hung from the pipe right above Ian. Erik leaned up against a heavy steel door marked with a small sign that read MORGUE, rubbing his head.

They were back—in the Lakehaven Psychiatric Hospital's basement, where they had begun.

Mendez got up and helped his wife to her feet. He wanted to leave, wanted to go home and hold his baby, rock her to sleep, feel her tiny breaths on his neck as she lay on his chest. He didn't want to take the chance of being sent away again.

Then he looked at Erik's face and knew that just couldn't be—at least, not yet. It still wasn't over. It wouldn't ever be over until they killed those things. He and Anita would never sleep another peaceful night or hold their baby or make love or eat waffles or anything without worrying, waiting, watching.... He couldn't go home until the Hollowers were destroyed.

"Are we...?" Ian stood, wincing from the pain in his back. He nevertheless extended a hand to Lauren to help her up. He noticed the noose, brushed it aside like it was crawling with bugs, and shivered. "We're back in the basement...aren't we? Are we really here?"

"Looks like," Erik said, getting to his feet as well. "Looks like they're done trying to break us. Ian, you still have the...you know, the artifact?" He looked around, saw what door he was leaning against, flinched, and moved away from it.

Ian patted his pants pocket. "Got it."

"You think it'll still work here? In our world?" Erik's voice was a conspiratorial whisper.

"Provided the words still self-translate," Ian answered in the same kind of whisper, "then yeah, I think so."

"Good," Erik said in that quiet, thoughtful, serious way he had. "No more fucking around."

"So where are they?" Lauren asked.

She was answered by the ding of the elevator door. It had reached their floor. They held their breaths, waiting for the doors to open, waiting to see what the Triumvirate would throw at them next.

The doors opened on an empty car. A breeze blew out of it, though, which had enough gust behind it to almost have substance. It made a whistling sound like a breath over a glass soda bottle.

They waited.

A chittering sound echoed in the basement, then died.

They waited.

"This is the end of things."

They jumped, their nerves frazzled, some throats choking out edgy little cries. The voice had come from behind them. They turned.

The Triumvirate stood there, *loomed* there, very tall.

Mendez saw Ian slide the artifact surreptitiously out of his pocket.

"We are done with you. Now you will die," the left one told them.

"No," Erik told them. "We are done with you. Get the fuck out of our world."

He looked to Ian and nodded, and Ian held up the artifact and began to read. Mendez didn't know if he was reading ancient Aramaic or the language, re-translated, of the ancient race who had written the words in the first place, but he kept going, loud and clear and strong, and as he did so, he began to change. It wasn't anything drastic, but Mendez, who by then had spent several very long, strange hours with the young man, could see the difference.

He glowed slightly, for one, and he looked taller, more muscular somehow. His body language was different, his posture different. It was almost as if the force of the artifact's creators was possessing him, guiding him, driving him through the incantation.

The Hollowers did not appear pleased by this sudden turn of events at all.

"Stop," the left one said.

Ian kept reading, his voice growing stronger, a chant picking up the rhythms of the cosmos.

The middle one made a motion with its glove, and with a savage growl, shot bolts of dark purple at Ian that fell to either side of his feet, causing the ground they touched to bubble and smoke.

Ian kept reading.

"Stop," the one on the right said. "Stop this." The basement around them stretched and yawned and creaked as if the whole thing might cave in on their heads. Babies cried from inside the morgue and the accusing voices of the dead bombarded them with vitriol and threats.

But Ian kept reading, right until the end. He lowered the artifact and stood his ground in front of the Triumvirate. And for seconds that seemed to stretch into years, they all held their breaths and waited.

There was a flash as a bolt of black lightning sizzled down, slicing the air, and the familiar heavy odor of ozone. The bolt folded in on itself as they had seen it do before, and then spread to a height of about six feet before pulling itself open. Around it and behind it, the air wavered as if heat were rising around it. Inside the rip, which struck Mendez as the opening of a throat leading to an endlessly hungry stomach, he could see nothing. He could hear, though. He could hear the storm of nonentity that used to be a universe tearing and shredding and crashing and rending far below.

"OhmyGoditworked," Ian breathed.

The heads of the Triumvirate turned in unison to the rip, then snapped back to Ian. Mendez could feel the hate radiating off them, pulsating off them in waves that burned with cold. He could also sense their confusion and alarm. He thought he sensed their fear. It gave him no small measure of satisfaction.

"What did you do?" they asked him, their three multi-voices tinged with hysterical tightness.

"I told you," Erik said. "We want you out of our world—for good."

"Stop. You must not do this." The one on the right tightened his glove into a fist. The air crackled between them. The middle one tilted its head at Ian and he cried out in pain. The metal figure fell from his hand and skittered across the ground. The Hollower on the right twisted its fist and the space that had crackled moments before began to open.

"No!" Anita shouted. She reached down and grabbed a chipped piece of concrete off the ground and threw it at the Hollower on the right. The rock crackled and disappeared with a small pop. There was a low hum, and then a flash from the space where the rock had been. It lanced out and hit Anita in the shoulder. She cried out and crumpled to the ground, breathing heavily. Mendez was by her side in a flash, checking the burnt cloth of her top and beneath it, the burn on her shoulder.

"I'm okay," she told him. "No worries."

"You think some trinket from a dead race is going to save you, when we can open up the gates of Hell and suffocate you beneath the flesh of demons?" The middle Hollower sounded angry for sure, but also uncertain. Mendez dared to hope they had done something right.

In front of the middle Hollower, a black schism tore the fabric of the basement air and began to open. Ozone choked Mendez's nasal passages.

"They can't come through, the others, they can't, can't," Erik muttered under his breath, not to anyone in particular. Mendez thought Erik was thinking of Dave then, and the rip the last Hollower had opened when it had threatened to call its kin in droves to destroy them. Dave had died that night, rather than let more monsters in to hurt his friends. Mendez frowned. Erik couldn't...just because Dave had.... But Mendez knew that look in Erik's eyes. Nothing was going to change his mind, either.

"Erik—"

"Tell Casey I love her."

"Whatever you're thinking, I—"

"Promise me."

"Erik, what—"

Erik dove for the metal figure and then charged the closest Hollower, the one on the left. With his left forearm, he rammed it in the gut, sending the line of them toppling backward through the rip. One by one that mouth swallowed them, and then Erik disappeared through the fluttering edges of the rip as well.

Mendez was at the rip in a second, reaching in and grabbing at Erik. His fist closed around clothing—the neckline of Erik's jacket and shirt. He was yanked forward. His other hand flailed, reaching for something stable, and found a chain hanging from a concrete support post. He could smell Anita's perfume behind him immediately and feel her arms around his waist, holding onto him. He didn't dare turn away from the rip, though.

The hand and wrist plunged into the alternate space grew painfully cold and stiff, but he held on. He could see the Hollower Erik had charged holding onto him by the forearm. Strangely, awkwardly, it held the glove of the Hollower below it, and that one held the glove of the Hollower below it. They didn't add any extra weight, so far as Mendez could tell—he was straining against Erik's weight, and that was it. But to bring Erik back through the rip would be to pull the train of monsters back through as well.

"Let me go," Erik puffed with strangled breaths. Even from where Mendez stood, he could feel the vacuum below tugging on the air of this world, drawing everything to it and chewing it up. "You have to...let...us fall."

"No," Mendez said. "You're going home to your wife." He pulled, but the fabric of Erik's shirt made a ripping sound. Mendez felt the slack in the fabric as Erik pitched forward. He let go of the post and grabbed at Erik under his arm with his other hand. Behind him, a train of grunts indicated that the others felt the strain of holding onto him, but their grip didn't loosen.

He could see the skin of Erik's forearm around the black glove turning white, then blue, then black. Likewise, a white frost spread like moss over each of the Hollower's fingers, then down the back of the glove and onto the sleeve. The frost moved quickly, and from the siren sound issuing forth from the depths of that dangling Hollower, it must have caused a great deal of pain.

Before the frost could reach the shoulder of the thing, Mendez saw the other glove spread its fingers, breaking its hold on the Hollower below it. There was a roar of surprise as two of the Triumvirate fell backward into the tearing, twisting darkness below. Mendez watched their forms until they grew small, at which point the substance of the chaotic storm beneath them tore them into little pieces. The death wail of their sirens lasted moments after, until the void swallowed the sound, too.

Mendez doubted the Hollowers were capable of anything even remotely like sympathy, but the Hollower with its icy death-clutch on Erik wailed when the last death notes of its comrades had faded away. It looked smaller somehow without the others making it whole.

Erik must have seen a chance in its diminutive moment of weakness, too. With his free arm, he pulled back and punched the Hollower square in the blank plane where a face should have been.

His fist, still clutching the artifact, sank into the Hollower's head, or else the head crumpled like paper around his fist. Immediately, Erik's fingers and knuckles turned purple and cracked, bleeding into the concavity of the Hollower's head.

The black glove let go of Erik's arm as Erik pulled his fist away, and then the last of the Triumvirate was falling, too, its own siren call long and loud as black frothed over black beneath it.

"No joda con nosotros," Mendez said to the shrinking form of the last Hollower, and yanked Erik back with all his strength. Behind him, Anita's small, strong hands held him tight and caught the momentum, pulling too, and behind her, Ian and Lauren held their ground.

Mendez and Erik toppled backward onto the hard ground of the hospital basement. Erik winced and straightened his purple, swollen, bleeding fingers, and released his grip on the artifact. Mendez crawled over to him and picked it up. He held it, an important instrument of a long-dead race from another dimension, a key to opening up the storm of black holes that had once been the Hollowers' home world And with a nod of encouragement from Erik, he tossed it through the rip and watched with satisfaction as it disappeared into the void. Then he collapsed next to Erik and lay there.

Only moments after, the rip crackled loudly and distorted, puckering and twisting, then sealed up with a pop and disappeared. A few seconds more and the ozone smell dissipated, the air smoothed out, and all trace of a rip ever having been there at all was gone.

Anita swooped down to hold him, and he saw the other two checking on Erik and his injured arm and hand. Lauren ran off to get bandages and medicines from the supply cabinet.

Mendez and Erik stayed there on their backs for a while, letting the others tend to them, and then Mendez started to laugh. It was a weak sound, almost just a cough, but it caught on. Erik started laughing, too. Anita and the others smiled, confused, but it didn't matter.

They had done it. They had sent the Triumvirate home.

Epilogue

Two weeks later, Ian sat on his mother's bed with the cell phone in his hand. All around him was the untidy evidence of his room re-do. Drop cloths covered the furniture too big to move out of the room. Small sample paint cans stood tiny sentinel around the baseboards. The plaster symbols had been knocked off and the wall scraped, sanded, and respackled where necessary. The newspaper had been peeled off the windows, and neither the Mayan can temples nor the box that had once occupied the space where Ian now sat were present in the room. He had thrown it all out, including her journals and news clippings. He wanted to remember his mother, but not those things. That part of her life—and his—was best left behind.

He did keep the collage. He found it captured all the things he *did* want to remember about her. And he kept the pictures of his parents on their wedding day. He'd even gotten frames for them, which he planned to hang when he'd repainted the room. He intended to paint it a bright color. A happy color.

It was a new life, a second chance. And he wanted to make the most of it.

His finger hovered over Lauren's name in his phone's address book. She was off that night. The thought of calling her made his heart pound almost audibly in his chest. He had to laugh to himself; he was more scared of calling the girl of his dreams to ask for a dinner date than he had been facing down man-eating monstrosities from another dimension.

His finger touched her name in the address book and her number popped up on screen.

But then, Ian had never been the type to swoop in and charm ladies. His battling inter-dimensional gods and monsters hadn't made him much less shy. He taught dead languages and had weird hobbies and a tendency to babble when he was nervous, usually about things most people didn't even understand, and—

Stop, he told himself. *You're better than you think, and on your way to being as good as you'd like to be.* She *had* told him to call her sometime, in their new life. She liked him. And Lord, did he ever like her.

But what if she said no? What if she had just been trying to be nice? What if—

What if a dimension opened up in your living room and swallowed you whole tomorrow and you blew the one and only chance you had to be happy?

He'd meant it as a mental joke, but it lost its funny right off the bat.

Still, it was a good point, in a figurative sort of way. If he'd learned anything, it was that uncertainty was the order of things, and that in terms of life's adventure, he wasn't so bad a guy to have along for the ride.

He took a deep breath, and dialed her number. He could feel his stomach tightening up with each ring, and when her voice on the other end said, "Hello?" he thought he might pass out. He managed to croak out a greeting.

"Ian! Hi!"

He was pleased to hear how happy she sounded that he had called. He relaxed a little as they made small talk. They talked about her patients—Mrs. Saltzman had confirmed to her that the doormen had gone away—and his classes, the summer session of which would be starting the following Tuesday. It felt right. Maybe it was corny, but he really did feel like he'd known her his whole life. No awkward pauses bogged down the flow of chatter between them. They finished each other's sentences with how much they had in common. And when she laughed, Ian felt buoyed by the airiness of it. He would have fought a thousand gods and monsters for the chance to hear her laugh again.

When they were almost an hour into the conversation, he screwed up his courage to ask her out.

"Hey, Lauren, I was wondering...I mean, do you think maybe you'd like to...well, that we could...." He took another deep breath. *A new life*, he told himself. "Would you like to have dinner with me?"

He could almost hear her smile from the other end.

"I'd love to."

The knot in his gut loosened. "Good! Tonight, at seven?" He smiled, too.

"Sounds perfect."

And the date turned out to be just that.

***

Mendez met Erik at the Olde Mill Tavern that night. When he entered the dim warmth backdropped by the crooning of Mick Jagger from the juke box, he saw Erik in his usual seat at the end of the bar, staring off distractedly over his Diet Coke. He looked smaller somehow, more withdrawn. Mendez stifled a frown and walked up to him, clapping him on the shoulder.

"Oh hey, glad you could make it."

Mendez noticed Erik had removed the bandage. The back of his hand showed patches of gray with stiff, reddish-purple skin around and beneath it. There was still a bandage over the patch on his forearm which Mendez had no doubt would be there for a while. The damage to the tissue had been extensive, and Erik would have a rough scar in the end to show for it. There was a sunken, shadowed look on Erik's face that Mendez hadn't seen since the days when Erik was using. He knew that wasn't what was making Erik look so haunted these days, though. It was like Nietzsche said about the abyss. Erik had stared into it, had almost fallen into it, in fact. That it looked back into him—that it looked out through his eyes every now and again, particularly when Erik seemed to be wool-gathering—well, that was to be expected, wasn't it?

"Hey, man. How've you been?"

Erik shook his hand and indicated the bar stool next to him. The bartender brought him another Diet Coke and he nodded his thanks. "I'm pretty good, man. Pretty good. How about you? How's Anita? Cora?"

Mendez sat. "Both good." To the bartender he said, "Corona please," then again to Erik, "Yeah, Cora's getting big. She can hold her head up on her own."

"Really?"

"Yup. Yup, Anita's pleased as all hell. And she smiles now—that's my favorite, seeing her smile. Nothing like it since...well, Anita's smile."

Erik took a swig of his Diet Coke. "That's great, man. I'm glad to hear it."

"You holding up okay?" he asked again.

"Yeah. Yeah, sure man."

Mendez, who was used to reading tones under tone and words between the lines, thought that might have been the only insincere thing he'd said so far, but let it go.

"And Casey?"

Erik beamed, blushing a little. "She's pregnant. Nine weeks. We found out yesterday."

"Really? Congratulations! That's great! When's she due?"

"March, looks like."

"I'm really happy for you both. Hey, Casey babysat for us—maybe we can return the favor."

The two lapsed into silence. Mendez found the same happened with Anita, when conversation even so much as skirted the edge of what had happened.

"You're gonna love being a dad," Mendez said.

"I hope I'm at least somewhat good at it."

Mendez smiled. "No worries, man. You go by instinct and do the best you can. Same as—" he stopped himself from saying "Same as you've done before, same as you've always done" and instead said, "Same as all dads do. You'll be fine."

Erik nodded. "Thanks." After finishing off his Diet Coke, he surprised Mendez by saying, "I'm scared. Of bringing a baby into this world."

"Well, I think all new parents are."

"No," Erik shook his head. "No, that's not what I meant. I mean this world, considering...what's out there. Beyond it." He turned to Mendez. "What if they come back?"

Mendez's glance swept around the bar, determined no one was listening to them, and said, "They can't. They were torn apart. I saw it."

"And others?"

"They won't. After what we did to the three strongest? Even the dumbest animals give up on a thing if they keep getting bitten. And really, if they won't come, what else would? What else even could?"

Erik looked at him as if he'd melted a weight off his shoulders. "You're probably right."

"You know it, man," he said, clapping a hand on Erik's shoulder. "You've been worrying about things for a long time. I think it's time you started enjoying yourself. You've earned it. Go home to your wife, and your baby growing inside her. Go home to your house. Let the worry go."

Erik nodded at him. "Seriously, man, thank you. I just...thanks."

"Any time, *amigo*. Any time." He finished off his beer and set the bottle down on the bar. "And now, I'm gonna hit the road."

"Really, Mendez? Want one more? Bird can't fly on one wing and all."

"Nah, I've got to get going. Anita's had the baby all day and I need to get back. Plus, I have a call to make that shouldn't really wait any longer."

"Okay, man, take care. Give the girls my best." Erik shook his hand again. Mendez was glad to see his grip was a little stronger than it had been when he'd arrived.

"You too, man. Take care." At the door, he glanced back once. Erik was staring off into the space over his drink again, but this time, he was smiling.

***

Mendez waited in the dark of his car in the parking lot of Olde Mill Tavern as the phone drilled off rings. He knew she'd still be up at this hour; she always was.

Another ring.

He'd waited until he was sure—as sure as he could possibly be, given the circumstances. He hadn't wanted to let her down, for Steve's sake.

Another ring. A brief flicker, not quite of panic or confusion, but something in his chest....

One more ring and then she answered. The flicker snuffed out. "Hello, Latin love machine. To what do I owe this late-night call? Shall I pour myself a glass of wine and get out my dictionary of phone sex terms?"

He laughed. "Hi, Eileen. How's my girl?"

"Good, baby. So what's up?"

"Just wanted to tell you," he said, taking a deep breath, "I made it right. No questions, no details. But yeah. I made it right. For Steve."

On the other end of the phone came a sigh of relief. "For Steve," she said in a heavy, contented voice, and Mendez guessed there were probably tears in her eyes. "Thank you. Thank you, Bennie."

"Good night, Eileen."

"Good night, sweetness."

Mendez started up the car and pulled out of the parking lot and onto the road. Inside the bar, there was light and noise and everyday folks drinking away the problems of the world. Outside, there was quiet in the cooling night, and a faint smell of ozone. The air crackled, and in a small clearing, the edges of the air fluttered in the light breeze. It was new, still tucked away from human eyes, one of many in the off-the-path places where the edges of universes brushed in the Convergence, wore thin, and tore open, but there were no Hollowers to pass through it.

No Hollowers, but there were others yet. Many others.

Made in the USA
Columbia, SC
18 June 2018